HENDERSON'S BOYS

ONE SHOT KILL
Robert Muchamore

Hodder
Children's
Books

A division of Hachette Children's Books

BY ROBERT MUCHAMORE

The Henderson's Boys series:

1. The Escape
2. Eagle Day
3. Secret Army
4. Grey Wolves
5. The Prisoner
6. One Shot Kill
7. Scorched Earth

The CHERUB series:

1. The Recruit
2. Class A
3. Maximum Security
4. The Killing
5. Divine Madness
6. Man vs Beast
7. The Fall
8. Mad Dogs
9. The Sleepwalker
10. The General
11. Brigands M.C.
12. Shadow Wave

CHERUB series 2:

1. People's Republic
2. Guardian Angel
and coming soon . . .
3. Black Friday

A Catalogue record for this book is available
from the British Library

ISBN-13: 978 0 340 99918 9

Typeset in Goudy by Avon DataSet Ltd,
Bidford-on-Avon, Warwickshire

Printed and bound by CPI Group
(UK) Ltd, Croydon, CR0 4YY

The paper and board used in this paperback by
Hodder Children's Books are natural recyclable products
made from wood grown in sustainable forests.
The manufacturing processes conform to the
environmental regulations of the country of origin.

Hodder Children's Books
A division of Hachette Children's Books
338 Euston Road, London NW1 3BH
An Hachette UK company
www.hachette.co.uk

Part One

16 May 1943–1 June 1943

By mid-1943, World War Two was turning in the Allies' favour. Hitler's armies had been knocked out of Africa, faced devastating setbacks in the eastern war with Russia and increasingly ferocious air raids by British and American bombers.

But Hitler still thought Germany could triumph. He believed that the alliance between Russia and the United States would be short lived and told his people that new and revolutionary German 'Victory' weapons would change the course of the war.

CHAPTER ONE

Fat Patty was a four-engined B-17 bomber, crewed by Americans, but assigned to a Royal Air Force special operations squadron. She'd been in the air for four hours, heading for France's Atlantic coast. There were three men in the cockpit. Seven more manned electronic equipment and gun turrets, plus two trained spies ready to parachute into one of the most secure areas of occupied France.

Fat Patty's crew were old hands. They'd dodged night fighters and anti-aircraft guns to insert agents deep in German territory and even made top-secret runs, dropping supplies to partisan groups in eastern Europe and refuelling in Russia before returning the following night.

Tonight's run was as easy as this work got. After

takeoff they'd flown down over Cornwall, then in a gentle southwards arc over the Atlantic, where no German fighter dared probe. The agents were to be dropped in countryside, a few kilometres from the port town of Lorient and its heavily fortified U-Boat[1] base.

Dale was the radio operator, but the crew called him Old Boy because at thirty-five he was ten years older than his pilot, and the rest were even younger. He rubbed gloved hands, pulled his headphone cup away from one ear and gave the girl squatting on her parachute a few metres away a big show of pearly white teeth.

'Gets damned cold up here,' Dale said, shouting above four propellers and a whoosh of air. 'Got a flask of coffee if you feel the need.'

The view down the metal-ribbed fuselage was gloomy. The only light came off illuminated dials and chinks of moonlight through the gun turret up front.

'If I drink too much I'll have to pee,' Rosie Clarke replied.

The closest thing to a toilet on board was a relief tube built into the fuselage, but even when it wasn't frozen up there was no dignified way a girl could use it.

'Better give it a miss then,' Dale said, smiling. 'How old are you? Seventeen? Eighteen?'

---

[1] U-Boat – German submarines were usually called U-Boats. The term is an abbreviation of the German word Unterseeboot, meaning submarine.

At sixteen, Rosie was young enough to be flattered when someone said she looked older. But while Dale seemed nice, she wondered if his question was a trick that would cause trouble when she got back to campus.

'I'd better not answer,' Rosie said. 'You know, security and everything.'

Dale nodded. He'd dropped enough agents to stop wondering what happened to them, but Rosie might stick in his head because she reminded him of his daughter. Rosie was nervous and kept the conversation going to help her mind settle.

'Where are you from?' she asked.

'Garfield County, Utah,' Dale said, before making a little laugh. 'I'll bet you've never heard of that.'

As Rosie nodded her stomach plunged. The pilot had pulled the bomber into a sudden upwards lurch and she had to put her hand against the floor to stop herself tipping over. They'd been skimming at two hundred feet to avoid German radar, but now they had to gain height to get a visual on their drop zone.

The two agents were to be met by a reception committee from the local resistance, who were supposed to switch on a battery-powered light beacon when they heard Fat Patty approach. Rosie's fellow agent Eugene came eagerly down the steps from the cockpit, crouching to save his head.

Eugene was a twenty-one-year-old communist who'd

run the anti-Nazi resistance around Lorient for almost two years. He'd been picked for the job by Rosie's commanding officer Charles Henderson and by most accounts he'd built a superb team of locals to gather intelligence and sabotage the town's heavily fortified submarine bunkers.

While the combat gear they wore draped awkwardly from Rosie's curves, Eugene's thick frame had been made for it. He was moderately handsome, but sharply angled eyebrows and slicked-back hair gave him a vampirish quality.

'How are we doing?' Rosie asked, in French.

'Just waiting for the beacon,' Eugene replied. 'I wanted to see the terrain from the cockpit myself. Last time I parachuted in, the navigator mistook the landing beacon for a German searchlight and I ended up walking twenty kilometres.'

Eugene had travelled to Britain to brief his superiors, learn the latest espionage techniques and most importantly to take a break from the mental pressure of working in Nazi-occupied territory.

For Rosie, this would be her first drop since completing parachute training two years earlier. After landing, her role was to serve as a back-up radio operator, and to train some of the younger members of Eugene's circuit.

'Take a step back, sweetheart,' Dale said, as he

removed his headset and stood up.

After squeezing past Rosie, Dale moved towards the rear of the plane and crouched over a hatch in the floor. Moments later a red bulb illuminated directly above his head.

'Beacon in clear view, commence drop in sixty seconds,' the pilot announced over an intercom.

The message sent everyone scrambling. Rosie and Eugene strapped on parachutes they'd been sitting on for most of their journey, then helped each other attach cumbersome equipment packs that buckled to their thighs. More supplies for the local resistance would follow on additional parachutes and the nose gunner had left his position to help Dale push them out.

'Twenty seconds. Wind north-by-north-east at two feet per second,' the intercom said.

Rosie glanced at Eugene, feeling like she was about to spew. 'I can't remember the winds. Is that blowing me left or right?'

'Gently left,' Eugene said. 'You're first. Remember your breathing. Get up by the hatch.'

As the red bulb died and the green next to it flicked on, Dale tugged on a rope handle and lifted a half-metre-square hatch out of the floor. Air currents ripped noisily towards the rear as buffeting made the fuselage shudder.

Eugene gave Rosie a friendly whack on the back as he

attached the static line hanging off her chute to a bar over the hatch.

'Drop positions,' Dale shouted.

The bomber flew at two hundred metres, going as slow as it could without stalling. But that was still over a hundred and fifty kilometres per hour, which meant every second moved Rosie's drop zone by forty metres.

She sat on the edge of the hatch, boots dangling over a black abyss and tense hands resting against the side. She looked up, catching angst on Dale's face. Eugene said something, but she'd pushed off before she understood it. She fell for two seconds before the static line tethering her to the plane snapped off, opening her chute.

The crack was reassuring. It's tough to judge the approaching ground in darkness, but if the pilot had got the height right, Rosie would be able to count to fourteen elephants before touching down. She saw the outline of a hill, but no sign of the landing beacon. As her chute opened she heard the crack of Eugene's line, followed by three more chutes loaded with equipment. At the same time, Fat Patty began a lazy turn, dropping back beneath German radar as she turned back out towards the Atlantic.

Rosie counted under her breath, 'Nine elephants, ten elephants, eleven elephants . . .'

The dark made it hard to see the ground, but a torch

beam hit Rosie and after a second's blindness she sighted trees coming up way too fast. On twelve elephants she yanked her left steering line, opening a vent in the top of the chute and tilting her sharply to the right.

A whiff of manure hit Rosie's nostrils as she got clear sight of where she was about to land. She'd cleared the trees, but there was a tall fence closer than she'd have liked and her boot thumped into it before she pulled up her trailing leg and made a gentle touchdown on its far side.

Two torch beams lit her up, casting shadows across her body in the shape of fence posts. She unbuckled the chute and scrambled forwards, ready to gather up the billowing chute before the next gust of wind caught it. She could see the other chutes landing nearby and then she heard a shout – in German.

Heart in mouth, Rosie rolled on to her bum and got her first proper look at the men behind the torches. Her eyes had adjusted to the gloom and it was hard staring into the torch beams, but the curved outline of two German army helmets was unmistakeable.

CHAPTER TWO

Lorient Gestapo headquarters was situated in a Roman-style villa, commandeered from one of the town's wealthiest residents. Obersturmfuhrer Huber sat at a desk in a sparsely furnished interrogation room. A second desk was meant for a typist to take notes, but it was one in the morning and nobody was available.

Huber was chubby, dressed in a grey civilian suit with a fancy pocket watch hung off a gold chain. He studied his nails uninterestedly as a uniformed guard dragged a girl into the room. She was around fourteen years old, extremely thin and dressed in grubby knickers and a blood-stained man's vest that almost reached her knees. Her eyes were badly swollen and she had dozens of burns and bruises.

'Still defiant?' Huber asked, watching the girl struggle

as the guard forced her into a chair. 'Edith Mercier, we've not had the pleasure of meeting before.'

Edith looked up, as the guard lurked behind, ready to strike. She'd not been in this interrogation room before, but they all had the same dim ceiling bulb and tang of bleach.

'Communist bitch spat in my face,' the guard explained. 'Earned herself a slap for her trouble.'

'Oh, Edith! Spitting isn't nice,' Huber said, smiling slightly. 'I just need you to answer some questions. Once that's done you can clean up. I'll find you something to eat and better sleeping arrangements.'

Edith's eyes were black marbles as she stared right through him.

'Where does the stubborn attitude get you?' Huber asked. 'You're just a girl. You're facing no serious punishment, but unless you wish to suffer more than you have already, you simply *must* give full details of the resistance scum you've become mixed up with.'

Edith kept silent as Huber signalled the guard with a raised eyebrow. She felt a hand clap the back of her skull as the guard thrust forwards and banged her forehead against the desk.

'Again,' Huber said.

Edith was dazed as the guard slammed her a second time. She twisted, slipping off the chair and stumbling sideways, but the guard pulled the skinny girl back into the chair and clamped a hand around a neck barely wider than his wrist.

'Where is Alois Clement?' Huber shouted, as Edith choked. 'When did you last see him?'

Edith gasped when the guard let go, but gave no answer. As punishment the guard snatched her wrist and twisted it agonisingly behind her back.

'This is all *so* unnecessary,' Huber said, as he shook his head gently. 'So, so unnecessary.'

'I don't know anything,' Edith shouted, when the pain became too much. 'I've never heard of anyone named Clement.'

Huber pulled a notebook out of his pocket and spun it across the desktop. 'You were carrying this with you when you were arrested.'

'Never seen it in my life,' Edith snarled.

'We've confirmed it's your writing. I know it's a coded list of names. I know you worked as a messenger for Eugene Bernard and witnesses tell me you regularly visited Alois Clement at the fishing port.

'Your witnesses are lying,' Edith shouted. 'You can't trust traitors.'

Huber leaned forwards. 'You'll tell me everything you know, or I'll make this the longest night of your life.'

'You're not even original,' Edith laughed. 'My last interrogator used that exact line. He got *nothing* from me and neither will you.'

'Who are you trying to save?' Huber asked. 'I've been in this room with many of your friends, Edith. They're happy to spill the beans, so why endanger your life by protecting them?'

Edith snorted. 'If you already know so much, why are you up in the middle of the night asking me questions? Why aren't you at home in bed, with your teddy?'

Huber was a professional interrogator, but didn't completely succeed in hiding his irritation. Edith knew she'd scored a small victory.

In Huber's experience the majority of people broke quickly under torture, often within minutes. About one third had the will power to hold out for a day or two, usually in order to allow a colleague or loved one to escape capture. Less than one suspect in fifty could endure pain as Edith had done.

'You were not a blood relative of Madame Brigitte Mercier?' Huber asked, picking a gentler tone as he signalled for the guard to back off. 'She was your guardian, yes?'

Edith had been through enough interrogations to know that her tormentor had changed tack to try winning her confidence. This bought her recovery time, so she always played along whilst being careful not to lose concentration and say something of value.

'I never knew my parents,' Edith explained. 'Madame Mercier adopted me when I was a toddler.'

'You worked for her?'

'I looked after her stables and ran errands for the girls who worked in her brothels.'

Huber nodded, trying to show some empathy. 'Sounds as if she was more like a boss than a mother. Having no *real* family must have been tough for you.'

'She treated me better than a state orphanage would have done,' Edith answered. 'At least until one of your goons snuffed her out in one of these torture chambers.'

'Madame Mercier's death was not intentional,' Huber said. 'She suffered a heart failure while under routine interrogation.'

'Bad news for you,' Edith said. 'She knew more than anyone.'

Huber bristled. He'd have liked to watch the guard bounce Edith off a couple of walls, but decided to have one last attempt at making an emotional connection.

'You lived at the stable, with Madame Mercier's horses?'

Edith was annoyed by the inference that Madame Mercier hadn't cared about her. 'And I suppose I'll do fine now I've got the Gestapo looking out for me?'

Huber rubbed his eye and took a moment to think up a response. 'Where are the horses now?'

This was something Edith didn't like to think about. She resented the fact that Huber had found a weak spot and failed to hide the lump in her throat.

'A little bird told me that it was an horrific moment for you,' Huber said, as Edith wondered who'd been talking about her. 'Your beloved horses burned to death, following a *British* bombing raid. You must have been devastated.'

Edith had run the stable for years and the death of the horses in a firestorm after a bombing raid had affected her more than anything, including Madame Mercier's death.

Huber looked at the guard, speaking gently as a tear left a salty track down Edith's cheek. 'Fetch her some hot coffee, and a bowl of hot water for her to wash with.'

The guard seemed surprised. 'Are you sure, sir? She might try something. She bit Thorwald's wrist so deeply that you could see the tendons.'

'Thorwald is a moron,' Huber said, as he shot to his feet. 'She's a little girl and I don't appreciate you questioning my orders.'

'As you wish, sir,' the guard said stiffly, before clicking boot heels and leaving the room.

Huber moved around the desk. Edith was horribly bruised and winced as Huber rested a hand on her shoulder.

'I can make things more comfortable for you, Edith,' Huber said. 'I just need something to work with.'

Edith glanced at Huber, then awkwardly at the notebook resting on the table.

'Everything in the book is written in a simple code that Eugene taught me,' Edith explained, as she reached out for the notebook. 'Can I show you?'

Huber was delighted. Younger investigators like Thorwald thought he was past it, but while they failed he'd cracked Edith in no time at all. Mentioning the burned horses had been pure genius.

Edith opened the notebook. 'This column is names. There are addresses, dates. The places where we met, and details of how much money I paid them.'

Huber nodded. 'Are all of the agents paid?'

'Yes,' Edith said. 'Eugene said it's important to put everyone in the circuit on a professional footing. Agents receive money, plus chocolate, coffee, and other treats when they get dropped by parachute. It's never a lot of money, but he says it shows them that the British and Americans appreciate the risks they're taking.'

This information wasn't news, but Huber felt it was too early to push hard and risk losing Edith's confidence.

'I'll need a pen to show you how the decoding grid works,' Edith said meekly. 'Once you have that, you'll be able to understand all the entries in my book.'

Huber slid a fountain pen from inside his jacket and unscrewed the cap. Edith's hand trembled, as she wrote three tiny rows of four letters.

'I'm sorry it's so messy. Thorwald bent back my fingers,' Edith explained.

'I'm sorry to hear that,' Huber said, as he leaned closer to the page and squinted at the minuscule letters

VIVE

LAFR

ANCE

Vive la France – meaning long live France – was a popular resistance slogan. As Huber realised Edith had been stringing him along, she thrust violently upwards, spearing the Gestapo officer's neck with the pen nib.

Edith had never received formal espionage training, but Eugene gave everyone who worked for his resistance group as much knowledge as he could, and one lesson that stuck in Edith's head was the one about going for the jugular vein if you ever get a good shot at someone's neck.

As Edith tore out the pen, a fountain of blood spurted half a metre from Huber's neck. He tried to scream, but the hot liquid was already flooding the German's lungs and he gurgled as he staggered backwards and collapsed over the typist's desk.

The Gestapo compound was well guarded, but it seemed a shame not to at least try escaping. Her bare foot skidded in Huber's blood as she headed for the door. She grabbed the door handle, but the guard was on the other side, about to enter with a coffee and a bowl of water.

Edith gave the metal bowl a shove, knocking the guard back and showering him with hot water. She made a couple of steps but the guard was too fast and too strong.

'Security,' he shouted.

Edith tried stabbing the guard, but he easily twisted the bloody fountain pen out of her hand, bent her fingers back painfully then smashed her head first into the hallway wall.

As Edith slumped to the floor unconscious, two uniformed men rounded the top of the staircase, while the guard stepped into the interrogation room and was staggered by the sight of Huber splayed over the typewriter and drenched in his own blood.

'Is he dead?' someone asked from behind.

'Look at him, you idiot,' the guard shouted. 'What do you think?'

CHAPTER THREE

One of the Germans shouted at Rosie in heavily-accented French. 'Stay down,' he ordered. 'Raise your hands *slowly* into the air.'

But in darkness, with fifteen metres and a fence between herself and the enemy, Rosie had no plans for a meek surrender. She unbuckled the equipment pack strapped to her thigh before ripping a small pistol from her boot and taking two wild shots into the torch beams.

'Eugene?' Rosie shouted, her boots churning soft earth as she started to run.

Rosie's shots hadn't hit anything, but they'd had the intended effect of making the two Germans wary of climbing the fence and coming after her. The moonlight lit billowing silk from the other parachutes, and gave her a clue where to find Eugene.

'Rosie, get down,' Eugene shouted.

It was good to hear Eugene's voice, but Rosie couldn't see where it was coming from as she scrambled up a slight hill.

'Get down,' Eugene repeated.

As Rosie hit the dirt, Eugene lit up a nearby copse of trees with the muzzle blast from a small machine gun.

'Get here, now,' Eugene shouted.

'What's going on?' Rosie gasped, as Eugene shoved her back against a thick tree trunk.

'They must have known we were coming,' Eugene said. 'I know this area well and I think we've come down a few hundred metres off target. If we hadn't, we'd have been surrounded.'

Rosie felt queasy, realising that she'd have landed at the German's feet but for her last-second tug on the steering rope.

'Are you fit?' Eugene asked.

'Leg bashed a fence, but it's not much,' Rosie said.

'The machine gun blast will make 'em wary, but we've got to move before they try and encircle us. They'll have seen five parachutes, so hopefully they'll think there's more than two of us.'

Eugene kept low as he led Rosie downhill. Besides the machine gun slung around his neck, he'd strapped on a large backpack that had been dropped on one of the equipment chutes. There were plenty of torch beams and

Germans shouting orders behind them, but as Eugene predicted they showed no appetite for a head-on charge into a potential machine gun ambush.

The pair kept up running pace for twenty-five minutes over five kilometres of countryside. They finally stopped behind a brick stable to catch breath and drink from a standpipe.

'Can you carry on?' Eugene asked.

'Just sweaty,' Rosie gasped, as she splashed her face and sucked water from the palm of her hand. For the first time in her life she was grateful for the fitness she'd earned on gruelling training runs.

'I've not heard any sign of Germans, but if they had sniffer dogs at the landing site they might still track us,' Eugene said.

'What do you think happened?' Rosie asked. 'How could they have been waiting for us?'

Eugene shrugged. 'If we're lucky, a local patrol stumbled into our drop zone and arrested a couple of members of our reception team. But for all we know the Gestapo have penetrated and destroyed my entire organisation while I've been away.'

'Why didn't the Germans spread out over a wider area?' Rosie asked. 'They didn't seem well organised.'

'Probably a lot of Germans in one place, because they overestimated the accuracy of our parachute landings. Or one of my people could have given a slightly inaccurate location under torture, giving us a fighting chance of getting away.'

'But we've been getting regular radio transmissions from your people,' Rosie pointed out.

'They could have captured my wireless operators and turned them against us,' Eugene explained. 'It wouldn't be the first time the Nazis have pulled that stunt.'

'So where to now?' Rosie asked, backing up as Eugene took his turn drinking from the tap.

'We'll get to a safe house with a radio before morning.'

'Could it have been compromised?'

Eugene shook his head. 'This is my personal safe house. Nobody knows about it. We'll wash, eat and rest. Then we'll start investigating. You'll have to transmit a message home explaining what's happened. Get them to re-check all transmissions coming out of Lorient in the last seven weeks and look for anything suspicious.'

*

Edith came to as a pair of strange guards dragged her down concrete stairs. She couldn't have been out for long because the corridors of the Roman villa were in uproar. She couldn't understand German, but angry sounds the same in any language.

'Is shit-head dead?' Edith asked, as her head rolled sideways.

Neither guard answered, but one of them gripped her arm extra tight. It hurt, but it was good to know that she'd pissed the Germans off. She wanted to hum something patriotic to see if she could really set them off, but her head was thudding and her jaw felt like a block of wood.

A cell door clanked. The space was bare concrete, except for a shit-crusted bucket. The guards threw Edith at a puddled floor.

Puddle of what? Edith thought, as pain ignited in every welt and burn.

'You'll hang for killing him,' one of the guards shouted, as the cell door banged, plunging Edith into complete blackness.

Pain and anger gave Edith a shot of energy.

'You'd have hung me anyway,' she shouted back. 'At least I took one of you bastards with me.'

Edith tried to get comfortable as the guards' footsteps faded out, but she was sore in a hundred places and the floor was hard. She put her back against the wall, tucked her knees up to her chin and stretched the oversized vest over her legs to try and stay warm.

She didn't want to give the Germans the satisfaction of hearing her sob, but from this dark spot, the only thing she could see was her own death.

CHAPTER FOUR

After invading in summer 1940, the Nazis forced hundreds of thousands of French peasants to abandon countryside in newly declared military zones running the length of the Atlantic coast. Three years on, buildings were disintegrating, swathes of farmland had returned to nature, and the Nazis had inadvertently created a perfect hiding place for their enemies.

All well-run resistance groups arranged safe houses, where you could hide out, or pick up essentials before going on the run. Eugene had made his personal bolthole in a deserted two-room farmhand's cottage. It sat on a hillock six kilometres from the centre of Lorient, with good visibility in all directions and two kilometres from the nearest major road.

Besides the equipment they'd arrived with, Rosie and

Eugene could draw on a radio transmitter, weapons and tinned food stashed in the surrounding fields.

Eugene had impressed his superiors in the two years since he'd taken control of the Lorient resistance group, and he'd impressed Rosie in the two days since their disastrous parachute drop. A lot of young men would have panicked and raged, but Eugene handled troubles with the calm air of an elderly chap solving *The Times* crossword.

For the first twenty-four hours, they'd laid low, staying in the dirt-floored cottage, except for a trip outside to dig up tinned food and retrieve a radio transmitter hidden in the roof of a nearby barn.

Rosie had transmitted a short message in encrypted Morse code, explaining what had happened on arrival, and asking for a review of all messages received from the Lorient resistance circuit over the past few weeks.

On the second morning – a Tuesday – Eugene set off before sunrise. The centre of town was too risky, but he'd made a mental list of people he knew in the suburbs and surrounding villages.

Some were active members of his resistance unit, but most were relatives of members, or sympathisers: people who'd turned a blind eye, or given some small assistance during a past operation.

Rosie stayed back at the house, waiting to pick up a radio transmission. She felt uncomfortable being alone, with no certainty about when – or even if – Eugene would return. After breakfasting on apples and pears picked from trees near the back door, she tried reading Eugene's battered copy of The Communist Manifesto.

There were two schools of thought on what would happen if the Allies won the war. Communists like Eugene believed a workers' revolution would sweep Europe. Others like Captain Henderson said the communists were idiots, who should visit Russia as he'd done and see what living under communism was really like.

Rosie was undecided, but The Communist Manifesto did little to help make up her mind. The text was dense and with so much on her mind her eyes skimmed words that failed to penetrate her brain.

When it got to 11 a.m., Rosie began setting up the aerial for her radio set. Like all radio operators she had a personal sked, with fixed times to send encrypted messages, and others when she had to listen to a certain frequency and pick up orders and responses to questions.

This system was secure, but meant that getting a reply to a question took two days, or even longer if storms or German jamming disrupted the signal.

By the time Rosie had stretched the wire aerial across the field behind the cottage and given the valves in the battery-powered set a few minutes to warm up, it was time to receive.

Just as you can recognise a person's handwriting, people transmitting in Morse code have their own distinctive signature, known as a *fist*. Rosie recognised the fist of Joyce Slater as she sat on the dirt floor by the back door, with the radio set alongside, pencil and paper in her lap and a cumbersome headset over her ears.

Joyce was Espionage Research Unit B's wheelchair-bound radio operator and something of an expert in code breaking and puzzle solving. The previous evening, Rosie had received a brief message, stating that there was nothing obviously wrong with the transmissions received from Lorient over the past seven weeks, but that a specialist was doing more detailed analysis. The fact that Joyce was the specialist cheered Rosie, because nobody would do a more thorough job.

The transmission lasted four minutes. The signal deteriorated a couple of times, meaning Rosie missed a few characters, but you never got them all. After pulling in the aeriel, and switching the set off to conserve the battery, Rosie hurried towards a table and began using a printed silk square, known as a one-time-pad, to decode the message.

The news was bad. Every radio operator in occupied territory slipped three-letter security check codes into their messages. According to Joyce's analysis, Eugene's chief radio operator had missed out her security checks on three occasions, beginning on 9 May. This should have been recognised as a sign that a radio operator might have fallen into enemy hands, but apparently it had been treated as a simple omission.

From 12 May onwards, the messages from Lorient all contained the correct security check, but Joyce now believed that someone was trying to impersonate the fist of the original operator, because there was a sudden tendency to elongate the last dot or dash in each letter, which resulted in certain letters getting mixed up.

Joyce's conclusion was that the Lorient circuit's chief radio operator had been arrested on or around 9 May. When forced to send false information by her German captors, she'd tried giving a warning by missing her security checks. From 12 May onwards, the original operator had been replaced by a German radio operator who was trying to imitate her style.

*

It was late afternoon when Eugene returned. Joyce's report only confirmed what he'd learned on the street.

'Everyone's terrified,' Eugene told Rosie, as he sat on a battered chair, with an intense scowl and a drumming foot. 'The few people I found barely spoke to me. In the end I had to turn nasty to get any information at all.

'Nobody knows how it went down, but the Gestapo must have had someone working inside my organisation for a long time, because they picked everyone up in a single swoop. Madame Mercier died under torture last Friday. They picked up the girls who worked in the laundry, my engineers in the U-boat yards, a few messengers, both wireless operators and people living at the last two houses they transmitted from. As far as I can tell, Alois Clement is the only person who escaped arrest.'

'I'm sorry,' Rosie said, as she approached Eugene. 'Would you like some wine? It'll help you calm down.'

Rosie passed over an enamel mug and Eugene downed it in three quick glugs.

'They've executed more than a dozen. A couple were shot, but most were hung at the gallows outside Lorient station and left on show.'

Tears welled in Eugene's eyes as Rosie put an arm around his back.

'I recruited most of them,' Eugene said. 'One woman spat in my face. Told me her daughter was tortured and raped before they hung her. She blamed me for leading her into it.'

'You know you're not to blame,' Rosie said. 'She's upset.'

Eugene wrung his hands and sobbed. 'It'll be worth it when the workers' revolution comes,' he said, though his retreat into communist propaganda sounded unconvincing.

'Can we try and rebuild the group?' Rosie asked.

'Maybe someone can, but not me. They'll have my

description, maybe even a surveillance photograph. They've arrested so many people that it would be like starting from scratch. Probably harder, because everyone's so scared.'

'Have you got any idea who the informant was?'

'Does it even matter?' Eugene asked. 'It's not the first resistance group to collapse. I doubt it'll be the last.'

'We'll have to leave then,' Rosie said. 'Sooner the better. We'll go to Paris, make contact with the Ghost circuit and they'll find us another task or a route home.'

Eugene made a kind of hissing sound, and Rosie backed up thinking that he'd found her remark insensitive.

'I still have one friend,' Eugene said. 'A German inside Gestapo Headquarters. Because of her position I never told anyone else about her.'

Rosie looked curious. 'How did you get to know her?'

'I met her when I was working in one of Madame Mercier's bars. She's in her forties. Husband crashed his plane over Poland, two sons killed on the Eastern Front, so she's no fan of the Nazis.'

'Did you have an affair with her?'

Eugene laughed. 'I'm half her age. She's just a lonely soul who needed someone to talk to.'

'And she knows you're with the resistance?'

'For the first few months that I knew her she thought I was a barman and I just picked up random gossip from her. When her second son died, it was clear how much she hated the war and I gradually opened her up to the possibility of helping the resistance. At first I worried that she might be manipulating me, but the information she's fed us has been far too valuable to be part of any ruse.'

'But she did nothing about the arrests?'

'If it had crossed her desk, I'm sure she would have found a way to tip one of my people off,' Eugene said. 'When I met her today she told me something else. Do you remember Edith Mercier, from when you were here two years back?'

'Vaguely,' Rosie said, giving a slight nod. 'Skinny bag of bones, lived in Madame Mercier's stable block?'

Eugene nodded. 'Apparently the Gestapo got what they wanted out of everyone. The ones they didn't hang in public have already been sent to camps in Poland or Germany. But Edith not only fought off two days of torture without saying a word, but apparently managed to take one of the Gestapo's senior investigators out with a fountain pen through the jugular.'

Rosie smiled a little. 'Good for her.'

'Not really,' Eugene said. 'Apparently they're putting on a show this Saturday. They're going to hang her in front of the station, along with the mothers of two young lads who worked for me inside the submarine base.'

The thought of execution brought a tightness to

Rosie's throat. 'Were the mothers involved with the resistance?' she asked.

'Not unless you count cooking their sons' dinners. But it's a powerful deterrent. People baulk when they know that their loved ones' necks are on the line as well as their own.'

'So is there anything we can do?' Rosie asked. 'There's only two of us. We can't take on the entire Gestapo.'

'The mothers are being held at a prison in town, I don't think there's anything I'll be able to do for them. But my lady friend has promised to try getting some information on Edith.'

'So we might be able to help her?' Rosie asked uneasily.

Eugene looked uncertain. 'There's an outside chance, but it won't be easy.'

CHAPTER FIVE

The blackness took away all sense of time. Edith wasn't sure whether to expect further interrogation or execution, but for two days the only attention she got was an occasional set of eyes peering through the slot in the door. When her thirst grew, she sucked beads of condensation off the cell wall and grew tempted by the urine sloshing in the filthy bucket.

When the door swung into the cell, light blinded eyes accustomed to pitch dark.

'Up against the back wall,' a female orderly shouted.

After biting one interrogator and killing another, Edith was regarded as dangerous, despite barely having the strength to stand. The orderly set down a tray of hard biscuits and potato peel and kicked it through the door.

'Can you get me a drink?' Edith begged.

She spent an hour sucking water out of the potato peel before the door opened again. She could hardly open her eyes, but recognised Thorwald, the circle-faced officer who'd conducted the first of her brutal interrogations. He sounded like he'd had a few drinks.

'Hear you're thirsty,' he said, as a bulbous guard standing behind made a boyish snigger. 'Seeing as you put that pain-in-my-arse Huber out of his misery, I'm happy to oblige.'

The big flunky laughed again as Thorwald twisted the nozzle of a powerful hose. Edith crashed to the floor as freezing water shot her in the belly. The cold hurt, but she balled up in the back corner, desperately wringing water from her soaking T-shirt into her mouth.

When Thorwald grew bored, he used the jet to knock over the slop bucket, sending a slick of urine and shit in Edith's direction. Then he stepped into the cell and sunk his boot heel into Edith's ribs.

'You haven't got long now,' he said, as Edith shivered. 'I needed stitches in my wrist, you little bitch.'

Edith fixed him with dark eyes. 'You'll all burn in hell,' she said.

Thorwald laughed. 'I'm not sure if they're going to shoot you or hang you. Either way, I'll enjoy watching.'

*

Eugene had given in to his emotions after returning to the hideout, but quickly reverted to type and began plotting. He offered Rosie an opt out: trying to save Edith was a huge risk, and she didn't have to take part because his action was grounded in his desire to help a member of his team rather than strict operational need.

'I'm not running away,' Rosie said. 'I'll do whatever you think is best.'

Tuesday night was cold for late spring. They had coal, but couldn't burn any in case the Nazis saw or sniffed the smoke. So they laid their sleeping sacks up close and snuggled together in the dark. Rosie gently brushed Eugene's fingertips and they held hands. She half hoped he'd try kissing her, but he had a mind full of things more important than girls.

The Gestapo's desire to execute Edith and the two mothers in public before the town's busy Saturday morning market at least gave them a few days to plan. They had all the weapons and explosives they'd need, plus large sums in French francs and German Reichsmarks which Eugene had brought with him to pay bribes and wages for members of his circuit. But they needed transport and an update on the latest security situation inside Lorient.

Unlike Eugene, Rosie's face wasn't known to the Gestapo. She had an impeccable set of fake ID and travelled over the bridge into town on Wednesday morning, under pretence of food shopping.

Eugene asked her to gather as much information as

she could about the gallows set-up outside Lorient station, as well as up-to-date details on security checkpoints and bomb damage to roads on the route between Gestapo headquarters and the station.

The town Rosie encountered was utterly different to the one she'd seen two years earlier, when she'd been radio operator for the small team that helped establish the Lorient resistance group. Back then the Allies had a policy of not bombing French towns for fear of killing civilians, but this had been abandoned and Lorient's huge submarine base made it a prime target.

Over the past year Britain and America had targeted Lorient with over a thousand bomber sorties per month, including several huge raids where hundreds of planes bombed the city in a single night.

The town's vast U-Boat bunkers were built from four-metre-thick concrete that could withstand direct hits from the largest bombs. But the area around the docks, which once contained bars, clubs, restaurants and the stables where Edith lived, had been repeatedly pummelled, before succumbing to a firestorm that killed more than three hundred and left nothing behind but soot-blackened walls jutting from mounds of charred wood and bricks.

Further inland, Rosie found streets that were less badly scarred, but there was hardly anyone around and a sense of dread had descended over the entire town.

There was rubble, broken glass, thousands of Nazi warning notices and the sickening view of dead resistance fighters twisting from the gallows outside the main station.

A huge hand-painted banner at the base of the gallows had swastikas at either end and the slogan: *Disobedience = Death.*

Rosie joined a small queue and used fake ration coupons to buy bread. Eugene had told her of a black-market butcher down a grotty alleyway, but there was no sign of him. An old woman in a shawl said the butcher was dead, then sold her four eggs out of her shopping basket before vanishing over a bombsite.

'So you're a laundress?' a Kriegsmarine[2] guard asked, studying Rosie's false papers as she tried to leave town. 'A laundress with dirt under her nails.'

Rosie baulked – her hands were filthy, but a laundress would usually have clean hands and skin blanched by hot water and laundry soap. It was details like this that cost agents their lives.

'My day off,' Rosie said uneasily. 'I was digging in my mother's garden this morning.'

Luckily the guard was young and Rosie was pretty. Lustful thoughts overwhelmed any chance of him making a link between the girl before him and the female

---

[2] Kriegsmarine – Name for the German Navy during the Nazi era.

parachutist he'd been told to look out for.

'I'll be at the Underground Club from seven tonight,' the guard said. 'I'll buy you a drink if you come and find me.'

He wasn't bad looking and Rosie giggled as he handed her documents back. 'Maybe I'll take you up on that.'

The guard looked pleased with himself as Rosie strolled across the main bridge out of town.

*

Lorient Gestapo was having a quiet week – mainly because they'd just wiped out the local resistance. Word about Thorwald hosing Edith down spread through headquarters and once it became clear that Edith was too weak to fight back the bored investigators had a good deal of fun slapping her around and choking her.

Edith expected more torment when Thorwald opened her door first thing Saturday morning. Instead he gave her milk to drink, before tossing her a tatty linen dress and unmatched wooden clogs.

'Gonna miss you, Edith,' Thorwald said. 'It's been fun having you around.'

Edith flinched as Thorwald threw a fake jab at her gut.

'Just kidding.'

But the kick behind the knees was real and Edith's body slapped the stone floor.

'Boot slipped,' Thorwald teased. As Edith moaned in pain, her tormentor's laughter turned to a bark, 'Now get that dress on before you *really* piss me off.'

After swapping the filthy vest for the dress and sliding her feet into the clogs, Edith limped blindly into the light outside her cell and needed the banister to support herself as she headed upstairs.

Her legs were feeble as her feet clacked across a marble-floored lobby, full of talking and women at typewriters. Some of them turned to stare: scarcely believing this scrawny teen had caused so much trouble.

Despite her pain, Edith was determined to walk unaided. As she stepped into the villa's courtyard and took her first outdoor breath in ten days, Thorwald signed her into the custody of the guard who'd been in the interrogation room before she killed Huber. Their ride was the rear compartment of a stately old Renault, with tasselled curtains at the windows.

'Drive on,' the guard ordered.

Edith knew they were taking her to die, but felt oddly calm. She'd known they'd execute her from the moment she'd attacked Huber. After five days of torment she just wanted it over with.

As the car rattled over cobbles she wondered if her destination was a firing squad at the town prison, or a more public demise on the gallows outside the train station. She marginally preferred the idea of hanging, imagining a last glimpse at some old friends and shouting something heroic that they'd all remember her by.

But Edith knew this was a fantasy. The Gestapo didn't have the manpower to deal with large crowds, so they performed hangings at dawn and left the bodies on display for the busy Saturday market.

The car ride gave Edith's eyes their first chance to adjust to daylight since the night she'd been arrested. It was a clear morning, hinting at a summer she never expected to see. She'd felt her wounds in the dark, but seeing her damaged arms and legs made her queasy and her dress was already stained with liquids oozing from her cuts.

The town had been bombed overnight. Edith hadn't heard anything, so it had probably been a diversionary raid designed to pull German night fighters away from a bigger attack somewhere along the coast.

Despite the raid's small scale, the driver had to take a kilometre-and-a-half diversion to avoid a street blocked with rubble, and they had to squeeze past fire crews dousing a smouldering roof.

'You'd better step on it,' the guard told the driver, in German.

'What am I supposed to do?' the woman replied curtly. 'Drive over rubble?'

'You didn't need to take such a long diversion,' the guard said. 'There are much quicker ways.'

Edith had learned a little German since the invasion, but not enough to follow a rapid-fire conversation. The guard grew even more irate as the driver took a left turn into a narrow street lined with bomb-damaged shops.

'Where does this one get us?' he shouted. 'You couldn't do worse if you were *trying* to take us off course.'

The driver slammed on the brakes, then turned back and scowled at the guard.

'Fine, I'll drive,' the guard said. 'You sit back here. But keep an eye on her. She may look weak but she's a terror.'

As the guard tugged on a cord to release the rear-door catch, the driver grabbed a tatty double-action revolver from the map pocket inside the door and shot the guard in the head.

Edith gasped as warm blood spattered her arm. Fearing that the driver would go for her next, she reached for the door handle, but a girl who'd sprung out of an alleyway opened it from outside.

'I'm with Eugene,' Rosie explained. 'Can you walk? We need to move quickly.'

CHAPTER SIX

While Rosie pulled Edith from the car, Eugene walked around the front and tried to calm the trembling driver.

'You did great,' Eugene said, as he looked at his ashen-faced German friend.

'I've never shot in anger before,' she stuttered, as she reached through the driver's side window and handed Eugene the revolver she'd used to shoot the guard. 'Now, get it over with.'

The German trembled as she stepped out of the car. On the other side, Rosie was appalled by the state Edith was in, breathing the stench of urine and infected wounds as she helped the younger girl limp into a cobbled pedestrian alleyway.

'I remember you,' Edith said, though her ears rang from the gun blast and she didn't catch Rosie's reply.

'Are you ready?' Eugene asked the driver. 'Show me the back of your left hand, as if you've held it up to shield your face.'

The driver smiled awkwardly as she held the back of her palm out to one side. 'The things we get ourselves into,' she said, managing an awkward smile as Eugene lined up the old revolver.

'You're completely sure?' Eugene asked.

'I agreed to your plan, didn't I?' the woman said, as her fear turned to anger. 'They won't believe me if I come out of this unscathed.'

Eugene moved the muzzle of the pistol to within half a metre of the outstretched hand and sent a bullet straight through it. The woman screamed and spun backwards, crashing into wooden boards covering what had once been a fishmonger's shop.

'Christ,' Eugene said, feeling awful as he holstered the pistol and cocked the machine gun slung around his neck.

'Edith's *really* weak,' Rosie shouted, from the other side of the car.

'Just get her clear,' Eugene shouted back. 'She weighs nothing. I'll piggyback her.'

It was a small town and they'd already made a lot of noise. The Germans would arrive within minutes, but Eugene still needed to strafe the car with machine gun fire to make it look as if it had been ambushed by a larger gang.

He worried that the bleeding driver was still too close to the car, so he tucked his hands under her armpits and dragged her a few metres back along the cobbles. Her face was streaked with tears and he felt horrible after all she'd done to help.

'I'm sorry,' Eugene told her. 'They'll fetch an ambulance for you.'

The woman gave Eugene a half-smile half-grimace. She was losing blood and close to passing out from the pain, but he'd been careful to put the bullet into a spot where it exited cleanly and was unlikely to do lasting damage.

'Get out of here,' she groaned. 'I'm suffering for nothing if you're caught.'

Eugene opened up with the machine gun. Bullets punched the car's bodywork, pinged off the engine block, burst tyres and shattered the windscreen. Then Eugene moved to the other side of the car and made sure he got a couple of extra bullets through the guard.

Eugene knew Edith had been knocked around, but it was worse than he'd expected and he gave Rosie a concerned look as he handed her the machine gun.

'Germans will get here any second,' Eugene said, as he crouched down low. 'Edith, I need you to put your hands around my back and hold on tight. OK?'

As Edith wrapped badly bruised arms around Eugene's neck, Rosie activated three time pencil fuses pushed into blobs of plastic explosive. She pressed the biggest charge under the bullet-shredded car's wheel arch. Hopefully it would kill the first Germans who arrived to investigate.

The second charge was a coin-sized disc with a miniature two-hour fuse. She pushed it into the blood-soaked pocket of the guard. It would make a big mess in the Gestapo mortuary if they didn't find it first.

Finally Rosie dumped the third charge in the alleyway. It had a five-minute fuse and half a dozen bullets tied around it. Anyone nearby would think they were being shot at when the plastic exploded and set off the bullets.

Eugene was already moving with Edith on his back. It fell to Rosie to carry a heavy backpack of guns, ammo and explosives, along with the machine gun and her own automatic pistol.

The escape route had been carefully planned. After jogging several hundred metres down the pedestrian alleyway, they heard the first police siren as they passed through an unlocked door and slipped across the floor of an abandoned machine shop. Next they went over a mound of rubble which had crumbled satisfyingly on to one of the Kreigsmarine's patrol vehicles during a bombing raid.

A startled mother and small boy stopped dead as Eugene and his bloody passenger charged on to the pavement right in front of them.

'Pardon, Madame,' Eugene said politely.

'Lorient resistance lives,' Rosie added, before raising a single finger to her lips. 'Keep your mouths shut.'

'Vive la France,' the woman replied weakly, before tugging the arm of her baffled looking son to resume their walk.

The first explosion and attached bullets echoed a kilometre away as Eugene led Rosie into another narrow alley. They were behind an apartment block, with rats darting through ankle-deep trash at their feet.

Edith had used this route hundreds of times while delivering messages for resistance and knew what came next, but Rosie gagged from the stench as Eugene cut down six concrete steps and opened a rectangular hatch covering a low brick archway.

He had to sit Edith on a step before crawling through the arch. A stream trickled below as he went down four metal rungs into the base of the brick-built sewer.

'Feels like home,' Edith joked weakly, as she pushed off a ledge and jumped into Eugene's arms. Rosie lowered the equipment before closing the hatch and climbing down herself.

Even with Edith clamped to his back, Eugene could stand up straight. During storms the sewer was flushed by rainwater running over a metre deep into Lorient harbour, but it had been dry for the past few days, allowing the stench of untreated sewage to build up.

Eugene's torch lit the way, sending rats sploshing for cover. Rosie felt sick and tried thinking of flowers or the smell of bread cooking, but her imagination broke down every time something unmentionable squelched under her boot.

'It won't be long,' Eugene said, when he looked back and caught the nausea on Rosie's face.

But it *wasn't long* in the same way that dentists tell you something *won't hurt* before putting you through an hour of complete agony. They were going gently upwards, against the trickle of sewage. Edith seemed slightly dazed, but also happy. She reminded Eugene that it had been her idea to start using sewers to move around town.

'Not just sewers,' Eugene said, making conversation to take Rosie's mind off her nausea. 'We knocked a few cellars together. The Boche[3] would put up a security barrier and we'd go into someone's house and emerge six doors down on the other side. Or sometimes even in the next street.'

'We had some scrapes, didn't we, boss?' Edith said.

'I'd expect more scrapes before we're out of this,' Eugene said.

There was enough tenderness in the way Edith spoke to Eugene to make Rosie suspect that she had a crush on him. And if the crush wasn't quite mutual, it was still

---

[3] Boche – Offensive term for Germans.

clear that Eugene was extremely fond of her.

In several spots the sewer had worrying cracks caused by bombing, and in one place the ceiling had partly collapsed. They had no choice but to squeeze beneath it, wary of bringing the roof down.

The final two-hundred-metre section was a circular stone pipe. They had to stoop, but it was easier on the nose because no sewage ran into this section of the pipe. At its mouth, the pipe emerged into a steep-sided ditch.

After clambering up an embankment, they found themselves amidst the rusty rails and overgrown tracks of a railway depot more than two kilometres from where they'd set off.

It had been a passenger train storage and maintenance yard before the invasion, but passengers weren't encouraged to travel into the secure zone around Lorient, so there were no trains left, and the only sidings in use were a pair that had been extended half a kilometre to serve a concrete mixing plant built by the Germans.

The mixing plant was visible over the tops of trees, though dark green camouflage netting had been stretched across to make it hard to see from the air. After a full three-sixty to check that nobody was in sight, Eugene dashed across a dozen rusted and overgrown tracks, before squatting down beside a disused signalling hut.

'What's the hold-up?' Rosie asked.

Eugene sat Edith against the side of the hut. He shook his arms and wriggled his fingers, while simultaneously rubbing his boots on the rough grass to clear the filth trapped in the soles of his boots.

'My hands have gone numb,' he explained.

Rosie was straining under the weight of the pack and machine gun. She thought about setting it down, but wasn't sure she'd have the strength to lift it up again. She settled for a long drink from her water bottle, and a vigorous attempt to scrape her boots.

This was also her first proper chance to look at Edith's injuries. All the agents in Espionage Research Unit B had done first aid training, but as she was a girl Charles Henderson had also sent Rosie away for a more advanced nursing course.

As far as Rosie could tell, a broken finger and the possibility of cracked ribs were as serious as Edith's injuries got. The bad news was that the sheer number of minor cuts, burns and bruises would slow the healing process. Several were already infected and a trip through a germ-filled sewer was the last thing she'd needed.

'Sorry, but I had to put her down or I would have dropped her,' Eugene said, as he screwed the cap back on his water bottle. 'Not too far to Madame Lisle's place now.'

CHAPTER SEVEN

Madame Lisle ran a small stud farm. Unlike most peasants, she'd been allowed to remain in the Lorient military zone because petrol was in short supply and several important Kriegsmarine officers had taken a liking to the practical, well-tempered horses she had a reputation for breeding.

Lisle was in her mid-sixties. She knew Edith, having been a lifelong friend of her guardian Madame Mercier. While not a resistance member, Lisle had helped in small ways and had even harboured a radio operator who'd been forced to go on the run.

Eugene had considered approaching Madame Lisle in advance, explaining their situation and asking to buy horses for the operation. But everyone was nervous after the brutal Gestapo crackdown and you couldn't be sure how anyone would react. So while he'd checked out Madame Lisle's property two nights earlier, making sure she was still around and had the kind of animals he needed, Eugene didn't speak with her until he arrived on her doorstep with Edith on his back.

'Edith, my god!' Madame Lisle said. 'The state of you.'

Shock turned to fright as she took in Eugene and Rosie's combat gear and she moved to close her front door.

'I have Germans visiting today,' she spluttered. 'You've got to go. It's dangerous here.'

The reaction was no surprise and Eugene wedged his boot in the door. 'I'm sorry to impose.'

'You cannot!' Madame Lisle shouted.

She was angry at Eugene barging into her front hall, but Edith's wounds and bloody dress were hard for a decent person to ignore. Madame Lisle's body deflated as she took a step back.

'They've been torturing people around here too,' she said anxiously. 'Four Gestapo came to my neighbour's house. Their boy is only thirteen. He's a bit simple, but they threatened to slice off his private parts if he didn't tell them what he knew about two friends who were in the resistance.'

'I know,' Eugene said soothingly, as he helped Edith into the hallway.

'The poor boy is up each night with cold sweats and

nightmares,' Madame Lisle said.

'These are tough times,' Eugene said. 'I promise we won't stay long.'

He took no pride in using his bulk to intimidate an elderly woman, but it was a matter of survival and there was nowhere else to get horses.

'Are you here alone?' Rosie asked. 'Is anyone working on the farm?'

'I have a stable boy, but he takes Saturday off.'

'We'll just be here until dark, Madame,' Eugene said. 'We need three horses and I'll pay whatever you ask. We've got a train to catch this evening and after that you'll never see us again.'

'Do you have a bath?' Rosie asked; breathing air tinged with the smell of horse piss, while realising she ought to have removed her sewage-smeared boots before stepping indoors.

'I've a tin bath but no coal. I've been chopping wood, but my back is terrible and that Michel is hardly worth the money I pay him.'

Eugene smiled as he showed off his bicep and sensed a chance to win the old girl over.

'Big strong arms,' he said. 'I can chop all the wood you need.'

Madame Lisle was on edge. She couldn't sit still and over the next couple of hours her mood flitted between sympathy and resentment. She helped Rosie scrub

Edith in tepid water, and found some bandage and iodine for her wounds, but she snapped at Eugene and didn't thank him for chopping wood and helping her feed the horses.

The German visitors were due at eleven and Madame Lisle led them upstairs. The first floor was the home's single bedroom. Photos of pet dogs and faded rosettes from horse shows were pinned around the dressing table.

While Eugene squatted by a small sash window, Edith lay on the bed as Rosie practised her nursing skills, cleaning the dirt out of wounds and putting in a couple of stitches with sterile thread from her first aid pack.

'I could shoot him dead from here,' Eugene said quietly, as he peered down at a horse trotting on the cobbles behind the house.

The grey-haired German in the saddle wore brown riding boots and a dark blue Kriegsmarine admiral's uniform. He was accompanied by the naval rating who worked as his assistant, while a driver waited in the open-topped Mercedes out front.

Edith hissed with pain as Rosie dabbed dark purple iodine fluid into a deep cigar burn on her shoulder blade.

'Sorry,' Rosie said. 'The wounds down your legs are already badly infected. I need to seal these up to stop it spreading.'

'I know,' Edith said, as a tear streaked down her face. 'I'm trying to keep quiet but it really hurts.'

Eugene watched as the German took the horse on a trot across the cobbles and the surrounding paddock. He was clearly an expert rider and when he jumped off, he gave Madame Lisle an enormous smile.

'You breed such beautiful animals,' the admiral told her, as he smiled under his great walrus moustache. 'The price as agreed, in Reichsmarks. Shall we go indoors to settle up?'

Eugene ducked below the window frame as the German turned back towards the house.

'Madame seems awfully friendly with the admiral,' Eugene noted warily.

Rosie dismissed the thought. 'He's an officer. He loves horses, of course she likes him.'

'Madame Lisle's horses *are* beautiful,' Edith said, sounding like she was a little bit out of it. 'If I ever got rich, they'd be the first thing I'd buy.'

Edith was weak and her whole body ached from being tortured, but after eating, drinking and washing she felt human for the first time in days. And the chance of life, after facing execution, gave her a sense of elation.

'I don't think this floor is very thick,' Eugene said, as he heard Madame Lisle and the officer chatting in the kitchen directly below. 'Put the iodine down and keep still for a bit. We can't risk another yelp.'

Downstairs, the admiral began counting out his money.

'Oh, don't be silly,' Madame Lisle said. 'I trust your word as an officer.'

The admiral laughed.

'When the Gestapo buy horses, I count *their* money,' Madame Lisle said. 'Those thugs practically steal them, the prices they force me to accept.'

'They're not gentlemen,' the admiral said, speaking in stilted but polite French. 'We'd have none of this trouble with resistance if the French people had been treated correctly. But what do I know? You and I hail from a gentler era.'

Madame Lisle gave a friendly laugh, but as that noise faded Eugene thought he heard the clatter of a diesel engine.

'Sounds like a truck,' Eugene whispered.

He crept across the bedroom to hear better, but there was no window overlooking the front of the house.

'Maybe it's to take the horse away,' Rosie suggested.

'You can't take a horse in a regular truck,' Edith said. 'You'd frighten it to death.'

Rosie's heart accelerated as Eugene picked up the machine gun resting on top of his backpack and edged towards the door.

'How can anyone know we're here?' Rosie whispered.

'A million ways,' Eugene said. 'If someone saw us going into the sewer they'd guess we'd end up near here. Or someone saw us coming out of the pipe and took cover. Or we passed someone working in a field.'

Edith was naked and Rosie threw over one of her own dresses. 'Get that on in case we have to run.'

As Rosie grabbed her boots and pushed her feet into them, Madame Lisle opened the front door. Out back, Eugene saw the admiral's assistant being startled by two armed Gestapo officers coming around the side of the cottage.

'They're blocking our exits,' Eugene said, as he took the safety off his pistol and threw the machine gun over his shoulder.

Rosie didn't have a weapon handy, so Eugene threw her the aged revolver that his Gestapo friend had used to shoot Edith's guard.

'Stay with Edith,' Eugene said. 'Don't come down unless I shout.'

The admiral was surprised to see Gestapo and shouted with the tone of someone used to being in charge. 'What the *devil* is going on here?'

'Gestapo business,' someone shouted back. 'Stand aside, these premises are to be searched.'

Training kicked in the instant Eugene and Rosie knew they were facing hostiles. They were trapped upstairs, so they had to make the first move.

Eugene rushed through the bedroom door, rounded the top of the stairs and aimed downwards. His first two shots hit the admiral in the back and as he crumpled another blast hit the Gestapo officer coming through the front door.

As Madame Lisle covered her ears and hurried down the hallway towards her kitchen, Rosie scrambled to the upstairs window. The old revolver wasn't the most accurate weapon and her first shot skimmed over the head of a Gestapo man heading for the back door.

The bullet disturbed the admiral's new horse, dragging the assistant holding her reins off his feet and bowling another Gestapo man over. As two more Gestapo officers scrambled away from the bucking horse, Rosie took advantage of the distraction.

Her first shot with the elderly revolver had pulled to the left, so she made a slight correction to her aim and popped off two shots. One Gestapo man was shot clean through the heart, the second was knocked unconscious by the bullet hitting his metal helmet square on.

With surprise still on his side, Eugene moved towards the front door. He shot the admiral's driver, then sprayed a dozen bullets into the admiral's Mercedes and the truck the Gestapo had arrived in. One Gestapo man was injured, while two more shot wildly towards the cottage as they ran for cover behind the car.

The machine gun needed reloading, but before Eugene backed into the hallway he ripped a grenade off his belt and lobbed it into the open-topped car. As he attached a fresh stick of bullets to his gun, Eugene heard someone shooting behind him.

It was the Gestapo man that Rosie had failed to stop coming in through the back door. Madame Lisle had grabbed a knife and sat cowering under her kitchen table. As the German passed without seeing her, he aimed his rifle at Eugene's back.

'Dirty son of a pig!' Madame Lisle shouted, as she plunged a jagged-edged bread knife deep into the German's calf.

The German squeezed the trigger as he fell, shooting Eugene in the right buttock. Nobody heard Eugene's excruciating howl because it coincided with the grenade exploding. The blast sent chunks of shrapnel in all directions, some of the hot lumps puncturing the uniforms of retreating Gestapo men.

Up in the bedroom, Rosie acted clinically, using her last bullet to shoot the admiral's assistant through the chest as he got up after being bowled over by the horse. Edith was weak, but she'd managed to open Eugene's backpack, pulling out a leather holster which held three grenades and an automatic pistol.

'Thanks,' Rosie said, throwing down the useless revolver before pocketing the grenades and taking the pistol. 'Get your dress on. Be ready to leave.'

Rosie's ears rang from the grenade blast, but she was more unsettled by the sudden outbreak of silence.

'Eugene?' she shouted, as she rounded the top of the stairs.

He was slumped against the wall of the narrow hallway, with his right leg twisted awkwardly under his body. The bullet had entered his buttock at an upwards angle and exited close to his belly button, taking his bladder and a huge chunk of his lower intestine with it.

The burst stomach left Eugene's pipe work spattered up the wall, and a smell of his ruptured bowels mingling with the gun smoke in the air. He was still conscious, and while Rosie's first thought was to help him, Eugene gestured frantically down the hallway.

The German who'd shot Eugene had fallen on his face with a kitchen knife sticking out of his calf. Madame Lisle had shown great agility for an elderly woman, jumping on the German's back, ripping out the knife and thrusting it back towards his stomach. But the soldier was much stronger. He'd gashed his right hand badly as he grabbed the blade plunging towards him. Now Rosie watched him turn the knife around and go for Madame Lisle's throat.

She was afraid of shooting the unfamiliar pistol and taking out Madame Lisle by mistake. She also had no idea who was still alive outside, so she feared a bullet in the back as she charged down the hallway.

Madame Lisle screamed as Rosie stepped over the blood pooled around the dead admiral. She took aim at the German. The bullet cavitated the top of his head, and took a huge chunk from the back of his skull as it exited. Rosie couldn't have aimed any better, but the German's final spasm had driven the kitchen knife deep into Madame Lisle's throat.

Lisle was losing blood fast. Rosie wanted to help, but more shots ripped along the hallway. As she took cover by backing into the kitchen, Eugene swung around with his machine gun.

He'd fixed the fresh clip on to the machine gun half a second before he'd been hit and he opened up, hitting a pair of Gestapo men coming across the front lawn towards the house.

Then it all went quiet again. Madame Lisle was past saving, so Rosie dashed back towards Eugene.

'Don't hang around,' he said.

Rosie tried to pull up Eugene's shirt to get a look at his wound, but he blocked her with a trembling hand.

'Get out of here. I'm going to die.'

Eugene was fiddling in a blood-soaked area around his belt. She realised he was going for his L-pill, which packed a fatal dose of cyanide.

'They might be able to keep me alive for a while,' he said. 'Taking this makes sure.'

Rosie straightened up, breathed deep and slumped against the wall in a state of complete exhaustion. The scene was carnage: gore splattered up the wall, boots swilling in blood. Part of Rosie felt blind panic. She had to get her mind back in focus.

Edith shouted weakly from upstairs. 'Hello?'

Just because it had gone quiet didn't mean that all the bad guys were dead. The vehicles out front were both destroyed. There were horses to escape on, but it would take time to saddle them up and sort Edith out. Time she might not have . . .

Rosie looked up the stairs and saw Edith in the bedroom doorway, wearing the dress but no shoes. 'I've got to go check the outside,' Rosie said urgently.

Everyone in front of the house seemed dead, and although Eugene was dying he was still poised with the machine gun in case something came out of the bushes.

Rosie went to the back of the cottage. She rolled the dead German off Madame Lisle's corpse and snatched his rifle, knowing it would do better than a pistol or a machine gun if she had to shoot at someone in the bushes.

She reloaded as she peeked out of the back door. The paddock looked idyllic, though the horses in the stable blocks on either side had been disturbed by the noise. There was no sign of the admiral's horse, though its path was clear from the chunks torn out of a hedge.

There were four dead Germans out back, but the one Rosie shot on the helmet was just knocked out. It seemed wrong to kill a man who was unconscious, but he could come round at any moment and she didn't have time to mess about tying him up.

After shooting him through the heart with the rifle, Rosie made a complete circuit of the cottage, keeping close to the walls in case one of the Gestapo men was hiding out in the bushes. Besides the admiral and his two companions, Rosie counted eight dead Gestapo.

Back in the hallway, Eugene was losing the fight. He'd gone much paler and tried saying something, but all he could do was shake and make a long croak. But his eyes showed Rosie his problem: his grip was weak and his lethal pill floated in the blood pooled between his legs

'They can't take me,' he finally muttered.

Rosie doubted Eugene would survive more than a few minutes, but despite being in agony he seemed anxious about being captured. She crouched down and picked the rugby-ball-shaped pill out of the blood.

'Do you want it?' Rosie asked, as tears smudged her vision.

Eugene parted his lips. His face felt cold as Rosie balanced the pill between his teeth and then pushed up his lower jaw to crush it.

'I let you down,' Eugene croaked.

As Rosie took the machine gun and made half a step back, the cyanide paralysed Eugene's breathing and his body began convulsing from a heart attack.

CHAPTER EIGHT

Rosie felt like breaking down. At least fourteen people had died in four crazy minutes and it might have overwhelmed her if she hadn't had to concentrate on helping Edith.

'I can't carry you far,' Rosie said. 'I'm not as strong as Eugene.'

Rosie stripped her equipment pack down to essentials: three grenades, pistol, machine gun, her ID, Madame Lisle's bandages and iodine plus the first aid kit, money, maps, compass, some food and refilled water canteens.

Rosie helped Edith down the stairs, then piggybacked her a dozen paces through the gore in the hallway and left her sitting on the doorstep at the back of the kitchen. There still might be Gestapo in the bushes, so Rosie didn't hang about as she belted across to the stables, with Eugene's blood-crusted machine gun slung over her shoulder.

There was a saddle room at one end of the stables, but Rosie had only ridden a few times and had never prepared a horse herself.

Which way round did a saddle go? How tightly? How would she know which horses were good for riding? Should they take one horse or two?

'I've got no clue,' Rosie confessed, once she'd dashed back to Edith. 'Do you think you can help?'

Edith had found a pair of Madame Lisle's rubber boots by the back door. They were slightly too big, but made walking on her badly scarred feet more bearable. She moved across to the stables with an arm around Rosie's back, but the sight and smell of horses seemed to rejuvenate her.

Friendly heads poked over the stable door and Edith gave two animals handfuls of fresh grass to keep them calm as she led them out and talked Rosie through fitting the saddles.

'You're sure you're OK to ride?' Rosie asked. 'It might get hairy.'

'If I can cling on to Eugene, I can ride a horse,' Edith said.

It took nearly ten minutes to get the horses ready. Edith asked for her own pistol and Rosie considered running back to the house to get one, but they heard a car approaching and cars only meant Germans, because civilians in the military zone weren't allowed petrol.

After giving Edith a lift into the stirrup, Rosie mounted her horse as voices sounded fifty metres away, around the front of the house.

'We were ambushed,' a German was saying. 'At least half-a-dozen guns blazing at us.'

Rosie gave her horse a little kick and said gee-up, but the animal regarded this with contempt.

'Not like that,' Edith said. 'A little higher up, and give it more of a snap.'

Rosie looked back anxiously, half expecting men to come running around the house aiming rifles while her horse stood rigid.

'Gee-up.'

This time Rosie kicked a little too hard and the horse shot off in an indignant gallop, almost knocking Rosie off backwards.

Edith was alarmed as Rosie's horse stormed off. 'Hard on the reins,' she yelled. 'Got to show her who's boss.'

Rosie pulled the reins more in hope than expectation. The horse came to a complete halt, but Edith had galloped up alongside, and the presence of Edith's horse seemed to act as a calming influence on Rosie's. After their jerky restart, the two animals began trotting side by side.

As the newly arrived Germans took in the full extent

of the carnage inside and around the house, the two teenagers vanished out of sight behind the stable block, then down a slight hill and on to a footpath that ran between the surrounding fields.

'We'll put a few kilometres in, then find a spot where we can hide out until dark,' Rosie said.

'I know all the tracks around here,' Edith answered, as Rosie noticed that blood was already seeping into the back of Edith's clean dress. 'But we should pick up the pace, are you ready for a gallop?'

*

Rosie never got comfortable in the saddle, but the pair rode for thirty minutes without incident. They skirted around villages to avoid being seen, but it was daylight and they still passed horses, carts, and even a gang of prisoners repairing roads, under the eye of grizzled French guards.

Fortunately there were no telephones out here and the local Gendarmes[4] didn't have radios. So unless they encountered men dispatched specifically to look for them, they'd be long gone by the time anyone realised that they'd seen Lorient's most wanted ride by.

When they reached the abandoned farms of the buffer zone, they found a stream where the horses could drink and settled down in the grass.

---

[4] Gendarmes – French civilian police officers.

Rosie was shocked by how much Edith was sweating when she helped her down off the horse. Edith drank water and nibbled some pieces of fruit, but she doubled over and vomited within minutes of eating them.

'Let it all come out,' Rosie said, as she held Edith's hair back.

'I can't get sick now,' Edith said, clutching her bony fists with frustration. 'I've got to fight it.'

Rosie tried to keep cheerful for Edith's sake, but her weakness was no surprise. Edith had barely eaten in a week and she'd spent days on a filthy cell floor while covered with open wounds. Rosie suspected that the vomiting and sweats were signs of an infection spreading into Edith's bloodstream.

'I feel dizzy,' Edith said. Then she sobbed. 'I was ready to die. No offence, but you shouldn't have tried to rescue me.'

Rosie didn't reply, but largely agreed. Eugene had known that the rescue was a huge risk. Perhaps if she'd stood up to him he'd be alive right now and so would Madame Lisle.

As the afternoon wore on, Rosie wiped Edith down to keep her cool and tried getting her to drink as much as possible. Eventually Edith fell asleep. After pulling Edith into the shade, Rosie pulled off her own boots and socks and spent a long time sitting with her feet in the stream.

Rosie kept vigilant for search parties as she washed the

outside of her boots and wiped the blood off the machine gun. Then she took the map of their escape plan from her backpack and felt miserable as she studied markings and notes made in Eugene's handwriting.

They'd planned to take photographs and make up a false identity for Edith while at Madame Lisle's house, then set off as soon as it started getting dark. They would then have ridden fifteen kilometres across country to a single-track railway which supplied coal to a power station at Moelan sur Mer.

War played havoc with train schedules, but Eugene had somehow confirmed that the power station was still operational and fed by a nightly delivery of coal. The train didn't stop, but was easily boarded when it slowed to a crawl on a hilly section of track near the village of Lisloch.

Eugene's plan had involved riding the coal train fifty or sixty kilometres to wherever it got to at daybreak. Then they'd have used their wits to make their way to Paris, but they'd hoped to find themselves in a lightly-policed rural area with immaculate documentation and all their major headaches behind them.

Rosie had no idea if she'd be able to get Edith aboard the slow-moving train on her own, she had no way of making up false documents and with a fever setting in, Edith urgently needed to see a doctor.

*

Rosie felt too edgy to eat, but she forced herself to nibble fruit and cheese as it grew dark.

'Time to wake up,' she said gently, as she crouched over Edith.

The skinny body had its head resting on Rosie's backpack. She nudged Edith several times, but nothing happened. Rosie was wary of inflicting pain and there was hardly any part of Edith that wasn't injured, but after a third nudge Rosie grabbed Edith's shoulder and rolled her on to her back.

'We have to leave or we'll miss the train.'

As Edith's body moved, Rosie felt an extraordinary blast of heat. Edith was like a little furnace. Her dress was soaking, and while Rosie didn't have a medical thermometer it didn't take one to see that Edith was burning up. She put her thumb against Edith's eyebrow and slowly raised the lid. The pupil reacted to the sudden change in light but she didn't wake up.

Rosie found the pulse in Edith's neck and counted fourteen beats in six seconds. You'd expect a hundred and forty beats per minute if you'd jogged a couple of kilometres, but Edith's heart rate should have been under half that after four hours' sleep.

Rosie felt overwhelmed by the responsibility that had fallen on her. The trickling stream was deafening and trees seemed to loom over her like ghosts.

CHAPTER NINE

The railway line bisected the landscape, making it easy for Rosie to find in the dark. She'd taken a single horse and ridden slowly. She was lucky not to sight trouble, because it would have been impossible to go faster with Edith slumped unconscious over the saddle behind her.

Just after midnight a fully-laden coal train began shaking the ground Rosie sat on. It wound down the hillside at more than twenty kilometres an hour, curving around a large S, designed to ease the gradient when it climbed back up.

Rosie squatted as close to the track as she dared. She'd imagined square-sided trucks like the wagons on her brother's clockwork train set, but much to her relief, these wagons carried coal in V-shaped pivot-mounted skips, enabling them to be emptied rapidly by tipping. At one end each wagon had a metal platform used to access and maintain the mechanism.

'I'm so thirsty,' Edith said weakly.

Rosie almost missed her voice over the clattering train, but dived into the trackside bushes where she was lying and allowed her to drink greedily from a canteen.

'You're doing great,' Rosie lied, stroking Edith's hair as she raised her head to stop her choking.

'I'm seeing funny shapes,' Edith said.

'It's the fever. You're delirious.'

The train seemed endless and by the time fifty coal wagons passed Edith had drifted back into unconsciousness.

Rosie had no idea how long it would take for the train to offload and steam back, but Eugene had expected it well before sunrise. She sat beside Edith, cradling her head and envying the carefree horse munching grass a few metres away.

It was near 3 a.m. when Rosie heard the first rumblings of the train heading back. Edith couldn't hold on, so Rosie aimed her bag on to the platform of a passing wagon, then grabbed Edith off the grass and needed all the muscle she'd built up in training to sling her over her shoulder.

Jumping aboard was precarious, but Rosie got a foot on a metal step and steadied herself by grabbing a metal rung used for climbing inside the container. After lying

Edith out on the metal platform and tucking her under the angled side of the coal skip to make her invisible, Rosie crawled along the ledge at the side of the wagon to retrieve her backpack from two wagons up.

She had no problem getting there, but the train crested the hilltop as she turned back. Noise and vibration grew as the train picked up speed. The pack made it hard to balance and she had to pull herself in desperately as overhanging branches thrashed the side of the wagon.

When the ordeal was over, her heart was belting. She was black with coal dust, and even more alarmingly the increased vibration had moved Edith's body several centimetres, leaving her head poking off the metal platform.

'Quite an adventure,' someone said.

Rosie jolted with fright as she saw two white eyeballs peeking over the end of the skip in the next wagon.

'You're better off using the foot holds,' a boyish voice explained. 'Climb through the skip and out at the other end.'

Rosie went for her pistol, making the eyes panic and drop back into the skip. 'How'd you get here?' she yelled. 'What are you after?'

'How'd you get a gun?' the voice asked back. 'Don't shoot me. I was trying to help.'

Rosie thought before answering. Someone this young was probably no threat, but unlikely to be travelling the middle of the night without company.

'What are you doing here?' Rosie asked.

'Nabbing coal,' the boy explained, his voice now echoing from deep in the skip.

'Are you alone?'

The boy considered this question for a few moments before answering. 'I'm alone. Will you shoot me if I stick my head back up?'

'Not unless you try something,' Rosie said.

But she felt vaguely ridiculous saying this, because the coal-black creature that swung its leg over the side of the truck was ten years old at most.

'I saw you jump on,' the boy said. 'Never hang off the sides like that. We're coming up to some tunnels. They'd have caught your luggage and minced you.'

Rosie nodded as the boy landed on the platform with a clank. He wore tattered trousers and boots held together with twine.

'I'm Justin,' the boy said, as he studied Edith. 'Your friend looks bad.'

'She's sick,' Rosie said. 'Are you running away, or something?'

'I would if I didn't have a mum and three sisters to feed,' Justin said. 'This is my work. I sneak into a loaded wagon on the way out. On the way back I work along all the skips, collecting the lumps of coal. Every wagon has a few bits that don't get tipped out.'

'Quite a scheme,' Rosie said.

'I can sell you coal if you want it,' the boy said, as he scratched his matted hair. 'I do OK, but the dust makes you itch like a *bastard*.'

Edith laughed, because it was kind of cute hearing this little lad swear. 'I don't need coal.'

'I could swap coal for food if you haven't got money.'

'You must come from somewhere,' Rosie said.

'Course,' the boy said. 'But you didn't tell me your name when I told you mine, which is being evasive.'

He made *evasive* sound important. As if it was the new word he'd learned in school the week before.

'I'm Rosie,' Rosie said, though she realised she should have lied. 'Do you ever get caught?'

'Loadsa times,' Justin said. 'The driver and guard let me be, but the railway police bash me up if they catch me.'

'Sounds rough.'

'Tunnel,' Justin said urgently, before taking a quick breath and burying his face inside his jacket.

Rosie didn't understand why until they plunged into pitch darkness. The blast of steam from the engine billowed around the tunnel, and air currents blew up a storm of coal dust off the wagons. She began coughing, then made things worse by rubbing her eye with a blackened finger.

Justin sounded exhilarated when they came out. 'You've gotta take a deep breath when you see a tunnel. It's actually fun once you get used to it.'

Rosie didn't see the appeal as she hunted blindly for her water and blinked the grit out of her eye. Then she remembered Edith and turned anxiously to see what the tunnel had done to her.

'Did your friend fall off the horse or something?' Justin asked.

Rosie couldn't tell whether the dust had affected Edith. But she was starting to realise that Justin might be more than an irritation.

'So where do you get off the train?' Rosie asked.

'She needs a doctor,' Justin said, as he went down on one knee and studied Edith more closely.

'I know she does.'

'You've got a gun,' Justin said. 'She's got whip marks on her arms, and that looks like a cigarette burn on her neck. Did you kidnap her?'

Rosie sounded irritated. 'Answer my question. Where do you get off the train?'

Justin smirked. 'You're not answering my questions either.'

Rosie put her hand on the gun. 'That's because I've got this and you haven't.'

'I suppose that's true,' Justin said, as he sat down on the platform cross-legged. 'I get off the train near my house. There's a water tower where the train has to stop and fill up. I live right by it.'

'She's going to die if I don't get her to a doctor quickly. Is there a doctor near where you live?'

'You can walk to the doctor in town.'

'She doesn't have documents,' Rosie said. 'Are there checkpoints?'

Justin backed up a little, scared, impressed and confused all at once. 'You're on the run from the Boche, aren't you? Tunnel coming up in a second!'

This time Rosie put a wet rag over Edith's nose and mouth before pulling her jacket up over her face. This tunnel was longer than the first and when they emerged there was a blacked-out town silhouetted in a valley below the tracks.

'I can pay if you help me find a doctor,' Rosie said, as she showed a ten-franc note.

Justin looked offended. 'You think I'd take money for helping a sick person?'

'And is your doctor a good person? Can we trust him?'

'Her,' Justin said, as he shrugged. 'I think she's OK. I went once when I went deaf and had to get my ear syringed. Mum was broke, but the doctor said pay something when you can. Have you ever had your ear syringed? It's *so* loud, cos they're shooting water right in your lughole.'

Justin's mix of street-smarts and boyishness lightened

Rosie's mood after bleak hours with nothing but dark thoughts for company. She reached into her backpack and passed over a stick of high-energy chocolate.

'Suck it or it'll break your teeth,' Rosie said. 'It's survival rations. Like they give to RAF pilots, in case they get shot down.'

Justin beamed as he peeled the foil off the chocolate and tried biting a corner off.

'Bloody hell,' Justin said, before bursting out laughing. 'Tunnel!'

CHAPTER TEN

Apart from nightly rides on the coal train, Justin didn't travel much. When Rosie quizzed him about where they'd be getting off he gave the name of somewhere that wasn't on her map and said that the local farmers sold goods at a market in Rennes. But he'd never been there himself, so he wasn't sure how long the journey took.

Still, anywhere near Rennes was well out of the military zone. Rosie had to take a punt on finding Edith a doctor who wouldn't report her to the Gestapo wherever she wound up, which made sticking with Justin at least as good a choice as any other.

It was near dawn as the train left its single track and merged into the regular railway. Rosie hoped they'd soon pass a station, which would give her a better fix on her location, but within a minute the wagons shuddered to a halt and the brawny steam engine began refilling its water tank.

'You've gotta run in case there's railway cops,' Justin explained quietly. 'Go down the embankment. I'll meet you at the bottom.'

Water gushed from the tower twenty wagons ahead as Rosie lobbed her backpack through trackside bushes. While she bent to pick Edith up, Justin had clambered inside a coal skip and began hurling out sacks, each filled with as much coal as he could lift.

The embankment was too steep to navigate with Edith over her shoulder, so Rosie slid down on her bum, left Edith at the bottom then went back for her pack. When she returned, two little girls were dragging coal sacks over a weed patch, while the youngest – who looked about three – stood with hands on hips gawping at Edith.

'Don't touch,' Justin said, before dumping his smallest sack of coal at the little girl's feet. 'Drag that back to the house, before I kick you up the bum.'

The girl knew the threat was a joke and poked her tongue out at her big brother.

Rosie picked Edith back up, while Justin burdened himself with Rosie's pack and dragged a coal sack with each hand. Home was a terrace of three tatty cottages, less than fifty metres from the tracks.

'Don't leave me behind,' the tiny girl ordered, making Justin look back and blow a big fart noise at her.

'I'm telling Mummy!'

'Tell her,' Justin said cheerfully. 'I don't care.'

The coal sacks were piled in the hallway as Rosie entered through the back door. A huge hole in the roof sent dawn light down a staircase sprouting moss, and Rosie noted that the three girls looked exactly like their big brother.

'Dump Edith in the armchair,' Justin told Rosie, then grabbed his oldest sister, who was eight. 'Agnes, run into town and get Dr Blanc.'

'Say that Justin is hurt,' Rosie added, as she put Edith down. 'Don't say anything about us being here.'

Agnes looked at her brother for confirmation.

'Do *exactly* what she says,' Justin said firmly.

'Who are they?' the girl asked warily. 'What will Mummy say?'

Justin pointed at Edith, then raised his hand threatening a slap. 'That girl could die. Just get Dr Blanc, and *don't* let that nurse fob you off, even if you have to bite her.'

As Justin knelt down to unlace his boots, he told middle sister Aimée to fetch him a bucket of water to wash with, then told little sister Belle that she was a good girl for helping bring in the coal, and gave her a square of the high-energy chocolate.

'Suck don't bite, and *don't* tell your sisters,' Justin said.

He then moved in to kiss Belle, but she backed off

yelling, 'You'll make me dirty!'

Rosie spoke as Belle squatted beside Edith's chair and took an experimental lick of the chocolate. 'Does your mother work?'

'There's a small German garrison not far from here,' Justin said, sounding embarrassed. 'Mum cleans for them, and does laundry and stuff. But she doesn't *like* them.'

'She says they're pigs,' Belle said.

Justin turned and spoke sharply. 'Belle, what have I told you about repeating things? If someone outside hears that you could get Mummy into trouble.'

Aimée was at the back door with a bucket of water, but Justin pointed Rosie towards it.

'Ladies can wash first.'

Aimée put her hand over her mouth and giggled. 'You being polite. That's a first.'

'I'm always polite,' Justin said.

'You never say *ladies first* to us.'

'Because you're not ladies,' Justin snapped back. 'Make yourself useful, cut us some bread.'

'I'm not your servant,' Aimée said, but still went into the kitchen to do it.

Rosie had given her only spare dress to Edith, so she couldn't change out of her combat gear after wiping down with cold water and a grubby cloth. While Justin took a more thorough wash, Rosie sprinkled Edith with cool water, took the farm boots off her feet and unbuttoned the back of her dress.

Dr Blanc arrived as Justin came back inside dressed in his good clothes. These were free of coal dust, but still appeared to have been worn through a great deal of muddy play. The doctor was a barrel of a woman, with a huge chest and bright red nose. She grunted when she saw Justin in perfect health, but forgot the deception the instant she saw Edith.

'When did she become feverish?' Dr Blanc asked, as she pulled down Edith's dress.

'Yesterday afternoon,' Rosie said.

'Christ, did they use her as a punching bag?' Dr Blanc said furiously. 'Someone did a half decent job patching her up. Was that you?'

Rosie nodded and half smiled. 'I did a six-week nursing course.'

'Good, you can give me a hand. I need her lying face down on the floor. She's running a very high temperature, but she's not sweating which means she's critically dehydrated. I need clean water, salt and sugar if you have any.'

Justin ushered Belle out of the room as Rosie swung Edith from chair to floor.

'I want to see,' Belle moaned.

Dr Blanc made heavy work out of kneeling down. As she pulled a bottle and length of rubber tubing from her leather bag, Justin fetched salt and water, while Rosie took the two sugar lumps from her emergency ration tin.

While Rosie shook the solution in the bottle, Dr Blanc pushed the rubber tube up Edith's bum.

'It's not pretty, but it's the quickest way to get water and minerals back in her system.'

Justin backed away looking queasy, while his three sisters intermittently peeked around the doorway. When the rehydration procedure was complete, Dr Blanc began washing Edith's body with cool water.

'Is she going to be OK?' Rosie asked warily.

'Did she have any health problems before this happened?' the doctor asked.

'None that I know of,' Rosie said.

'We'll keep her cool and hydrated,' Dr Blanc said. 'She's young and healthy, but there's nothing I can do about the infection. It's a matter of keeping her comfortable and waiting to see if she has the strength to fight it off.'

*

Dr Blanc hurried off once she'd done all she could to help Edith. Rosie couldn't travel outside in combat gear, so she negotiated the purchase of a shabby dress belonging to Justin's mum, for a price that would easily buy two replacements on the black market.

After she'd shared Justin's breakfast of egg, fake coffee and coarse black bread, a horse and buggy organised by

Dr Blanc arrived. Joseph the driver was the doctor's handsome son and he carried Edith outside and laid her out over straw in the back of the buggy.

Rosie felt uneasy putting so much trust in strangers, but Dr Blanc seemed reliable, and with Edith fighting for life there was little choice.

'Where are we heading?' Rosie asked, as the horse moved down an unfinished path between tightly spaced cottages.

'To my brother's house,' Joseph said. 'There's a lot of families around here. They're decent people, but the right information in a Gestapo officer's ear can earn your husband or son repatriation from Germany, so it's best not to waft temptation under their noses.'

'What about checkpoints?'

'We'd have to be very unlucky,' Joseph said. 'There's nothing of strategic value around here. You can go a month without seeing a German.'

'Justin said there was a garrison.'

'More of a geriatric ward,' Joseph said. 'You only get posted out here if you're no use anywhere else.'

'So does your brother have family?' Rosie asked.

'He's an army doctor.'

'A prisoner?' Rosie asked.

Joseph nodded, and Rosie's paranoid side linked the fact he was a prisoner with the comment about rewarding informants by sending prisoners home.

'I was studying medicine in Le Mans, but the Gestapo shut my academy down after a student protest,' Joseph explained, as the buggy picked up speed. 'Now I'm living out of sight, hoping the Compulsory Labour Service doesn't track me down and pack me off to Germany.'

'Aren't doctors exempt?' Rosie asked, as they turned on to a narrower track.

'But I'm not a doctor yet. And even doctors get sent to Germany. They've got more wounded soldiers than German doctors can care for. And what about you?'

'What about me?' Rosie asked defensively.

Joseph laughed noisily. 'Well, there must be a good story. Not many girls your age turn up on a coal train, with a machine gun in their backpack and an unconscious friend who's been tortured half to death.'

They both glanced behind as Edith's body rumbled.

'That'll be water coming back out the way it went in,' Joseph explained.

'I'm with the resistance,' Rosie said. 'But frankly, the less you know, the safer you'll be.'

CHAPTER ELEVEN

Joseph Blanc lived in a large brick house that belonged to his older brother. It was several kilometres from the railway and surrounded by farmland.

The house had the rare luxury of a coal-fired water heater and after a hot bath Rosie used the water to wash out her underclothes. But she kept her pistol within reach, because she'd been taught never to trust anyone and people who showed kindness were among the most likely to betray you.

Being alone with Edith had been frightening, and Rosie was relieved seeing her in a proper bed in an upstairs bedroom. Joseph repeated the hydration and once in a while they wiped Edith down with cool water, but the unconscious body gave no clues about the battle being fought by her immune system.

As Rosie napped, Joseph cooked chicken and potatoes. It was the best thing Rosie had eaten since landing in France and they shared a bottle of wine over the meal. When Dr Blanc arrived at the house shortly before 9 p.m. she found the two of them sitting on a rug playing draughts.

Although the wine made her a touch drunk, Rosie soon found herself in serious conversation with the buxom doctor.

'I have a resistance contact in Paris,' Rosie explained, as she sat across from the doctor, who was eating chicken leftovers with bread and cheese. 'We didn't get a chance to prepare identity documents for Edith before the Germans stormed in, and I could only carry the absolute essentials after Eugene was shot. The blank identity documents and miniature camera were in his pack.'

'So you want to leave Edith here and travel to Paris?' Dr Blanc asked.

'Tomorrow, if that's acceptable,' Rosie said.

'I telephoned the station and got details of tomorrow's trains,' Joseph added.

Dr Blanc nodded. 'I can see the sense in that. There's nothing you can do to help Edith by being here.'

'I expect I'll be gone for two or three days,' Rosie said. 'I'm not short of money and I'd be happy to leave enough to pay for any treatment.'

'There's nothing to pay,' Dr Blanc said. Then she leaned forward conspiratorially. 'Are your resistance colleagues well connected?'

'Please don't take offence, doctor,' Rosie said warily, 'but the less I say the safer it is for everyone.'

Dr Blanc accepted this, but pressed gently. 'I have two reasons for asking. Firstly, there's a drug known as penicillin. It's impossible to get supplies around here, but it might be available on the black market in Paris.'

Rosie had seen stories about penicillin in newsreels and newspapers. 'Isn't that the *miracle drug?*' she asked.

'Everyone's heard of it, nobody can get it,' Dr Blanc explained. 'The Germans produce it in small quantities, but it's only made available in their military hospitals. Edith is extremely sick and a vial of penicillin would tilt the balance of probabilities in her favour. The second reason I ask is this.'

The doctor reached into her medical bag and produced a crumpled grey notebook. Rosie caught Joseph's expression, and he apparently had no more idea what it was than she did.

'Two Germans came to my doorstep after Easter,' Dr Blanc began, as Rosie reached across and took the notebook. 'It was all rather gothic. We drove out several kilometres into woodland. Pitch dark, rain lashing the car. They took me down into a bunker – a vast underground warehouse. There were a great deal of military supplies in storage, everything from bombs to boxes of grenades.'

'You're talking about the old army storage bunker,' Joseph said, interrupting his mother. 'You never told me you'd seen a patient out there.'

Dr Blanc gave her son a look of surprise. 'How do you know about it?'

'When Frédéric and I were boys we used to explore in the woods. It was built as an ammunition store during the Great War. There would always be a soldier guarding the perimeter and boys would sneak up and throw acorns or chestnuts at him.'

'Then you know more about it than I do,' Dr Blanc said. Then with a half-smile, 'And apparently my sons were not as well behaved as they led me to believe at the time.'

'I haven't thought about that old place in years,' Joseph said. 'The soldiers used to get cross and shoot their guns, but they knew we were kids and always aimed high into the trees. With so much bombing now, I can see why the Germans would want to make use of it.'

As Joseph spoke, Rosie flipped through the notebook and saw pages of tiny writing, plus equations and intricate pencil drawings of gyroscopes and clockwork mechanisms. There were also pages of maps, with dashed lines plotting what looked like the course of a ship. It all looked like the work of one man, who was quite possibly bonkers.

'My patient was a suicide attempt,' Dr Blanc continued. 'A well-spoken Frenchman who'd cut his wrists. Luckily he'd made the classic mistake of cutting across the vein and hadn't lost too much blood. There seemed to be other Frenchmen there. I saw very little, but got the distinct impression that they were scientists being kept underground in some sort of research facility.'

'How did you get the notebook?' Rosie asked.

'I was there for some hours stabilising the patient. I asked to use the bathroom and it caused a minor fuss, because the toilets in the bunker were foul and there were no facilities for ladies. The Germans were apologetic and sent an elderly Frenchman to clean a toilet for me. As he passed me in the hallway, the cleaner pressed the notebook upon me. He told me it was valuable. He said to hide it in the bottom of my bag and get the information to someone on the outside.'

'But you didn't try passing it to anyone until now?' Rosie asked.

Dr Blanc shook her head. 'This is a remote area. I've heard the resistance spoken of in BBC radio broadcasts, but you're the first time I've physically encountered any sign of it.'

Joseph and Rosie were both intrigued by the story

– but in Rosie's case her fascination was tainted by doubt. Had she really just *happened* to meet a doctor who was in possession of a dossier smuggled out of a secret laboratory?

The tale had the whiff of a plot concocted by the local Gestapo. Perhaps Dr Blanc had offered to swap information for her older son who was a prisoner of war in Germany.

But despite the chills shooting down her back, Rosie had no choice but to play along. If Dr Blanc had visited the Gestapo, they'd almost certainly be watching the house. And the only reason they hadn't arrested Rosie already would be that they hoped to discover more resistance members by tracking her movements.

'I'm no scientist,' Rosie said, as she looked back at the book. 'You're both doctors. You probably understand more of these equations and drawings than I do.'

Dr Blanc nodded. 'There's a certain manic quality to the entire notebook. I've tried to understand it, but I can't tell if it's a secret weapon or the insides of a cuckoo clock. All I have to go on is the apparent desperation of the man who passed it to me.'

Rosie nodded, as she noticed that the doctor had a rather disgusting way of cramming chicken into her mouth with her porky fingers.

'I'll make contact with my liaison in Paris tomorrow,' Rosie said amenably. 'The book weighs nothing and it can be passed up to my superiors for proper analysis.'

'I do hope it proves valuable,' Dr Blanc said, as she rose out of the armchair while wiping greasy fingers on a napkin. 'When did you last check on the patient? I might go upstairs and take a look at her.'

*

There was no change in Edith's condition. Dr Blanc headed home to her rooms above her surgery in town and Rosie retired to a comfortable attic bedroom some time after eleven. She'd not had much sleep, but sat in candlelight studying the notebook.

Her first instinct was that the whole thing was a Gestapo-engineered hoax. But if it was a hoax, the seventy-two sides of writing and drawing must have been prepared well in advance of her arrival. And if the Gestapo wanted to follow her back to Paris and see who she met, why give her the notebook when it would only serve to make any trained agent suspicious?

Perhaps she'd become part of some sophisticated plot. Maybe the book was genuine and Dr Blanc and Joseph were the decent people they appeared, but it all seemed fishy and churning it in her mind brought no great revelation.

Whatever the truth, Rosie's doubts about her hosts meant that she had to act as if she was going to be tailed when she left. And the best way to avoid that was to change her route and time of departure.

After dressing quietly and packing her things, Rosie left her bag by the front door then sneaked back upstairs to check on Edith. Joseph had kept her hydrated and changed her position every so often to prevent bed sores. Because of the fever, she was naked with a rubberised sheet beneath her that could be wiped if she urinated.

The window was open, but the smell of sweat clung to the air. Rosie watched Edith's expressionless face and felt tearful. She had to leave, but hated the possibility that Edith would die, or that she'd win the battle taking place inside her body, only to be shipped back to Lorient for execution.

Rosie couldn't stick around, because Joseph would know she was leaving the instant he saw her fully dressed. If the house was under German surveillance they'd be watching the front door for sure and there might be someone at the back.

Rosie found paper and pencil and scrawled a note which she left on the kitchen table.

Joseph
Changed plans for security reasons.
Hope to be back soon.
Please look after Edith, <u>whatever</u> happens.
Rosie.

She had second thoughts about underlining *whatever*.

And what if they were honest people and took offence at her sneaking off? But she'd been through all the possibilities a hundred times already. Rosie had to forget repercussions and focus on getting away.

After grabbing her pack, Rosie picked a small side window for her exit. She felt guilty trampling a narrow vegetable plot, then athletically vaulted a crumbling wall and dropped on to the overgrown track that marked the boundary between the house and the surrounding fields.

Rosie took a forlorn look backwards at the open window of Edith's room, glanced around looking for any sign of surveillance and then began wading into a field of knee-high wheat. After fifty metres, she dived down on her face and began crawling in a different direction.

Following five minutes on hands and knees, Rosie crawled out on to a road and started running back along the route that the horse and buggy had taken earlier on. There would be no passenger trains for hours, but she reckoned she could pick up the coal train when it stopped by the water tower. She'd ride inside one of the coal skips for a while, then bail out and switch to a passenger train heading towards Paris before it got too light.

CHAPTER TWELVE

CHERUB campus, three days later.

It was 5:30 a.m. and still dark as a United States Air Force policeman strolled lazily out of a guard hut next to a wooden barrier. There was a motorcycle ticking over, its rider's leather suit getting pelted with big blobs of rain.

'Dangerous night to be out on that thing,' the big American said.

'I've been driving back and forth for half an hour,' the rider said. 'I'm trying to deliver a package for the Royal Navy Espionage Research. But I can see that's not you.'

The American laughed as he put his hand to his brow to keep the rain out of his eyes. 'You've got the right spot, but I'll need to see your security clearance.'

The rider took his gloves off and fumbled inside his jacket for a security pass.

'Looks good to me,' the American said, barely looking at it. 'You gotta ride up three hundred yards. At the fork, you branch off left. You'll see an old school building with a cottage next door. Might have to rattle some windows to get them out of bed this early.'

The motorbike didn't like the rain and the engine stuttered as the rider passed under the gate. The fork was a gap between trees which he almost missed. A muddy track led him up to the school building, where a crack of light escaped around the edges of a black-out curtain in the main door.

A lightning bolt turned the world blue as the rider put down his kickstand and he was surprised to see a pretty young woman in Royal Navy uniform rolling towards him in a wheelchair.

'I believe you have a package for me, Aircraftsman?'

The rider looked confused as he unlocked a metal storage box behind the saddle. 'I have instructions to deliver this into the hands of First Officer Slater.'

'Which would be me,' Joyce Slater said. 'And just because I'm in a wheelchair, it doesn't mean you don't have to salute me.'

'Sorry, ma'am,' the rider said, as he gave a mildly sarcastic salute. 'I'll need to see your identity badge before I can pass this across.'

Joyce wasn't the kind of person who gave a damn about saluting, but it pissed her off when people looked at the chair instead of the stripes on her uniform. She signed a receipt for the small waterproof packet, and turned her chair around.

'Would you like me to wheel you anywhere, ma'am?' the rider asked.

Joyce ground her teeth. 'I'm perfectly capable,' she snapped. 'And I made hot tea for you inside. You're welcome to warm up and use the facilities before riding back.'

'Yes, ma'am,' the rider said. 'A cuppa would be most welcome.'

As the rider walked into the school building, Joyce wheeled herself quickly towards a prefabricated Nissen hut and entered via a wooden ramp. Third Officer Elizabeth DeVere – known to all as Boo – was already under the curved metal roof, lighting an oil-burning heater.

'Good morning, ma'am,' Boo said, as Joyce wheeled past a radio transmitter the size of a filing cabinet and threw the packet on to a large planning table.

'Have you seen Captain Henderson?' Joyce asked. 'He'll want to see this immediately.'

'He's up and in uniform,' Boo replied. 'I think he's bringing a couple of the boys down to help with analysis.'

As Boo spoke she used a tea-towel to dry the outside of the waterproof pouch. She then slid out a small, seventy-two-page grey notebook.

'Real or fake?' Joyce asked as she wheeled up to the table. 'Fancy a bet?'

*

Captain Charles Henderson was slightly disgusted by the aroma of teenage boy as he crossed the first-floor dormitory room with a white drill stick tucked under his arm.

'Wakey wakey,' Henderson said, as he gave fifteen-year-old Marc Kilgour a good poke. 'Hands off cocks, feet in socks!'

As Marc groaned, Henderson turned and ripped the covers from the next bed, exposing Rosie Clarke's skinny fourteen-year-old brother, Paul.

'Bloody hell,' Paul moaned, as Marc stretched into a lazy yawn. 'What time is it?'

'For you two, it's time to get up,' Henderson said, as he looked around at the room's other occupants, PT and Joel. 'Whereas you two clearly need your beauty sleep.'

Marc and Paul pulled on shirts, trousers and army boots before dashing to the bathroom. Henderson began a lecture as they peed.

'Rosie arrived in Paris two days ago with a mysterious grey notebook. It either contains valuable scientific information, or is part of some fiendish Gestapo plot. A preliminary assessment made in Paris indicates that the notebook might contain valuable intelligence.

'The notebook was immediately taken by train to

Switzerland in a false suitcase compartment. From there, the package was put aboard a British diplomatic flight. The flight landed at Croydon aerodrome just after midnight and was immediately brought here by motorbike. First Officer Slater will co-ordinate a detailed intelligence analysis.'

By this time the boys had finished urinating and Henderson was leading them down the stairs.

'Our first task is to make photographs of the notebook's entire content. I want you two to deal with this. Develop the films and print eight sets of photographs. Images and prints must be of reference quality, every word must be legible. I want them printed and dried, and ready for distribution to any additional intelligence experts who need to see them. Is that clear?'

'Crystal clear, sir,' Paul said. He was delighted because he'd rather spend time developing photographs than go through the usual campus morning routine of a three-mile cross-country run followed by physical jerks in the gymnasium. 'Did you get any other news on my sister?'

'Obviously we're restricted to brief Morse code transmissions. All we know is that Rosie is in Paris, being looked after by Ghost's resistance circuit.'

As Henderson and Paul swept past a sodden motorcyclist drinking tea and warming his hands over a radiator, Marc went in the other direction towards the kitchen.

'Where are you going?' Henderson barked. 'You haven't got time for breakfast.'

'I was going to put on a large saucepan,' Marc explained. 'We'll need warm water for developing.'

'Yes, excellent thinking,' Henderson said. 'I'll see you in the radio shack.'

'Good morning, Captain,' Boo and Joyce said, when Henderson led Paul into the hut.

Both girls had been selected for intelligence work because they were exceptionally bright. Joyce was a Cambridge maths graduate who was regarded as one of the best code breakers and intelligence analysts in the country. Boo was younger and had joined the Royal Navy directly from a posh finishing school.

Henderson saw that the girls were going through the pages quickly, trying to form an initial impression.

'What have we got?' Henderson asked.

'I'm making lists,' Boo said as she wrote rapidly. 'I've been through and picked out all the names in the text. If these men are real scientists, we should be able to find references to them in French scientific journals.'

'I don't have a huge knowledge of electronics, but these drawings seem to be for some kind of electronic system that takes inputs from magnetically charged gyroscopes,' Joyce said.

Henderson stepped up to the notebook. He wasn't a scientist, but he had some technical knowledge because his pre-war job with the Espionage Research Unit had involved spying on Britain's European rivals and getting hold of their military secrets.

'If this is what I think this is . . .' Henderson said, before tailing off as he slid the notebook away from the girls.

'And what's that, sir?' Joyce asked.

'Before the war, the French had a project to develop a pilotless flying bomb. It was navigated by magnetic gyroscopes.'

Paul looked aghast. 'That's absurd. How can anything fly without a pilot?'

'It's not absurd at all,' Henderson said, as he flipped through the pages. 'We already have magnetic torpedoes that can find a ship's hull and acoustic torpedoes that home in on the sound of the propeller. Why not an aerial bomb that can guide itself to a target?'

Henderson's eyes flicked across to one of Joyce's notes, at the top of which she'd written FZG-76.

'Why did you write that down?' Henderson asked, as Marc came into the hut holding a bag of photographic equipment. 'What is it?'

'It rang a bell,' Joyce said. 'I've fixed quite a few undecipherable messages, and I've seen references to FZG-76. It's a secret project. I remember references to launch ramps somewhere in Denmark, so definitely some kind of flying object.'

'So,' Paul began thoughtfully, 'it looks like drawings and notes relating to this pilotless aircraft slash bomb thingy. But none of us knows enough about the technology to tell whether it's valuable information or a useless crock.'

'But knowing what we're looking at is a big help,' Henderson said. 'I'll get on to the Air Ministry and try to pin down an expert on pilotless bombs. Boys, I need you two to set up the photography and get those images ready, so we can send them off to whoever needs to look at them. Girls, excellent work so far. Keep writing down your observations.'

'No library will be open yet, but when it gets to nine, we can call Mavis Duckworthy at the University of Cambridge library,' Boo said. 'They keep complete sets of all the major French scientific journals and she can check the background of the scientists named in the book.'

'I also want us to start thinking about the bunker where this secret laboratory is supposed to be,' Henderson said. 'I'll try and see if there's any aerial surveillance images, and I'll put out some discreet feelers to see if anyone with the Free French[5] or the

---

[5] Free French – A London-based group, led by General Charles de Gaulle. He refused to accept France's surrender in 1940 and by 1943 many French colonies were under Free French control.

French Section of SIS[6] knows anything about the history or layout of the bunker where these men are supposedly being kept.

'And remember the first golden rule of intelligence work. Speed is important, but accuracy most important of all.'

---

[6] SIS – Secret Intelligence Service. The official name for the British intelligence organisation that is now more commonly known as MI6.

CHAPTER THIRTEEN

Breakfast was put on hold and three other lads were enlisted to help as the campus kitchen became a darkroom. By 10 a.m., more than two hundred freshly developed sixteen-by-twelve-inch photographs were strung out to dry across the tiny school gymnasium.

Two hours later a small Air Ministry passenger plane landed at the American airfield on the far side of campus. The photographs were larger and easier to read than the original notebook and the kids were sent upstairs before two professorish looking brothers named Hughes were let into the gym to inspect them.

At first the brothers had the air of people greatly put out at being ordered away from their London office. This changed to brief jubilation, before they started arguing furiously over the interpretation of one of the drawings.

Henderson interrupted. 'Gentlemen,' he began firmly, 'The life of at least one agent depends upon an accurate assessment of whether this is genuine intelligence or misinformation fed to us by the Germans. Can we concentrate on that before you bicker over details?'

The younger Hughes turned to Henderson. 'This notebook is the work of a French scientist named Maurice Jaulin. His drawings have been published in American Aeronautics magazine. The style is highly distinctive.'

'Could he be working under duress?' Henderson asked. 'The Germans have a history of hatching elaborate plans to throw our intelligence services off the scent.'

'These *have* to be genuine,' the younger Hughes said.

'Have to be,' the older Hughes agreed. 'We know that the Germans have been testing a pilotless flying bomb in the Baltic under the codename FZG-76. The maps in your notebook show the trajectories of test bombs.'

The younger Hughes tapped one of the hanging prints. 'You see here? This map shows the trajectory of a dozen test flights and where they landed. Now, if you look at a later page you see the map from a more recent batch of tests. The flying bombs plotted here end up much closer to the intended target, because they're gradually refining the guidance technology.

'The Danish resistance has tuned into radio tracking signals sent by test bombs as they fly, giving us maps similar to these. But this notebook gives us far more detailed information on how the bomb's navigation system is constructed, and on how the system has been refined during the development process. There's also information about the bomb's launch and propulsion systems which is entirely new to me.'

'But you've only just seen these drawings,' Henderson said. 'What if you start trying this stuff in your laboratory and none of it works?'

The Hughes brothers both shook their heads.

'This is full of things that make you say, *My god, why didn't I think of that?*' the younger brother explained. 'The drawing on page six gives details of how the pilotless bomb gauges distance flown. The system is ingenious, and you only have to look at it to see that it's an extremely valuable scientific idea.'

'Can we take these photographs back to London?' the older Hughes asked.

'With my compliments,' Henderson said. 'It's important that you don't reveal the source of this intelligence, because it would compromise my agents working in France. But you both have *Most Secret* clearance.'

The Hughes brothers laughed as they began excitedly unpegging a set of photographs from the drying lines.

'We shan't get much sleep for the next few nights,' Hughes younger said. 'This is *extraordinary*.'

'Gentleman, if you'll excuse me,' Henderson said. 'I

hope you have a safe return flight. Unfortunately I have urgent matters to attend to.'

Henderson rushed out and bumped into Paul and Marc, who'd been listening outside the door.

'Good job with the photographs,' Henderson told the boys as he headed towards the radio shack. 'The intelligence appears to be good. Depending on the transmission sked, we should hopefully be able to get that information back to Ghost's people in Paris by this evening.'

'So Rosie can go back to the west and get Edith?' Marc asked.

'If she's not dead already,' Henderson said bluntly. 'And now we know that there really is a bunker laboratory where French scientists are developing German secret weapons, I suppose our next job is to find some way to put it out of action.'

*

The Paris resistance had set Rosie up with a one-room apartment four storeys above a wine merchant's shop. The first night she slept like the dead, but after that she'd been kept awake by nightmares. The parachute landing and the shootout at Madame Lisle's house had been traumatic, but it was hauling Edith's comatose body about that plagued her subconscious.

Every trip outside posed the risk of encountering a checkpoint or a detailed document inspection, so Rosie followed protocol and stayed in her room. There was no radio, but there were shelves of books and a delivery boy came by every morning with fresh bread, a bottle of milk and enough food to keep her going.

By the third night, the four walls and the smell of cigar smoke creeping up from the apartment below were doing Rosie's head in. She sat with the window open staring at stars. It was after curfew and Paris seemed eerily quiet until two cars approached.

A chill shot through Rosie as they stopped outside. Eight black Mercedes doors opened near simultaneously, spilling a mix of German army and Paris police on to the pavement and cobbles.

Rosie felt lucky not to have been asleep. She kicked out a loose piece of skirting, grabbed the pistol hidden behind, then put it down on the end of the bed as she pulled a dress over her head and slid her feet into sandals. These were part of a new wardrobe to replace her combat boots and the ill-fitting dress she'd bought from Justin's mum.

There was no fire escape, so Rosie's pre-planned escape route was up to the fifth floor and out over the roof. The men were stomping up the stairs as she tucked her gun into a small leather bag and opened the door, but as she peeked into the hallway there were several shouts followed by men kicking a door two floors below.

Nobody went higher than the second floor, so Rosie

backed into her room. Within seconds there were shouts as two men were dragged from the apartment. Rosie walked back to her window and saw the first young man getting pulled into the street, dressed only in his undershorts.

He might have been a criminal or someone involved with the resistance, but as he only looked about eighteen Rosie thought it most likely that he'd been hiding out to avoid compulsory labour service in Germany.

The second person dragged out was more boy than man and looked slightly comical in baggy pyjamas. Despite small stature he roared abuse and landed a punch as a policeman tried shoving him into the car. This wasn't a wise move, because within seconds he'd been knocked down and had three cops laying into him.

'Traitor scum,' a woman shouted from a second-floor window. 'They're good boys. How can you betray your own people?'

The volley of words was followed by the contents of a piss pot. Rosie was amused, but backed off from the window in case they thought it had come from her.

As the policemen shook urine off their cloaks, two Germans charged back inside. Rosie heard a loud scream as the woman who'd thrown the pot – presumably the one who'd been sheltering the two young men – was bundled down the staircase.

Halfway down she managed to kick at another door.

'Don't think I don't know who told 'em, you fat old dog,' she shouted.

Rosie caught first sight of the woman as she came out on to the pavement. She was old enough to be the grandmother of the two men she'd been sheltering, but this didn't stop the largest of the Germans swinging his baton full force into her ribcage. Then a couple of the piss-soaked policemen took their revenge, stomping the elderly woman as she balled up on the ground.

It was sickening and Rosie backed away from the window with her fists bunched. But it was also a reminder of why she was here, and that people like Eugene were dying for a good reason.

CHAPTER FOURTEEN

Rosie woke with a start four hours later. Someone was thumping on her door, and her first thought was Germans. But two double knocks and a single was the safe signal and she opened the door bleary eyed, assuming that her delivery boy had arrived early.

In fact it was Maxine Clere. Rosie had known Maxine before she'd become the legendary Paris resistance leader known as Ghost. Two years living under constant threat of arrest had made Maxine thinner and greyer, but she was still six feet tall and beautiful.

Ghost's resistance circuit was the largest in France, centred on Paris but with operatives as far north as the Channel coast. While Eugene's circuit in Lorient was one of many smashed by the Gestapo, Maxine's much larger operation had seen many members arrested, but tight security meant it had stayed intact.

The core of this success lay in the fact that Maxine had made her 'Ghost' persona so elusive that even senior members of her own circuit had never met her, and some even questioned her existence.

Rosie wanted to say something momentous and congratulate Maxine on building up a resistance circuit that had saved the lives of hundreds of airmen and done untold damage to German operations. But she was drowsy and could only manage a rather dumb, 'You're up early.'

'Irregular hours,' Maxine said warmly, as she pulled Rosie into a hug. 'Sometimes I hardly know if it's night or day.'

'I never expected to see you personally,' Rosie said. 'The legendary Ghost.'

Maxine laughed. 'You can stop that bullshit! The enigmatic reputation is useful, but my importance is overestimated. If a Gestapo sniper shot me dead right now, my circuit would barely miss a beat.'

Perhaps this was true, but Rosie was too tactful to mention that the Gestapo would be far more likely to torture Maxine than to assassinate her.

'Have you heard from Britain?' Rosie asked.

'All good things,' Maxine said brightly. 'The notebook is a document of extraordinary intelligence value. Much too valuable to be part of any Gestapo trap.'

Rosie gasped with relief as she sat back on her bed. The risks she'd taken weren't in vain and Edith wasn't in the hands of German stooges.

'I should travel back to the west as soon as possible,' Rosie said. 'I have no idea how Edith's doing and the way I disappeared in the dead of night must have seemed rude.'

'They'll understand,' Maxine said, as she pulled an envelope from her tatty handbag.

'Blank identity documents. There are no photographs of Edith anywhere on file, so there's a miniature camera, squares of photographic paper and developing chemicals. Most importantly of all, six vials of penicillin.'

'Was it easy to get hold of?' Rosie asked.

'We get it in air drops of American medical kits,' Maxine explained. 'We use it to blackmail Germans stricken with gonorrhoea. Penicillin is the only cure, and they'll do anything not to have to go home to their wives and explain their giant, swollen balls.'

Rosie giggled at the thought, but her mood darkened when she thought of Edith.

'I just hope Edith's still alive when I get there,' Rosie said.

'There's a train in three hours. I assume you're happy to return?'

'Of course. Why wouldn't I be?'

'You've been through a tough few days,' Maxine said.

'There'll be no black mark against you if you say no, but I'd like you to take this operation to the next phase. You're only sixteen, but you've been well trained by Henderson and you can operate a radio independently.'

Rosie looked curious. 'What's this next phase?'

'We need information about the bunker,' Maxine said. 'I can provide a camera and film. We need to know the layout, the security arrangements, the number of men on guard, the number of scientists in the bunker, the location of the laboratory. I expect others will be sent in to help you, but to begin it will be down to you and any locals you feel able to trust.'

'I suppose we can now say Joseph and Doctor Blanc's loyalty is beyond question,' Rosie said. 'They'd probably be willing to help.'

Maxine nodded. 'A doctor is likely to be well connected. But just because she's on our side, doesn't mean she's discreet. And you've got to make it clear that you're the boss, no matter *what* your age and gender.'

'What's the longer term aim?' Rosie asked.

'That depends what you find out and on subsequent decisions taken in London. The bunker could be bombed and destroyed. If it's heavily reinforced, it may have to be sabotaged from the ground, or mined for information if we can get someone on the inside.'

'Right,' Rosie said, as she interlocked her fingers. 'There's a lot of decisions to make.'

'Only one to begin with,' Maxine said. 'Are you up for this or not?'

Rosie had dropped into Lorient with an unglamorous mission to help train members of Eugene's resistance circuit and act as a back-up radio operator. Maxine was offering something a lot meatier.

Part of Rosie wanted to take the easy route and head back to Britain. But she'd always felt that she had to work harder than the boys on campus to prove her worth, and even then she still found herself being pushed into traditionally female roles. This was her chance to put nursing courses and back-up radio operator jobs behind her and prove that she could take command as well as any man.

'It's what I've trained for,' Rosie said determinedly. 'I've already made connections in the area and if I don't take the risks, someone else has to.'

*

The Nazis kept Paris railway stations under close watch, but the Ghost circuit had good connections amongst railway workers.

Rosie made her five-hour train journey in first class. She carried nothing but clothes and toiletries, which made her much less stressed than when she'd gone in the opposite direction a few days earlier.

A young German officer with three missing fingers flirted until mercifully he left the train at Laval. On arrival in Rennes Rosie showed her immaculately counterfeited documents to a Gendarme manning the end-of-the platform checkpoint. Then she walked to a cafe two streets away and sipped vile acorn coffee until the stoker from her train dropped a bag under her table, then disappeared before she could even say *thanks*.

It was twelve kilometres to the house where she'd left Edith and the only way out was on foot. Luckily it was dry without being too warm, and despite aching feet Rosie burst into a run as the elegant house came into view. Was Edith dead or alive?

Rosie tugged on the doorbell, but nobody answered. After a circuit of the house, she forced the same small side window she'd escaped through a few nights earlier. Her landing on the drawing-room floor was painful and she clutched a palm as she raced upstairs.

Edith was alive, but still unconscious. Some of her bruises had turned from red to grey, but the infected wounds down her leg looked worse. Her temperature was high and both ankles were puffed up.

Rosie sat at the bottom of the stairs rubbing her aching feet as Joseph's buggy pulled up outside. He gave her a hug and apparently bore no grudge over the way she'd disappeared, or the fact that she'd broken into his house.

'I half expected you not to be there when I woke,' Joseph said. 'You looked wary when my mother showed you the dossier.'

Rosie helped him carry baskets of freshly-pulled potatoes and carrots into the kitchen.

'Edith looks much the same,' Rosie said.

Joseph shook his head. 'I've been trying to force feed her using a stomach tube, but she brings most of it straight back up. And if she's not eating, she can only get weaker. The worst of the infection is in her legs. We're close to the point where the only option will be to have a surgeon amputate them, but I doubt she's strong enough to survive the operation.'

Rosie looked shocked. The thought of someone Edith's age losing her legs was almost worse than her dying. 'Could penicillin still help?'

Joseph looked excited as Rosie unclipped her case and took out six carefully-wrapped glass vials.

'Miraculous,' he shouted. 'I've studied its effects in medical school, but I've never actually seen it. And this looks like enough for several patients. My mother has another comatose patient who picked up an infection after giving birth. Can we use some for her?'

'As long as there's enough for Edith,' Rosie said.

'Of course,' Joseph said. 'I'll get my medical bag and prepare her first dose.'

CHAPTER FIFTEEN

Once Edith had been injected, Rosie began making soup with fresh veg, while Joseph went back out on the buggy with two vials of penicillin, trying to track down his mother.

After a day's work Dr Blanc always rode out to eat an evening meal prepared by her son. She was complimentary about the soup, though in truth Rosie had done little but boil up vegetables, with salt and garlic as the only available sources of flavour.

Mother and son were both pleased to hear that the intelligence was valuable. And since they both knew who Rosie was there seemed little point hiding her next objective from them.

'I've brought a small camera,' Rosie explained. 'I need to get out to the bunker and take photographs. I'll also need to conduct longer term surveillance: watching who arrives, who leaves, what equipment goes in and out.'

'It might be risky going into the forest with a camera and no clear motive for being there,' Joseph said. 'I suppose you might be OK at night.'

Rosie shook her head. 'I'll need good light for photographs.'

'Tricky,' Joseph said, 'although boys have always played in the forest. I have no idea how near to the bunker you can get, but if it's well guarded I'd bet some of the local boys would have tales of being kicked out.'

Dr Blanc nodded in agreement. 'Joseph was too well fed to hunt as a boy, but my brothers hunted in those woods back in the 1900s. Most families are short of food right now, so I'm certain trapping and hunting are popular.'

'Can you think of any boys you might speak to?' Rosie asked.

'Perhaps,' Dr Blanc said. 'But I'm seen as an authority figure. They'd probably think they were in trouble and deny everything.'

Rosie nodded. 'And it's not right for you to go around asking questions. If something happened at the bunker and the Germans began an investigation, any interest you've shown might create problems for you.'

'How about your little mate who brought you to us in the first place?' Joseph asked.

Rosie smiled. 'Justin,' she said brightly, feeling slightly stupid that this idea hadn't already occurred to her. 'He's bright and he already took a great risk to help me. I'll go and find him in the morning.'

*

Low sun punched through the attic window as Rosie rubbed her eyes and picked up the chamber pot under her bed. As her bare feet made the first-floor landing boards creak she heard a soothing version of Joseph's voice coming out of Edith's room.

'Hello?' Rosie said curiously, as she leaned through the door.

'Good morning,' Joseph said brightly.

Edith's head turned slightly as Rosie stepped inside. Her eyes were open and Joseph had her propped on a pillow, while he sat on the edge of the bed feeding her small mouthfuls of scrambled egg.

'It really is a miracle drug,' Rosie said. A mist of tears blurred her vision as she put the pot down and rushed up to the bed. Edith's eyes were only part open and her lids were crusted with yellow muck, but she smiled when she recognised Rosie.

'If the bacteria are susceptible, penicillin can wipe out an infection in a few hours,' Joseph explained. 'I checked her temperature before I went to bed and I saw it had begun to drop. Rather than go to bed I brought a chair in and slept in here to see how things developed.'

The teaspoon of egg chinked against Edith's front teeth.

'Your throat hurts because I put the feeding tube down,' Joseph explained. 'But you must eat to get your strength back.'

'What time did she wake up?' Rosie asked, as she gently held Edith's hand.

Edith made a little moan of pain as she swallowed some egg.

'Good girl,' Joseph said, before turning to Rosie. 'She came around briefly at 2 a.m., then again at six. Chances are she'll keep drifting in and out for a little while yet.'

'Is she getting better?' Rosie asked.

'The penicillin seems to have dealt with the infection in her blood. I'll keep injecting her to make sure it fully penetrates the infected wounds, but it looks good.'

Edith had understood and smiled as she gripped Rosie's hand a little bit tighter.

'Provided she's a good girl and keeps eating her eggs,' Joseph said, as he raised a spoon. 'Open wide.'

*

Rosie was in a good mood as she rode into the village on one of the Blanc family's horses. She had a good memory for places, but she wasn't certain that she'd knocked on the door of the right cottage until eight-year-old Agnes opened the door.

'You look much prettier,' she told Rosie, as three-year-old Belle peeked out of a doorway in the background.

Rosie remembered that the last time Justin's sisters had seen her she'd not washed or slept in days and was covered in coal dust.

'Is your mummy here?' Rosie asked.

Agnes shook her head. 'She's at work.'

'What about Justin?'

Agnes nodded. 'He's sleeping.'

'Can I speak to him?'

'Is it important? He gets really cross if we wake him up.'

Rosie had thought Justin might be asleep. She'd even considered dropping by later, but was keen to make progress. Agnes led her up mildewing wooden stairs, beneath the gaping hole in the roof and into a small musty room. The window was blacked out and Justin was curled up on a straw-filled mat, snoring gently.

The arm and leg poking from Justin's rough blanket were bruised from carrying coal and in this state he seemed more childlike than the cocky lad she'd met on the coal train.

'Are you going to wake him?' Rosie asked.

Agnes backed up to the doorway and shook her head warily. 'I'd rather you did it. He might bash me.'

A big cockroach scuttled out of the way as Rosie crouched down and gently rocked Justin's shoulder.

'Bloody hell,' he moaned, as he rolled over. 'What?'

There was a smell of earth and feet, but Justin was young enough for Rosie to feel slightly maternal about his boyish blue eyes and scrambled hair.

'Do you want coal?' he said irritably, as he glowered at Agnes. 'Why can't she do it?'

'It's the girl you brought on the train, stupid,' Agnes snapped back. 'She asked to talk to you.'

Justin did several long blinks and rubbed glue out of his eye before apparently recognising Rosie. 'You look really different,' he said. 'How's your friend now?'

'Fingers crossed,' Rosie said, 'she seems to be getting better.'

'Great,' Justin said. 'What's so important that you had to wake me up?'

Rosie looked at Agnes, 'In private, if you don't mind.'

Agnes looked put out, but a stern look from Justin sent her stomping back down the stairs.

'You don't look too great,' Rosie said. 'Are you sick?'

'I'm always knackered,' Justin said. 'My mum earns next to nothing, and the coal train runs seven days a week, so I work it seven days a week. And even when I'm asleep, I get woken up by the girls. Or by someone wanting coal.'

Rosie felt even guiltier about waking Justin when he sat up, revealing a big red welt that ran from his upper arm and across his chest.

'Railway cops,' he explained, as he grabbed a grubby

shirt off the floor. 'Two nights ago. And the bastards stole my whole night's coal.'

'Sorry to hear that,' Rosie said, then she began to explain about the bunker in the woods and how she needed to get close to it and take photographs. For security, she didn't mention Dr Blanc's role or the notebook. She just said that her boss in the resistance had asked her to get information.

By this time Justin had woken up enough for some of his cockiness to return. He scratched his chin with black fingernails before speaking.

'What's in it for me?'

Rosie smiled. 'It's for France. You said you hated the Boche when you met me on the train the other night.'

Justin shrugged. 'I don't much like 'em. If the Brits and Yanks sweep into town tomorrow, what difference will it make to me?'

'Didn't you say your dad was a prisoner? You'd be better off with him at home, wouldn't you?'

Justin shrugged. 'He's a drunk.'

Rosie realised concepts like freedom and patriotism didn't mean much to a ten-year-old who spent his life picking up coal scraps to earn enough money to keep his family from going hungry. But Rosie had money and resistance leaders like Eugene and Maxine paid people for their work.

'How much do you earn selling coal on a good night?

Whatever it is, I'll pay you the same whenever you work for me. And I can get you some treats. I bought chocolate with me from Paris.'

Justin raised one eyebrow. 'I'll cop another beating if I'm caught on the train. What will I get if I'm caught helping the resistance? And what will they do to my mum and the girls?'

Rosie saw Justin's point, but decided not to offer more. It was good to put things on a professional basis and reward people who helped the resistance, but offering large sums of money encouraged greed and led to suspicious behaviour when they spent it.

'If it's just about money, I can't trust you,' Rosie said, pretending that she wasn't bothered either way. 'I can tell you've got a good heart. You could have earned a fortune turning me and Edith in, but you did the right thing and sent for Dr Blanc.'

Justin went quiet, and stared at his filthy toes poking from the end of his blanket.

'You can't tell my mum because she'll whip me. And the girls tend to speak without thinking, so keep them out of this too.'

'OK,' Rosie said, still not sure what Justin was offering.

'I know a lot of kids who hunt in the forest, but what you really need are people who you can trust not to go running to the Germans, right?'

Rosie nodded. Justin was smarter than any ten-year-old ought to be.

'There's two guys about your age who spend a lot of time in the forest – Didier and Jean,' Justin explained. 'They're from Rennes, but they went on the run when they got called up for labour service. They're proper rough. I was scared the first couple of times I met them, but I trade my coal for their meat and they've never tried to rip me off.'

First Joseph, then the men in the apartment below in Paris, and now these two – Rosie was starting to feel that every young man in France was hiding out to avoid compulsory labour service in Germany.

'Sounds ideal,' Rosie said. 'I'll pay whatever you would have earned by selling coal. Is that a deal?'

Justin nodded. 'Those boys move around, so we may have a job tracking them down. But they usually come into town once every couple of nights, selling hares or rabbits to the butcher's shop near Dr Blanc's surgery.'

CHAPTER SIXTEEN

Rosie was in a rural area, with clumps of cottages sprawled out over family smallholdings. The local centre was a cluster of businesses where three dirt tracks joined the cobbled route into Rennes. This strip had no official name, but everyone called it *the junction*.

Along with Dr Blanc's surgery and the butcher's shop, the junction had a grocer, a bakery, a farm supply store and a blacksmith. A church with sprawling graveyard stood on higher ground a couple of hundred metres further along.

Locals walked or came by cart, while a vehicle from the German garrison passed through once or twice per day. It was the type of place where everyone knew each other and would gossip over anything unusual, so Rosie and Justin kept look out from an overgrown section of the graveyard. This gave them a vista over shop fronts on both sides of the road and multiple escape routes if anyone came near.

Monday was a waste of time, and Tuesday was early closing, but patience was rewarded on Wednesday when two furtive lads sprang from a field and bolted over the cobbles. They both carried poles hung with rabbits on each shoulder.

Rosie agreed with Justin's assessment that they were about her age, possibly a couple of years older. Didier was tall and broad, with a tiny lower jaw and huge rat-like front teeth. Jean was short, but built tough with chunky limbs and bright red hair.

A girl who worked as the butcher's apprentice met the pair in front of the shop, as Rosie scrambled deeper into the graveyard so that she could still see the action. After a quick look and a sniff at the dangling rabbits, the girl took the poles inside, then quickly peeled off paper money and handed over a small cloth sack.

'We need to start moving,' Rosie told Justin. 'If they cut back through a field we could lose them.'

Approaching Jean and Didier anywhere near the shops would guarantee curious onlookers, so Rosie planned to follow them out of town. After giving Justin a leg-up over the graveyard's stone wall, she vaulted it herself and followed him through long grass.

As they reached the shops, Jean led Didier up an

alleyway between the baker and blacksmith's. Rosie was anxious not to lose them after their long stake-out, but stopped Justin from breaking into a run because it would then be obvious that they were chasing.

Rosie and Justin reached the uncultivated land behind the bakery as Jean and Didier stepped over a gate into a cow pasture fifty metres further on. Crossing open ground risked the boys spotting them if they looked back, but they'd started to run and she had to take the risk.

She reached the gate with Justin a few metres behind, then peered down the line of a tall hedge, where she was relieved to see that the two boys had slowed to a brisk walk. After following for several hundred metres, Rosie and Justin dived for cover in the hedge as Jean took the sack off his back and used a pocket knife to pull the cork from a bottle of red wine.

*

Five kilometres and two bottles of red wine later, Didier and Jean stumbled into a dilapidated cowshed that hadn't housed an animal in years. There was a crash of metal, followed by howls of drunken laughter.

Rosie had said little during the walk, but her expression told Justin that she was having doubts about using the lads as her guides.

'There is another boy who hunts,' Justin whispered, as they crouched at the base of a tree. 'He might help us, but he's mouthy.'

Rosie gave her head a little shake, then told Justin to stay put while she crept up to the long shed. The sides were vertical wooden slats and she peeked through. The boys had only colonised one corner, and had some fairly nice kit: fold-out beds with proper mattresses, a rug on the dirt floor, a pile of books and gas lamps fixed to the wall.

As Rosie moved around the building, she was less impressed to find grass spattered with animal blood, an undisguised washing line and black patches left by regular fires. Anyone approaching the shed from this end would immediately know that someone was hiding out.

'Need a piss,' Didier shouted from inside.

'Have one for me too,' Jean said, before howling with laughter at his own joke. 'I drank too fast. It's all spinning!'

The accents intrigued Rosie. They looked a rough pair, but spoke more like the sons of lawyers than the sons of peasants. This hint at their background, plus the stash of books, made her hopeful that she could whip them into shape with some common-sense advice.

But it was starting to get dark and it didn't seem like a brilliant idea to approach two drunken strangers, so she decided to return in the morning.

Didier's urine noisily splashed grass as Rosie crept back towards Justin. She was at the corner of the shed when her canvas pump caught in a rabbit snare. As the wire pulled tight it cut into her ankle. She successfully stifled a yelp, but her stride was off balance. Her hand shot out instinctively, but while it saved a fall her palm had thumped the side of the shed.

Inside Jean turned towards the source of the noise. 'Didier?' he shouted. 'Is that you back there?'

Rosie studied the trap anxiously. The snare had been anchored to a nearby bush and the trailing wire was pulled tight. She took out a pocket knife, but the flat blade skidded over the wire.

'What have we got here?' Jean asked, as he moved around the side of the hut, while hurriedly pushing his bits back inside his trousers.

As Didier came around the other side of the hut, Rosie pulled her sleeve over her hand then wound the wire around and ripped it away from the bush. This left her ankle in the wire loop with a metre of wire trailing freely behind.

'This is better than catching a rabbit!' Didier said, as he grinned foolishly.

Rosie felt a little scared with two drunken lads coming towards her from either end of the hut.

Jean saw less of the funny side and barked, 'Who are you? Why are you snooping around here?'

Justin ran out of the bushes waving his arms. 'Don't hurt her. She's with me.'

Jean glowered at Justin. 'Did you follow us from the

butcher's shop? How dare you follow us, you little brat.'

Justin dived for cover as Jean chased him into the bushes.

'Hey, you big bully,' Rosie shouted.

Justin kicked and spat as Jean carried him out of the bushes, then plonked him on his feet and knocked him back hard against the wooden hut.

'I told you to stop,' Rosie shouted. 'He's just a kid. I asked him to help me find you.'

Didier moved closer to Rosie. Apparently toothbrushing facilities out here weren't great because his breath was rank.

'How did you manage to follow us?' Didier demanded.

Rosie laughed. 'You're amateurs. You don't double back on yourselves, you get drunk, you walk slowly. And this hut is surrounded by blood and cinders.'

'We've survived out here long enough,' Jean said, as he gave Justin a little slap across the cheek.

'The only reason you've survived is that nobody's been out here looking,' Rosie said. 'And if you touch him again . . .'

'I think we should forget all about this,' Didier said, slurring his words as he closed right up to Rosie and cupped his hand around her breast. 'You're really pretty, aren't you?'

Rosie glowered. 'You have *three* seconds to take that hand off my tit.'

'Or what, darling?' Didier snorted.

'Two,' Rosie said.

Justin looked really worried. 'She's got friends,' he blurted. 'If you hurt us they'll come and find you.'

'One.'

'Oh, I'm scared, Justin,' Jean said. 'Cocky little shit-pants.'

'Zero,' Rosie said, as Jean gave Justin a harder slap on the cheek. 'I *told* you to leave Justin alone.'

Rosie grabbed two handfuls of Didier's shirt and gave him a powerful head-butt across the bridge of his nose. As he stumbled back, she kicked him in the guts and he landed on his bum before tilting backwards into a tangle of branches.

Jean could have backed away, but he didn't think Rosie was a threat, so he was still rooted to the spot as she launched a high back kick. Her muddy heel hit the squat teenager square on the lips.

As he teetered, Rosie went into a boxing stance and went for the gut, winding Jean with three hard punches before getting a hand behind his neck and bashing his head into the side of the hut.

'Bloody hell!' Justin shouted, scrambling away as Didier crawled out of the bushes with a bloody nose and thorns bedded in his arms.

Didier didn't have the appetite for an attack on Rosie, but Jean was more aggressive. He came at her like a wild thing with thick arms swinging. Rosie stuck her hand into a small shoulder bag and ripped out an automatic pistol as she took half a step back.

'Do you want your head splattered up the side of this cowshed?' she shouted, as she clicked off the safety. 'Put your fat little hands in the air.'

As a gawping Jean did what he'd been told, Rosie swung the gun around so that Didier got a good look down the barrel.

'Don't shoot me,' he begged, as he threw up his hands.

Rosie looked at Justin. 'Are you OK, mate?'

He nodded, but was shocked and awed by what he'd seen Rosie do.

'Since you two have behaved like pigs, I'll treat you like pigs,' Rosie said. 'Get down on your hands and knees, and crawl back into the shed.'

Justin stifled a smile as the two lads crawled through the bushes, around a corner, past the cinders from the fire and through a cracked wooden door into their den.

'You don't move unless I tell you to move. You don't speak unless I ask a question. And don't think I won't shoot you because I'm just a girl. I'm well trained and I'll execute you both in a heartbeat.'

As her two little pigs looked up, Rosie squatted on one of their filthy beds while Justin stood awkwardly in the doorway. They had a collection of hunting gear kept in good condition, but Rosie's eyes were drawn towards the books, which included several anti-German pamphlets and a copy of *The Communist Manifesto*.

'Which one of you read this?' Rosie asked.

They were reluctant to admit anything with a gun pointed in their face. Didier's nose was dripping blood into the dirt.

'I had a copy once, but I never finished,' Rosie said, trying to sound friendlier as she picked up one of the anti-German leaflets. 'I can't believe you've survived this long while being this stupid. They're desperate for men in the factories, you know? If they catch you, they'll ship you off to Germany. But if they catch you with communist literature and resistance pamphlets, they'll pass you over to the Gestapo, who will torture you. Only a *total* moron would leave this stuff lying around next to their beds.'

Rosie threw the pamphlet and *The Communist Manifesto* at Justin. 'Start a fire and burn these.'

As Justin walked outside, Rosie considered her position. She'd had no option but to fight and there was no harm in showing Jean and Didier who was the boss, but young men tended to have big egos and they'd hate her if she humiliated them for much longer.

'If I put this gun back in my bag, are you going to be civil?'

'Sure,' Jean said grumpily.

'He's got half a bush sticking out of his arse,' Rosie

said, pointing at Didier. 'Help him get the thorns out.'

'Who taught you to fight?' Didier asked, as he stood up and wiped his dirty palms down his trousers. He didn't seem so drunk now, probably because the beating had generated an adrenaline kick.

'I was trained by the resistance,' Rosie said, deliberately not giving details. 'You're on the run, and I can see from your literature that you want the Germans out of France as much as I do. My question is, do you want to run around the forest catching rabbits and getting pissed, or have you got the balls to make a difference?'

It was a loaded question – what red-blooded teenage male would turn down a pretty girl asking for help?

'What is it you want?' Jean asked.

Rosie loosened the bloody wire embedded in her ankle and pulled it over her shoe as she spoke. 'Justin brought me out here because he said you know the forests around here better than anyone.'

This wasn't strictly true, but after knocking the boys down, they needed some flattery.

'Are you interested in the bomb bunker?' Didier asked.

Rosie half smiled, as she clamped a handkerchief over her bleeding ankle. 'Well, the resistance would hardly be interested in the trees and the squirrels, would it? Why do you call it the *bomb* bunker?'

'That's what they store there, isn't it?' Didier said.

This was news to Rosie, but she hid her surprise well.

'You've seen trucks of bombs going in and out?' Rosie asked.

'You see Luftwaffe men loading them on to trucks,' Jean explained.

'Can you get up close to the wire?' Rosie asked.

'You'd be pushing your luck to get up really close. We'd never set traps around there, but there's an old guard we've gotten to know. He likes his rabbit meat and he swaps it for tinned stuff out of the bunker: jam, beans, fruit.'

'I need a guide to take me up there tomorrow,' Rosie said, as she pulled out a small camera. 'I need a good set of photos. They need to be taken in daylight from all angles.'

'It's risky,' Didier said.

Jean shook his head. 'Not *that* risky, as long as you go the back way. Stay well clear of the road and the main footpaths. Except for an occasional patrol, the guards stay behind the fence. And if they spot you from inside the wire it's easy to duck into the trees.'

'No tracking dogs or anything like that?' Rosie asked.

'Not that I've ever seen,' Jean said.

'This is a down-payment,' Rosie said, as she took two ten-franc notes from her shoulder bag. 'The resistance doesn't just take. Whenever you work for me, you'll earn a small wage. We can also help you with documents, accommodation and ration books if you ever need them. When more people come here to help me, you'll receive training and weapons.'

Both lads smiled, but as they reached for the money, Rosie snatched it away before taking a grave tone.

'If you're caught, you'll be tortured and killed. You *have* to follow my orders and if you betray the resistance, we'll be every bit as ruthless as the Gestapo when we catch up with you. If you say no now, I'll walk out of this shed and you'll probably never see me again. But once you take this money, there's no stepping back.'

This time the lads hesitated. Didier took his money first and Jean a couple of tense seconds later. Rosie picked an open wine bottle off the rug and took a slug before passing it to Didier.

'I drink to the resistance,' Rosie said.

'And to France,' Didier said enthusiastically, as streaks of red wine drizzled down his chin.

Part Two

12 June 1943–3 July 1943

CHAPTER SEVENTEEN

'I've got nineteen boys and one girl in total,' Captain Charles Henderson explained as he led a man in US Army uniform through the hallway of the old village school on campus. 'Three are currently deployed in France, one in the French colonies and one in Switzerland. At first a lot of people sneered. *What's the point of training kids?* But now those same people call me up, desperate to use my agents.'

'Is there a shortage of adult agents?' the American asked. He wore thick-framed glasses and the brim of his cap barely reached Henderson's nose.

'It's become impossible for males of military age to live openly in occupied France without being scooped off the street and sent to work in Germany,' Henderson explained. 'But I've got bilingual twelve- to sixteen-year-olds who are fully trained and ready to drop.'

The American was momentarily distracted by a glass cage with a fist-sized spider inside it, but before he could comment Henderson had led him through swinging doors into a small school hall. There was a good deal of grunting and pained expressions as a dozen shirtless boys grappled on crumbling rubber mats.

'Attention,' the Japanese combat instructor Takada shouted as he made a sharp clap.

Red-faced lads in baggy white shorts lined up, with feet apart and hands locked behind their backs. The only motion came from heaving chests and the sweat streaking down their faces.

'Marc, Luc, Paul, Sam, get your kit on and meet me out front in one minute,' Henderson said, not quite shouting. 'The rest of you, get back to it.'

As Takada paired off grapplers who'd lost their partners, Marc, Luc, Paul and Sam exchanged *what are we in for* looks as they pulled on freezing muddy combat gear in which they'd run seven kilometres earlier that morning.

Marc and Luc were fifteen, similar height and solid build, but where Marc was blond and dashing, Luc was dark, hairy and thuggish. Hard training had given fourteen-year-old Paul a bit of muscle, but he still looked as though a stiff breeze would knock him over. At twelve, Sam was the baby of the group, but he'd trained with older boys for two years and always fought hard, even when he was outmatched.

'Get a bloody move on,' Henderson snapped, as the boys paced out into a drizzly June afternoon. 'Go to the firing range at a jog. And Sam, do that boot lace up properly before you trip and crack your head open.'

Hearing that they were going to the firing range was a relief: shooting guns was a lot less taxing than running with packs, swimming the lake or most of the other reasons for which they could have been dragged out of the gym.

When campus was first set up, shooting practice took place on an open field. But Espionage Research Unit B now had use of a swish new range built by their USAF[7] neighbours. There was a wooden armoury building, linked to a partially-covered pistol shooting range. The much larger rifle range was in the open, with rows of sandbagged shooting positions and targets ranging from tin rabbits to the buckled snout of a fighter that had been written off on landing.

For this morning's exercise a selection of man-shaped paper targets had been set out at varying distances. Each figure had a Hitleresque moustache and target rings on the chest with tiny swastikas in the bull's-eye.

'Listen up, boys,' the American began. 'I'm Staff

---

[7] USAF – United States Air Force.

Sergeant Hiram Goldberg, United States Army. Captain Henderson tells me that you four are his best marksmen. Over the next ten days, my job is to push those skills to a much higher level. Now, which one of you four thinks he's hot stuff?'

There was a second's silence before Paul spoke, 'Marc's probably the best shot, sir.'

Marc knew he was best, but scowled at Paul for putting his name forward. Sam nodded in agreement with Paul, while Luc, who hated Marc's guts, just stared into space.

'Let's see what you've got then, young man,' Goldberg said. 'Targets are lined up at forty-yard[8] distances: eighty, one-twenty, one-sixty and so forth. Take a rifle, lay yourself down and aim for the furthest target you feel confident about hitting.'

There was a strict safety procedure for picking up a strange weapon. Marc couldn't remember half of it and expected Goldberg or Henderson to yell as he grabbed a No 4 Mark 1T British army rifle, fitted with a telescopic sight.

'You're familiar with the weapon?' Goldberg asked.

'Yes, sir,' Marc said.

'Take your shot slowly, it's not a race,' Goldberg said, as Marc lay on his belly in the short grass. 'Which target are you going for?'

---

[8] Yard – One yard equals 91cm (or a little less than a metre).

'Number three, a hundred and sixty yards,' Marc said.

After checking that the cartridge was full and pulling the bolt to load a bullet into the chamber, Marc focused the optical sight on the target, made tiny corrections for wind and trajectory and pumped a bullet straight into the target, missing the swastika by less than five centimetres.

'Not bad,' Goldberg said, smiling as he studied the target through binoculars. 'Now, double your range.'

'Sir?' Marc said curiously.

'Three hundred and twenty yards,' Goldberg explained. 'Take it slowly. Give it your best shot.'

Marc pulled the bolt, ejecting his spent cartridge. He then reloaded, steadied the gun and held his breath before taking another shot.

It was too far for Sam and Paul to see where Marc hit, but they both saw the target quiver and erupted in a little cheer. Goldberg seemed less impressed at a bullet that had merely grazed the paper target's outer edge.

'Now double up again,' he said. 'The furthest target. Six hundred yards.'

Marc glanced back at the other boys. 'I'll have a go, but I barely hit the last one, sir.'

Marc swung his rifle towards the furthest target. At this range, the minutest jiggle of his rifle sent the view through his sight from one side of the target to the other. Even if he could get a steady view through the sight,

Marc knew he'd have to aim off – adjusting for the wind, and the fact that bullets fly in a curved arc, not a straight line.

This was beyond Marc's skills, so he pulled the trigger and hoped for the best. As he was shooting over the length of five football pitches, only Goldberg with his binoculars got any idea where the bullet landed.

'You blew up a tuft of grass more than thirty metres shy,' Goldberg said. 'Trajectory decays rapidly at distances over four hundred metres. What are your chances of hitting the target if I give you another shot?'

'Remote, sir,' Marc said. 'If I correct any more, I'll be aiming above the target, so I'll have no reference point.'

'Would you bet me a dollar that I can hit from that range?' Goldberg asked.

Marc laughed. 'I'd have thought not, sir. But since you're our instructor and you're willing to bet, I'll keep my money off the table.'

Goldberg laughed. He gave Marc the binoculars before taking the rifle. 'Watch that target.'

As Marc stared through the binoculars, Henderson and the other three boys watched Goldberg perform an intricate ritual. He began by lying flat in the grass, making minute adjustments to his position. He then altered his telescopic sight, took a long white feather from his pocket and studied the movement of its fronds to judge the wind.

There was deliberateness to his movements, as if he was slowing time and cutting out the rest of the world. After a final adjustment, Goldberg held his breath and gently squeezed the trigger.

'Whoa!' Marc said, as he watched the swastika bull's-eye get torn in half. 'That's *impossible*.'

To prove the shot was no fluke, Goldberg reloaded the bolt action rifle. His second shot was weaker, but still only missed the bull's-eye by two inches. The third flew perfect and punched a hole through the centre of the swastika.

As Goldberg stood up, Marc passed the binoculars to Henderson, who briefly inspected Goldberg's handiwork before passing them along to Luc.

'Who wants to learn how to do that?' Goldberg asked.

'That was awesome,' Sam said keenly. 'Who wouldn't want to learn how to do that?'

'It's a mixture of skill, practice and mental arithmetic,' Goldberg said. 'Anyone with a steady hand and half a brain can shoot at six hundred yards. The best Russian snipers can shoot accurately to over one thousand yards. But that's only half of the story.'

For dramatic effect, Goldberg paused, spread his arms out wide and took in a broad sweep of his surroundings.

'Right now it's light. Your target is easily visible, there's no rain and a steady wind. Most importantly, there's no enemy sniper ready to blow *your* brains out if you poke your head up too high, or let him catch the sun reflecting in your telescopic sight while you're looking for him.

'So I'm not *just* going to train you how to shoot. I'm going to train you how to shoot in the dark, when it's lashing with rain, when you've been running all day, and you're hungry, muddy, and so exhausted that your heart is pounding and you can barely hold your eyes open and your gun upright. These next ten days will be tough. At the end of them, you'll either be a damned good shot or you'll be walking with my boot wedged permanently in your butthole.'

CHAPTER EIGHTEEN

Five and a half days after Sergeant Goldberg first escorted the boys to the firing range, the quartet had a night-time exercise in a forested area five kilometres from campus.

With the help of eighteen-year-old trainee PT and training assistant Kindhe, Goldberg had spread eight firing points over ten kilometres of steeply sloped woodland. The boys worked in pairs. They had four bullets for each target, and had to alternate between sniping and target spotting.

Besides shooting accuracy, the boys would be assessed on how quickly they navigated between targets and the safety of their chosen shooting positions. Marc and Luc hated each other, so from day one, Marc paired with Paul and Luc with Sam.

It was two in the morning, with limited moonlight as Paul threw down a kit bag. It was his turn to shoot and he found a good bracing point for his rifle in the fork of a tree.

According to their map, the boys had to locate a circular target between four and seven hundred yards from their aiming point. It was a warm night and Marc's T-shirt and combat jacket stuck to his back as he knelt on one knee, scanning darkness through high-powered binoculars.

Their bodies ached. They'd not been fed since lunch and their feet had been in boots for twenty hours. To make matters worse they were behind the schedule set by Goldberg and they'd just run two kilometres flat out to make up time.

Marc blamed Paul for selecting an easy footpath, rather than a steep-but-direct climb from the previous target. But Marc kept his trap shut, because Paul had to start controlling his breathing and getting his heart rate down to control four shots.

The rifle scope only magnified by three times, so it was Marc's job to find their target with binoculars. It took ninety seconds of methodical sweeps before he sighted a yellow ship's lifesaver ring chained to a tree trunk on the opposite side of a valley.

'Acquired,' Marc said, sticking to the language Goldberg had taught them to make describing target locations easy. 'North-east, aiming down twenty degrees. Two trees, with a willow growing out almost horizontally in front of them.'

'I see them,' Paul said, as he peered through the scope. 'Setting range.'

Paul's telescopic sight had a split-focus device that enabled him to gauge distance to his target. As he turned the focusing ring, Marc watched swaying treetops.

'Same wind we've had all night,' Marc said. 'Coming from your left at less than five knots.'

As the target was down in a valley, Paul suspected that the wind would be lower than up in the trees. But his real concern was that he had to shoot down at the target. To aim this low he couldn't lie flat. He had to brace, with one knee against the trunk and his right shoulder taking the weight of his upper body.

The technique Goldberg taught for sniper shooting was a form of self-hypnosis. Paul had to cut himself off, imagining he was in a dark space, listening to his own breathing getting slower and slower. He closed one eye as he pulled the bolt to load a bullet.

So still that he could feel the pulse in his neck, Paul shut down until the target through the crosshairs was the only thing in his world. He decided to trust his instincts on the wind and corrected a little less than Marc's figure suggested.

At this range, moving the gun by a millimetre would

move the spot where the bullet hit by half a metre. Even the trigger squeeze had to be smooth if you wanted to hit your target.

The instant the bullet cracked, Marc bobbed up from the undergrowth and checked with the binoculars. The target was intact, but a chunk of tree bark had been blown out of the trunk less than a hand's width away.

'Minor correction right,' Marc said.

Paul swore under his breath: it was a decent first shot, but he'd not made enough of a correction for the lack of wind in the valley. A break would shatter his concentration, so he pulled back the bolt, lined up, held his breath and took the second shot three seconds after the first.

'Nice one, mate,' Marc said, as he viewed a huge hole punched in the left-hand side of the life preserver. 'Let's have two more of those.'

Scoring a first hit lowers a sniper's stress level because it means you've mastered the wind and range. Paul's third shot made a hole a few centimetres above the second, while his final shot was right on the edge.

'You've done some damage, but I can't tell if it was bark splinters or your bullet that hit the ring,' Marc said.

'Two and a half out of four,' Paul said, as he stood up. 'Could have been worse at that range.'

As Paul pulled a cloth from his jacket and began wiping smears of his sweat off the rifle, Marc glanced at a pocket watch, then at their map. The shooting had gone well, but they were still behind schedule.

'Looks like the last aiming area's less than a kilometre away,' Marc said. 'Mostly downhill, although we've got to cross a stream.'

'How deep?' Paul asked warily.

'Wish I knew,' Marc said, as he peeled the binocular strap from around his neck.

Marc would snipe at the final target, but as he took the rifle from Paul both lads were dazzled by yellow light.

'Why can I see you?' Sergeant Goldberg shouted, as he crawled out of the undergrowth with a powerful torch in one hand and a section of camouflage netting worn like a cape. 'What are you playing at?'

'We're checking the map ready for our run to the final aiming point, sir,' Marc said.

'I'm not blind,' Goldberg said, as he aimed the torch beam right into Marc's eyes. 'But what were you told about this terrain?'

Marc's mind was a blur. He was dripping sweat, exhausted, hungry and his feet were so blistered that he was dreading the pain when he took his boots off.

'Well?' Goldberg shouted, as the beam made Marc's eyes tear over.

'We were told to treat the terrain like enemy territory at all times, sir,' Paul said weakly.

'Enemy territory,' Goldberg repeated, as he rapped his

knuckles against Marc's skull. 'That means you keep *low* at all times. That means you take cover. It certainly doesn't mean that you stand still on open ground, staring at your map and talking in voices that I can hear from my hiding spot twenty-five yards away. Both of you, get down. I need to see thirty push-ups.'

Marc started pulling the strap of his equipment pack off his shoulder, which made Goldberg's eyes bulge.

'Did I tell you to take that off, lad?' Goldberg roared.

Marc was strong. If he'd been fresh he'd have knocked out thirty push-ups in as many seconds. But his arms began shuddering at twenty-two.

'Twenty-four,' Goldberg shouted, when Marc collapsed. 'Crack on! Did I say twenty-four?'

Paul had taken his pack off to shoot, but even without extra weight his gangly arms meant push-ups were always hard. He only got to thirteen before collapsing in the dirt.

'I can't,' Paul gasped, as Goldberg moved close and blitzed him with the torch beam.

'Can't what?' Goldberg demanded.

'Do any more,' Paul said.

If it hadn't been dark, Paul would have seen Goldberg turning red.

'What's the last word out of your mouth every time you address me, boy?'

Everything clicked into place. 'Sir,' Paul said. 'I'm

sorry, sir, I'm just tired, sir.'

'It's warm and dry,' Goldberg shouted. 'This is *nothing*. Real sniper teams eat, piss and shit in freezing-cold rat-infested holes for days on end, waiting for one Nazi head to pop up. And you *dare* moan that you're tired after a little overnighter in the forest?'

Goldberg switched off his torch and for a few moments there was nothing but the sound of two boys gasping in the dark.

'Shall we carry on now, sir?' Marc asked breathlessly.

'Sam and Luc started ten minutes after you so that they didn't reach the aiming zones at the same time. They overtook you before the fourth aiming point. They're already heading back to campus for a shower and bed.'

Paul and Marc exchanged solemn looks. Goldberg wasn't bad and the tough guy act was what they expected from a training instructor. But learning they'd finished behind their rivals after working so hard was a kick in the gut.

'Captain Henderson is giving the four of you an 8 a.m. briefing,' Goldberg said. 'I was in these woods preparing well before you two got up, and now I need my bed. So you two can forget aiming point eight. The exercise ends here and now.'

As they'd already lost, Paul and Marc were happy not to have to carry on.

'You've got *nothing* to smile about, soldiers,' Goldberg said. 'There's no bed on campus for you two tonight. You can sleep out here, then make your own way back in time for the captain's briefing. Is that clear?'

'Yes, sir,' both lads replied.

'Bloody, shitting shit!' Paul cursed, once he was certain Goldberg was well clear. 'It's gone two now and it's over an hour's walk back to campus from here.'

Marc knew he'd have been faster with anyone but Paul as a partner, but he said nothing because they were good friends and it wasn't Paul's fault that he'd been born weedy.

'It's warm and dry, so I'm not buggering about making a shelter,' Marc said. 'And it may not be comfortable, but I'm knackered so a few bugs and a bit of damp won't stop me sleeping.'

CHAPTER NINETEEN

Luc was usually a scruff, but he'd polished his boots and put on a clean white shirt, knowing it would make Marc and Paul feel even worse.

'You've got twigs in your hair,' Luc taunted, as his rivals came into the classroom used for mission briefings. 'Man, I slept *so* well last night. Did you sleep well, Sam?'

Sam liked Marc and Paul. He'd have happily stayed out of the teasing, but Luc was a bully and he couldn't risk upsetting his powerfully built training partner.

'Yeah, I slept well,' Sam said, half-heartedly.

'I was so muddy when I got in last night,' Luc continued. 'I didn't want all that dirt clogging the shower, so I wiped the worst of it off on stick-boy's bed sheet.'

Marc ignored the pain in his blistered feet as he

booted a chair out of the way and lunged towards the desk Luc sat on.

'If you've touched either of our beds, I'll kick the crap out of you,' Marc shouted.

Paul put a hand on Marc's shoulder and pulled him back. 'Don't rear up. That's what he's after.'

'Pippa cooked a good breakfast this morning too,' Luc said. 'Scrambled egg, black pudding, three slices of bread. Ain't that right, Sam?'

Sam looked down at his muddy boots. 'They might have saved you some.'

'I'm not even hungry,' Marc said. 'We found plenty of fruit and berries on our way here this morning.'

This was a total lie.

'How many points out of thirty-two did you two get?' Paul asked.

'None of your business,' Luc said.

Marc sensed a chink in Luc's armour: if they'd shot well he'd have been shouting from the rooftops.

'What did you get?' Marc asked Sam.

Sam shrugged. 'There's a couple where we didn't see our exact score. But I reckon it's somewhere between sixteen and eighteen points.'

'It was easily more than that,' Luc said. 'I shot at least ten. I bet when Kindhe collects our targets it'll be more like twenty.'

Sam looked doubtful, but didn't contradict his

partner. 'How many did you guys get?'

'About twenty,' Paul said. 'It would have been more, because it was Marc's turn on the last target. He only missed two shots all night.'

Luc wasn't keen to dwell on scores, because Marc was easily the best shot of the four. 'I wish you'd sit over the other side,' he told Marc. 'You smell like you slept in something that came out the back of a cow.'

'Well at least I've never wet my bed,' Marc shouted.

'I didn't wet my bed,' Luc said furiously. 'I had really bad flu. I passed out.'

Marc smiled. 'Bed pisser!'

Luc jumped off the desk and grabbed the lapels of Marc's combat jacket. Marc went for a kick in the balls, but only banged his shin on a desk because Luc had spun him around and was trying to splay him over a desktop.

'Let go, moron,' Marc shouted.

As Luc slugged Marc in the gut, Paul ran to the front of the classroom and grabbed the big wooden blackboard ruler. It made a very satisfactory crack as it hit Luc over the back of the head.

'You wait, stick-boy,' Luc shouted. 'I'll break you when I've dealt with this arsehole.'

Chairs and tables grated against the floor as Luc landed another punch on Marc, while Paul tried to lock his arms around Luc's waist to drag him away. The door swung open and Third Officer DeVere – more commonly known as Boo – charged into the tangle of flying limbs.

'Pack it in, now,' she roared. 'The captain will be here any second and you'll all be for it.'

Boo was taller than the two fifteen-year-olds but not as strong. With Paul's help she got Luc off Marc, just as Henderson came into the room holding an armful of briefing papers.

'This is unacceptable,' he shouted.

After putting his papers down, Henderson charged towards the boys. He picked the blackboard ruler off the floor and there was a whooshing sound, followed by a crack as Marc took an almighty swipe across the front of his thigh.

As Marc yelped, Henderson's second swipe caught a rapidly retreating Luc across the buttocks. Paul braced for a whack himself, but luckily Henderson had only seen him helping Boo break the fight up.

'Sit down, all four of you,' Henderson barked. 'I'm sick of you two constantly fighting. I'm starting to think a damned good Royal-Navy-style flogging is needed to straighten you out. If I see this again, I give you my word that that's what you'll get. Understood?'

'Yes, sir,' the boys chanted.

'Now, sit down.'

Paul drew pleasure from the pained expression Luc wore as he sat on his freshly thrashed arse. Henderson hadn't been messing about – the blow to Marc's thigh had drawn blood, and he was still wincing with pain as Henderson moved his papers to the front of the room, then got Boo to help pin photographs around the outer frame of the blackboard.

'In contrast to what I've seen here this morning,' Henderson began, 'Sergeant Goldberg tells me that all four of you have made good progress during the first five days of sniper training. I know you're wondering why you've been undergoing this training, and as you've now reached the halfway point I felt you deserved an explanation. Boo will begin the briefing with some background information. Sam, don't hide up there at the back, come up front so that you can see the photographs properly.'

Boo began talking as Sam shuffled between tightly packed desks towards the front.

'As some of you know already, a few weeks back Rosie Clarke stumbled upon a notebook containing remarkable intelligence relating to a secret German project known as FZG-76.'

Boo paused to make a rough outline drawing on the blackboard. It looked like a bomb, but it had small wings and a tail with what looked like a giant golf tee mounted on it.

'As Hitler feels the weight of Allied pressure, he's been making an increasing number of statements about

"Victory" weapons which he claims will turn the war back in his favour. We believe that FZG-76 is one such victory weapon and it will probably be the first of them to be used in anger.'

'So what is it?' Sam asked.

'Good question,' Boo said cheerfully, as she tapped her stick of chalk against the diagram. 'Put simply, it's a bomb that flies by itself. There's a propellerless engine of unknown design built into the tail, a big cargo of explosives in the middle, and in the nose there's a gyroscopic system that guides the flying bomb to its target.'

The four boys looked at each other in disbelief.

'It'll never work,' Marc said. 'A plane with no propeller and no pilot. How does it even get off the ground?'

'I'm afraid it's flown already, Marc,' Boo said, which was enough to make Luc mumble that Marc was a dickhead. 'The resistance in Denmark has been picking up radio signals transmitted by FZG-76 test units for over six months. Triangulation of these radio signals leads us to believe that the units fly faster than any British fighter and that the accuracy of the self-guidance system is improving.'

'So when will they start bombing us with them?' Paul asked.

'Indications are that FZG-76 is still in prototype phase.

Mass production is probably still three to twelve months away. What we're really interested in is the guidance system, here in the nose.'

Boo chalked a big white X on the nose of her crudely drawn bomb.

'The notebook Rosie recovered suggests that much of the work on the guidance system for this new weapon is being undertaken by a group of French scientists. They're currently being forced to work against their will in an underground bunker west of Rennes. Our job is to stop these highly-skilled scientists doing their job.'

Luc smiled as he raised an invisible sniper rifle. 'So we've been training so that we can hide in the bushes and blow their heads apart when they come up for exercise, or whatever. Sounds like a good laugh. You can count me in!'

Paul looked uncomfortable, while Marc shook his head before jumping at a chance to prove Luc wrong.

'Don't be a moron, Luc,' Marc said. 'If we wanted the scientists dead we'd just plant a massive bomb and blow the place sky high.'

'Don't call me a moron,' Luc growled. 'I'm not the one who slept in the woods and stinks like a tramp.'

'All right,' Henderson shouted, as he slammed the big ruler against the blackboard. 'You two are going *exactly* the right way about earning that flogging I promised. But Marc's assessment is basically correct. You've been training for a sneak raid on the bunker. The reason sniper skills are required is that besides the research lab and a dozen scientists, Rosie Clarke has confirmed that the bunker is being used as a storage depot for Luftwaffe bombs. You'll need to shoot straight, because if this raid turns into a fire fight, there's a good chance that a stray bullet will set off enough bombs to blow up a small town.'

'Why put important scientists in such a risky location?' Paul asked.

'We questioned this too,' Boo answered. 'The first reason we can think of is that bunkers with rooms large enough to hide a laboratory are rare. There are probably less than a dozen similar bunkers in France, and while there are many large bunkers in Germany, the level of Allied bombing means that space inside them is always going to be desperately short.

'The second reason is political. As you can see from the photographs, the base is patrolled and run by the Luftwaffe, who use it to store their bombs. But according to our sources in Denmark, the FZG-76 project is classified as long-range artillery. Its development is controlled and funded by the German Army.'

'So the Luftwaffe and the army are like a couple of kids fighting over a shared bedroom,' Sam said.

Boo smiled and nodded. 'That's what we suspect.'

Henderson pointed to the photographs before

speaking. 'Rosie Clarke has befriended a couple of lads who know the area around the bunker well. With their help, she's made an excellent job of photographing the base and studying security and movements in and out over the past few weeks. She estimates that the base is manned by a team of around ten elderly Luftwaffe guards, plus five soldiers who guard the scientists.

'The resistance in Paris have sent Rosie a wireless operator, who has been in daily communication with us. She's using a small team to keep the bunker under surveillance, and our picture of bunker operations is improving all the time.'

'So how exactly do we attack?' Paul asked. 'I can't see more than a couple of guards in any of those pictures. Which means the rest of them will be underground.'

'The details of our plan will be refined over the next few days, as Rosie feeds us more information,' Henderson explained. 'At this stage, I want you four to concentrate one hundred per cent on mastering your sniper skills. On the last day of the course, Sergeant Goldberg will conduct a final test. The two boys who score highest will be picked for the mission.'

Marc and Luc eyed each other warily. Marc was the best sniper and Sam the weakest, but second and third places were a toss up between Paul and Luc.

Sam raised his hand warily, and posed the question on everyone's mind. 'Captain, what happens if the two boys who finish top don't get along?'

'Candidates in this unit will be picked for missions based solely on their abilities,' Henderson said curtly. 'Anyone who is incapable of putting personal differences aside for the duration of a critical mission has no place inside Espionage Research Unit B.'

CHAPTER TWENTY

Four days later.

The lads began their penultimate day of sniper training on the USAF shooting range. The paper targets were now set at hundred-yard distances, starting at three hundred and going up to a thousand.

Sergeant Goldberg spent much of the morning working one-on-one with each boy, making tiny adjustments to their shooting technique. The tolerances for long-distance shooting are extraordinarily fine, so a tiny change in body position or breathing technique can add a hundred yards to the range over which a sniper can shoot accurately.

Goldberg's biggest breakthrough came with Sam. The No 4 rifle was a long weapon, and Sam was at full stretch when he shot. Goldberg rectified this by replacing the wooden stock on Sam's rifle with one from a more compact version of the No 4 developed for commando operations.

Changing a sniper's weapon so late in the course was a risk, but after a few rogue shots Sam began hitting targets at five to seven hundred yards. Nobody took score, but by the time they broke for lunch Sam's smile looked like it had been glued on.

'I'm real competition for the second slot now,' Sam said, as the quartet downed an unappetising lunch of tinned beef stew tipped over mashed potato.

Paul smiled. Marc liked anything that reduced the possibility of his having to do the mission with Luc. Inevitably, Luc himself looked annoyed.

It all came out after lunch, when Sam went upstairs for a pee and Luc bundled him against the tiled wall.

'What's your problem?' Sam shouted.

'I thought we were partners,' Luc said. 'I've carried half your kit for the best part of two weeks.'

Half was an exaggeration, but Luc had carried some of Sam's stuff because he was faster and much bigger.

'We've always been fighting for the same job,' Sam said.

'You're younger,' Luc said, as he gave Sam another shove. 'Your time will come, but this is my mission.'

Sam didn't want to make an enemy of a thug like Luc. 'If I throw a couple of shots, you'll owe me a big favour.'

'That's fair,' Luc said, nodding. 'I'll beat someone up for you, or whatever.'

Sam's jubilant mood was gone as he walked down to a ground-floor classroom for their afternoon session. He tried telling himself that he hadn't expected to make it on to the mission when he got out of bed that morning and his situation was no worse now. But he hated the fact that he'd let Luc get his way.

The classroom-based afternoon session was all about calculations. Over normal distances, shooting is about taking a good aim and pulling a trigger, but for sniping the steadiest hand and perfect technique are useless unless you're also able to grasp the physics of a flying bullet.

'Range six hundred and forty yards north-east,' Goldberg said, as he rapidly chalked figures on the blackboard. 'Wind gusting three to seven knots, heading south, temperature eighty degrees, humidity high, target eighty metres above the firing position.'

The trainees each had pieces of chalk, a handheld slate and a selection of pre-printed range tables.

'Time,' Goldberg said, after about forty seconds.

The four boys held up their slates, each with figures for vertical and horizontal aim-off chalked on them.

'The good news is that you've all got similar figures,' Goldberg said. 'The bad news is that you're all going to send bullets ploughing into the dirt well short of the target. High humidity makes air more dense, which means?'

Sam raised his hand. 'The arc of the bullet is less pronounced and the denser air makes the trajectory decay faster, sir.'

'Correct,' Goldberg said. 'So why didn't you take that into account in your calculation? Assuming you don't have a barometer handy, how can you judge humidity?'

Paul raised a hand, 'You can expect high humidity after rainfall, sir. Humidity is more likely to be high if you're near to large bodies of water . . .'

Goldberg interrupted. 'I didn't ask *where* humidity was, I asked how you judge it.'

Paul hesitated. 'The amount you sweat is a clue, and if you fog a piece of glass such as the back of your scope, or breathe on a cold mirror, rapid evaporation means that humidity is low, sir.'

'Good,' Goldberg said. 'But it's going to be different depending on which mirror you use. Your breath will have less moisture in it if you're breathing heavily. So if you're in a climate where it's hot and humidity is likely to affect your shooting, you've got to practise. Find a barometer with a humidity gauge, test your mirror under different circumstances.'

Sam raised his hand again. 'Can you get little humidity gauges that you can carry around, sir?'

Goldberg nodded as he walked towards Marc, who'd

apparently lost concentration. He flicked Marc's ear, before grabbing all the velocity and distance charts on his desk.

'When you're working in near dark, you can't stand around looking at charts, or squinting at a mercury bar on a tiny humidity gauge,' Goldberg said. 'A good sniper knows the underlying physics so well that he *feels* his shot. Senses the wind, temperature and humidity, and rattles off the maths as easily as you'd do your two times table.

'That level of skill only comes with years of experience. So when this course ends tomorrow I want you to keep memorising your charts. Take your weapon out and practise regularly, in rain, snow and heat. Is that clear?'

'Yes, sir,' the boys barked.

'Right,' Goldberg said. 'New calculation. Range one thousand three hundred and thirty feet. Shooting north, wind twenty-two knots, gusting south by south-west. Target is eighteen yards above your shooting position, and you're lying in thick snow, with your breath visible.'

*

After a morning of shooting and an afternoon of brain-numbing maths, Goldberg had devised an evening potato hunt that would raise morale, while testing the four recruits' stealth and camouflage skills.

A sack of potatoes had been distributed in the area around the old village school, Henderson's cottage and the nearby church graveyard. The trainees worked alone and had to collect as many spuds as possible, while Goldberg had mustered more than a dozen staff and fellow trainees to hunt them.

If a trainee was caught, they had five potatoes taken out of their sack and had to run back to a starting position near the campus gates before resuming the hunt.

The first round of the game only lasted ten minutes, at which point Henderson's wife Joan emerged from their cottage and began yelling. She was trying to get her two-year-old to sleep, but it was proving impossible because he kept running to the window every time he heard something exciting going on outside.

After that little glitch, all potatoes were moved away from the Hendersons' cottage and the game resumed. When ninety minutes running around in twilight were up, Paul surprised everyone by winning. His cunning strategy had been to hide all the potatoes he'd collected until the end of the game, which meant he didn't have to worry about losing five of them every time he got caught.

Goldberg had thrown himself into his role as a hunter, and his uniform was wet and streaked with grass stains as he walked up to the dormitory rooms on the first floor. All the kids who'd taken part were in high spirits, and a new battle had broken out with pillows, flying boots and balled-up socks as they got changed for bed.

'I've enjoyed working with you four,' Goldberg told his trainees, once they'd gathered around. 'People your age learn fast, which makes my job easier. There's going to be one final exercise tomorrow morning. Kindhe and I are driving out early to set up four shooting points in the woods.

'You'll each work alone, four shots per target and you'll lose a point if you don't reach each shooting zone within twenty minutes. I want you at the front door ready to shoot at 9 a.m., so I'd suggest you all get a good night's sleep. The two trainees who score highest will parachute into France with Henderson.'

CHAPTER TWENTY-ONE

The Group A dorm was full of snores and nasal whistles as Marc opened one eye and peered at his bedside clock. It was 2:30 a.m. He rolled out of bed, dressed in underpants and grubby from all the running around he'd done the previous evening.

After sweeping his boots, shirt and trousers from under the bed, Marc did a furtive three-sixty glance before dashing through the open door, along the hallway and down to the ground floor. The main door creaked alarmingly as he pulled it open; then he ran on bare, blistered, feet to the side of the building.

Marc leaned against a cold wall as he stepped into his trousers. He did his shirt up in the wrong button holes, pushed grit-covered soles into his boots and dashed off towards the graveyard with his laces trailing behind.

Cutting across the graveyard brought him out on to a path, and he reached the armoury after a three-minute jog. It seemed empty, but he nervously circled the building to make sure.

The main door was padlocked, but it was an easy climb over a shoulder-height fence on to the pistol shooting range and once he'd dropped into the compound the door between the pistol range and armoury had no lock at all.

The armoury hut was split in two. One half was behind a locked steel mesh, with boxes of ammunition and unissued service weapons stacked on shelves. The larger half had slotted wooden gun racks along the walls, coat hooks, a few benches and three large workbenches, each with built-in slots for the lubricants, polishing cloths and brushes used to clean weapons.

In most cases these guns kept in the armoury were the personal property of shooting enthusiasts in the USAF, so almost all of the weapons lived in bags or wooden boxes. The four trainees' sniper rifles were stacked near the main entrance in zipped canvas bags.

Marc and Paul's guns were next to each other, and Sam's was distinctive now that it had the shorter stock, but it was Luc's weapon Marc was interested in. He felt a twinge of guilt as he unzipped Luc's rifle and laid it across the nearest bench, but Luc was a nasty piece of work and Marc reasoned that this mission would be better off without him.

Every gun comes with its own cleaning and maintenance kit, but Marc ignored Luc's kit and took a small screwdriver from a wooden drawer beneath the worktop.

A rifle is more accurate than a short weapon such as a pistol because its long barrel is bored with a spiral pattern that spins a bullet. Marc expertly removed the bolt handle and receiver from Luc's gun, then jammed the screwdriver into the near end of the barrel and roughed up the surface with the sharp end.

The scraping left several silver gouge marks in the oiled metal, so Marc dripped gun oil on to a cloth and smeared it over to disguise them. The result wasn't invisible, but while you'd have had to look hard to find the scratches Marc hoped they'd be enough to reduce the spin of the bullet leaving the gun and make Luc miss a couple of his more difficult shots.

*

As usual Pippa the cook fed her French boys with a hearty English breakfast. The four lads on the sniping course were nervous and sick of each other's company, so Luc sat alone, Sam joined his big brother Joel, and Marc sat with PT.

Marc had seen Paul get out of bed, but didn't see him again until he walked into the toilet. Paul was emerging from a cubicle, looking weak, with the tang of sick hanging in the air.

'You OK?' Marc asked.

'Nerves,' Paul said weakly, as he put his mouth under a cold tap and rinsed.

'I'll bet you do better than you're expecting,' Marc said, grinning and half tempted to tell Paul what he'd done the night before.

'It's doing well that I'm scared of,' Paul confessed.

Marc looked baffled. 'I don't understand.'

'Goldberg's had us shooting car tyres, alarm clocks, paper targets, dead chickens and rugby balls,' Paul said. 'But if I get the mission, it's going to be real people I'm seeing through my scope.'

'You can do what it takes,' Marc said. 'You killed Germans and saved Rosie's life in Lorient two summers back.'

'This is different,' Paul said. 'Lining up someone a thousand feet away and executing them. It's cold-blooded. Part of me hopes Luc does beat me this morning. This job suits a cruel bastard like him.'

Marc looked crestfallen. 'How can you start this up?' he blurted. 'People always call you a wimp, but I never thought it was true until now.'

Paul looked wounded and Marc immediately felt bad.

'Try your best today and we'll talk this through afterwards, yeah?' Marc said.

Paul was used to people calling him a wimp, but Marc

was his best friend so this was different. He opened his mouth to speak, but no words formed so he barged Marc and stormed towards the stairs.

Marc yelled from the top landing, 'Paul, I'm sorry.'

But Paul ignored him and Marc felt like crap as he headed off to the armoury to get his weapon.

*

The atmosphere stayed tense as Goldberg drove the quartet out to the woods in a canvas-sided Royal Navy truck. The boys set off from the starting point at ten-minute intervals so that they didn't reach the shooting zones at the same time. To minimise the chances of catching each other up, they went in order of speed, with fastest runner Marc going first, then Luc, Sam and Paul last.

Until now all the training had been in pairs because snipers most commonly work that way in the field. Marc enjoyed being able to move without Paul holding him back and reached his first shooting zone after an eight-minute uphill run.

It had rained heavily that morning and his thighs grew soggy as he settled into a firing position where a boulder served as cover. As it was daylight, he had an easy time spotting a pair of circular targets set at four-eighty and six hundred yards.

The instructions stapled to his map said he had to take two shots at each target. Goldberg's point system only distinguished between hit and miss, but Marc still took pride in two hits on the centre of the nearer target.

A wind gusted strongly into his face as his first shot at the more distant target punched the earth several metres short. He corrected upwards by half a degree to compensate for the wind and got his final shot dead on.

The route to the second shooting zone involved doubling back, and Marc and Luc exchanged grunts as they passed on a steep slope. Marc got slightly lost on his way to the second target, but scraped inside the twenty minutes he needed to avoid losing a point.

The firing position for the second target was down at a sharp angle, but he still hit with four out of four. He missed two shots on the third target, but the range was over seven hundred yards and he was the only one of the four trainees who could regularly hit targets over that sort of distance.

The final shooting zone was more than five kilometres from the third. Rather than kill himself trying to run it in under twenty minutes, Marc walked, trading the loss of a point for being in good shooting condition when he arrived.

The final target was two hundred and fifty yards away, but the shooting position was a muddy riverbank and late morning sunlight reflecting off fast-moving water meant he saw nothing but golden blurs when he tried using his split-image rangefinder.

Marc was concerned. There was no certainty he could hit the target without a clear view through the scope and if it clouded over when the other lads arrived they'd have four easy shots. He looked up hoping to see a cloud heading towards the sun, but the only thing in the sky was birds.

Luc had tried to beat the twenty-minute arrival time and burst through the undergrowth between two large trees as Marc sent his first shot a few inches wide of the target.

'Sir?' Luc shouted, sounding a touch desperate.

Marc broke out of his sniper state, to look around. Henderson and Goldberg were walking uphill towards the shooting zone.

'Sir, I'd like another go.' Luc said. 'There's something wrong with my gun.'

'What makes you say that?' Goldberg asked.

'I've not hit a thing,' Luc said. 'Might have caught the edge of one target, but that was more a fluke than anything.'

Marc's nerves jangled as he turned back to his scope and tried to focus. He'd hoped that the scratches he'd made in the barrel would cause two or three missed shots and be dismissed as Luc having a bad day. But if Luc had missed all but one target, there was sure to be an investigation.

Marc's second shot was a near miss, but a minor

correction sent the third and fourth flying into the centre of the rectangular target.

'Good morning, sir,' Marc said, standing up as Henderson stepped up to him.

'How did it go?'

'I hit eleven out of sixteen, sir,' Marc said, trying to sound confident. 'Minus one for arriving late at the last target.'

'Sounds good,' Henderson said. 'I'd be surprised if that isn't enough to book your ticket.'

As Marc spoke he kept one eye on Goldberg, who'd begun inspecting Luc's gun.

'I expect it's dirty,' Goldberg said unsympathetically. 'I've warned you enough times. You've nobody to blame but yourself.'

Sam came scrambling out of bushes from the opposite direction to which Marc and Luc had arrived, which brought a smile to Henderson's face.

'Why are you coming from that way?'

'Got lost, sir,' Sam said, breathlessly.

'How's the shooting going?'

'Can't get it right today, sir,' Sam said. 'I've only hit four from twelve. And I'm late to this shooting zone, so I've lost a point for that too.'

'See if you can make it up here then,' Henderson said.

'Luc's scored one or zero,' Marc said. 'Claims there's something wrong with his gun.'

Marc expected to see a grin, but Sam looked worried as he found a shooting position a couple of yards left of the one Marc had taken. Sam had deliberately missed a couple of shots on the assumption that it would be enough to ensure he finished behind Luc. But if Luc had scored one or less, then all his misses had done was gift second place to Paul.

As he'd already beaten Luc, Sam saw no reason not to try his best. He didn't need binoculars to identify the target, but was surprised when he looked through his telescopic sight and saw nothing but golden blurs. It was the first time he'd encountered problems with reflected light, but he remembered something that Goldberg had said on the second day of the course.

After a quick rummage in his kit bag, Sam pulled out a leather pouch filled with optical filters and screwed a polarising lens to the end of his scope. The polariser was designed to cut out light coming from a specific direction, and by looking through the scope and rotating the filter, Sam was able to eliminate all the reflections.

The filter also cut out a lot of regular light, so the image through Sam's scope was gloomy, but still better than anything you'd see when shooting at night. As Marc kicked himself for not remembering the filter pack, Sam aimed his rifle at the target and made four clean hits.

'That's more like it,' Henderson said, as he gave Sam a slap on the back.

'Seven out of sixteen's not great,' Sam said, as he wondered if it would be enough to beat Paul.

While Sam had been shooting, Goldberg had rolled a piece of canvas out on the ground and begun disassembling Luc's rifle.

'A bullet seems to have partially disintegrated inside the chamber,' Goldberg said stiffly. 'You've ruined the barrel. You're lucky you're not in the army, because this weapon is useless and you'd have been docked at least three month's wages.'

'There was no dirt in there, sir,' Luc said, sounding uncharacteristically shrill. 'I spent half an hour cleaning that weapon last night. It was *spotless*.'

'Then how could this have happened?' Goldberg shouted, but his expression changed as he raised the barrel up to his eye and looked down towards the disc of sunlight at the far end. 'Did you try dislodging a bullet with something sharp?'

'No, sir,' Luc said.

'Explain this to me then,' Goldberg said, as he passed the weapon across. 'Bullets move fast, they leave long straight trails. How did those great wiggly gouges get there?'

Marc gulped as Luc looked down the barrel.

'Sabotage, sir!' Luc shouted indignantly. 'I cleaned that gun last night, running through with a soft clean cloth just like you showed me. Those scratches weren't there, I swear on my dead mother's grave, sir.'

'That's a serious allegation, Luc,' Goldberg said. 'Are you certain you want to stick with it?'

Luc glowered furiously at Marc. 'I know this was you,' he roared, before charging towards Marc.

CHAPTER TWENTY-TWO

Marc dived out of the way, but still caught a glancing punch across the upper arm and stumbled into low branches. Henderson charged in and pulled the boys apart.

'Pack it in,' he shouted. 'What's going on?'

'There's unusual damage to the barrel,' Goldberg said. 'Luc isn't the best at keeping his weapon clean, but I've never seen markings like that inside a barrel before. It certainly looks like sabotage.'

Henderson snapped his head around and stared at Marc. 'Well, was it you?'

'No, sir,' Marc said. 'Those guns aren't locked up. Anyone with access to the armoury could have done it.'

'I suppose,' Henderson agreed. 'But I find it a hefty coincidence that Luc's gun should be sabotaged the night before your final exercise.'

Goldberg spoke. 'To be fair, Captain, Marc was the best shooter by far. It was the other two who had most to gain by ruining Luc's chances of finishing second.'

'Marc hates me,' Luc blurted. 'He doesn't want me on the mission with him. Sam and Paul are both too gutless to try something like this.'

'I'm not gutless,' Sam shouted angrily.

Henderson turned towards him. 'So did you sabotage Luc's gun?'

'No, sir,' Sam said. 'But we've been partners all week. I don't like him having a go at me.'

'Well, it has to be one of you,' Henderson said. 'If I don't get a confession, I'll wait until Paul finishes shooting and then get Kindhe up here. He'll make the three of you do PT for two hours, and then I'll ask again. If nobody confesses, you'll do another two hours. And this will keep going until one of you does the decent thing and owns up.'

Paul came up a path looking exhausted and confused. 'What's all the shouting about?'

Luc pointed at Marc. 'Ask your girlfriend.'

Marc was a decent person. He couldn't live with the idea of Sam and Paul being forced to do drill so he took half a step back from Henderson and raised his hands.

'It was me,' he said weakly. 'I sneaked out to the armoury in the night.'

Luc broke into a huge smile as Henderson grabbed Marc's neck, shoved him back against a tree trunk and slapped him full force across the side of his head.

'Are you completely stupid?' Henderson shouted. 'Guns aren't toys, you know? The bullet that exploded in the chamber might have blown his ear off. You're an absolute bloody idiot.'

Henderson gave Marc two more brutal whacks before yanking him out of the trees and giving him a kick up the arse that sent him sprawling face first into the undergrowth.

'I said I'd flog the pair of you if things flared up again,' Henderson roared. 'It might be the only thing to sort you out.'

'I'm the victim here, sir,' Luc shouted indignantly.

Henderson didn't like Luc, but in this instance he was right.

'OK,' Henderson said, after a moment's silence. 'This is *extremely* serious. I need to think about this whole mess before making any decisions. Sergeant Goldberg and I will ride back to campus in the truck. You four can have a jolly good think as you walk back and there'd better *not* be any fighting between you. When you arrive on campus, form a line by the main door and stand to attention. Do not move until I'm ready to come outside and speak with you.'

'What about my last four shots?' Paul asked.

'There's no point,' Henderson snapped. 'This has descended into a farce.'

*

Whilst Henderson plotted missions, devised training programmes and attended secret intelligence briefings, Superintendent Eileen McAfferty was actually the commanding officer of Espionage Research Unit B. She was the one who haggled over budgets, made sure there was food on the table and procured everything from plastic explosives to disinfectant and boots for growing boys.

McAfferty's Glasgow accent always grew stronger when she was cross. 'I always leave disciplinary matters to you,' she told Henderson firmly. 'But I want it on record that I'm dead against any boy getting flogged.'

The captain and superintendent were in their shared office, immediately off the hallway of the old village school.

'I was flogged as a naval cadet,' Henderson said. 'Never did me any lasting damage.'

'That's a matter for debate,' McAfferty said. 'They're only boys. It's barbaric.'

'I was younger than Marc and Luc,' Henderson said. 'They'd make us bend bare-assed over this old vaulting horse, crusted in dried blood. The other cadets were made to cheer every time you took a stroke.'

McAfferty smiled slightly. 'You're hardly winning me

over with that description.'

'And I promised Marc and Luc they'd be flogged if there was any more trouble between them.'

As Henderson spoke, McAfferty rifled through a tray of letters. She pulled one out and took on a sly expression as she held it up.

'I had this through from SIS headquarters in London,' McAfferty said, before reading a short section aloud. '*The risks of serious security breaches are such that it is no longer acceptable for senior officers with detailed knowledge of British intelligence operations to work inside German-occupied territory.*'

'How does that have any bearing on Marc's behaviour?' Henderson asked.

McAfferty smiled. 'I know you're keen to drop into France on this operation. But after reading this letter, I can't help wondering if I ought to run your plan past headquarters first.'

Henderson bristled, but also smiled a little. 'And I suppose this is only likely to occur if Marc or Luc gets a flogging?'

'You're being pig-headed,' McAfferty said, deliberately ignoring Henderson's question. 'And you've always been fond of Marc.'

'Marc's a great lad, but he's been utterly stupid in this instance,' Henderson said. 'If you're not going to allow a flogging, what am I supposed to do?'

McAfferty thought for a couple of seconds. 'The root

of all this is that Marc and Luc can't stand each other. Back in Glasgow, the head of my brother's school used to give boys who couldn't get along a set of gloves and stick them in a boxing ring.'

'That's common enough,' Henderson laughed. 'The PE masters at my grammar school did the same to lads who squared off on the football pitch.'

'I'd say they're evenly matched,' McAfferty said. 'Let 'em knock the hell out of each other for a few rounds.'

'They might even learn to respect one another when it's over,' Henderson said.

*

After two hours standing outside, followed by regular afternoon lessons and a roast dinner, Sam and Paul found themselves sat against the wall by the open rear doors of the school hall.

'We could ask Henderson who's going on the mission,' Sam said.

'Ask if you want to, but he's in a terrible mood,' Paul said. 'PT reckons Henderson was having a blazing row with McAfferty in the office earlier.'

'It's bound to be Marc and Luc,' Sam said. 'Have them fight it out. Tell them to hug and make up then pack 'em off on the mission with Henderson.'

Paul didn't sound convinced. 'Those two loathe each other, so I wouldn't bank on them making up. I've never really understood the logic behind making boys square off.'

'I'd rather stand in the ring than get flogged in front of everyone,' Sam said. 'And even if we don't get on the mission, I reckon it's gonna be a bloody amazing fight. You coming inside?'

Sam led Paul into the hall, which still had the muggy aroma of roast lamb and boiled veg. There was no proper boxing ring, just a square made from eight rubber training mats which had been nailed to the floorboards to stop them slipping.

Everyone wanted to see the fight, and even the two cooks had stayed late to watch. At one end of the hall, Marc was having a pair of thinly-padded brown boxing gloves pulled over taped-up fists. Luc was a lone wolf at the other end, sitting on the food-serving counter in shorts and white plimsolls with his gloves already fitted.

'Square up,' Kindhe shouted.

The big African instructor would be referee, even though his take on the rules of boxing wasn't entirely conventional.

'I'm the boss,' he told Marc and Luc, shaking his enormous fist in their faces as the crowd sizzled with anticipation. 'Any nonsense and I'll splatter you into next week.'

Henderson sat with two-year-old Terence on his lap. McAfferty and Boo had seats close to the mats and space was made for Joyce's wheelchair, but everyone else was on their feet.

'Four rounds of three minutes,' Kindhe said, as he pointed to Henderson who was holding a small brass bell. 'Ready when you are, boss.'

As Marc and Luc glowered at each other in the centre of the mats, Sam's brother Joel shouted, 'Get him, Marc.'

The other boys and even most of the staff were on Marc's side and a cheer went up in his favour. Neither fighter wore a mouth guard, and Luc gave the crowd a scowl.

'Your mums are all slags,' Luc shouted.

That sort of language wasn't used in front of ladies, and Henderson flirted with the idea giving Luc a slap. But he wanted to see the fight as much as anyone, so he put the bell in Terence's little hand and told him to give it a good shake.

CHAPTER TWENTY-THREE

The crowd might have been cheering Marc, but if they'd been forced to bet most would have had their money on Luc. Within a second of the fight starting, Luc's glove had smashed Marc backwards. Follow-up jabs pounded his gut and kidneys as Marc buckled and went down on his bum.

'Come on, Marc!' Paul shouted. 'Put some oomph into it.'

Marc had the metallic taste of blood in the back of his mouth as he looked up at his opponent. Luc had thighs like logs, and his defiant stare told everyone that their booing was just spurring him on.

Kindhe was giving a ten-count. 'Four . . . Five . . . Six . . .'

Part of Marc wanted to stay down and save further

punishment, but pride won out and there was a roar as he got up.

'You OK?' Kindhe asked, as he looked into Marc's eyes, before giving the signal to resume fighting.

Marc had learned a brutal lesson: Luc was too strong to stand up to over four three-minute rounds. For the next minute and a half Luc became a charging bull throwing punch after punch; Marc was the bullfighter ducking and backing off.

In a proper boxing ring Luc could have cornered Marc against the ropes, so when Marc backed off the rubber mats for a third time Kindhe gave him a warning. Two more and he'd be disqualified.

Close friends like Paul stayed loyal to Marc, but those hoping for action had tired of Marc's tactics by the time Henderson rang the bell to end the first round. Marc retreated to a stool at the edge of the mat, and PT moved in with a bucket and sponge to wipe the blood dribbling out of his nose.

'He's too strong,' Marc gasped, as he watched Luc flexing his biceps at a taunting crowd at the opposite side of the ring.

PT didn't respond.

'Well?' Marc asked. 'What's your advice?'

PT twisted his lower lip awkwardly. 'I've never boxed in my life. But if I were you, I'd probably try to avoid getting knocked out.'

'Thanks, brains,' Marc said, shaking his head as Kindhe called the fighters back to the centre.

'You're dead meat,' Luc growled as he jumped high and pounded his gloves together.

As Terence rang the bell, Luc swung a punch. Marc ducked and slammed Luc with an uppercut to the kidneys. The crowd broke into a huge cheer, but within moments Marc was back to bullfighter mode, skipping in a backwards circle.

'Get moving!' someone shouted.

Marc was more interested in staying conscious than in entertaining the crowd, but Kindhe was losing patience with his tactic of stepping off the mats. Halfway through the round, Kindhe gave Marc a shove back into the ring.

'You've got to stop that,' he bellowed.

Marc tripped over his own foot as he lurched forward and Luc caught him with a left-right combo to the head, followed by a low blow.

Marc felt a horrendous ache between his legs as he sprawled out over the mats, groaning. Kindhe pushed Luc back and gave him a warning, then allowed a few seconds for Marc to recover.

'How's your balls?' Luc taunted.

Luc had grown so used to Marc backing off that he threw a wild punch as the fight resumed. Marc ducked, bobbed up and smashed Luc hard in the jaw. The crowd went bananas as Luc stumbled backwards, catching a glancing blow to the head and a perfect shot in the solar plexus.

Somehow Luc stayed upright and surged back with a couple of glancing blows as the bell rang for the end of the second round.

'Much better,' PT said, as Marc sat down.

'Must be your brilliant advice,' Marc replied, as his balls touched the wooden stool, giving him a painful reminder of the low blow.

As PT wiped his chest with the sponge, Marc noted that Luc wasn't posturing any more. He'd gone straight to his stool and breathed hard while instructor Takada shoved a wodge of iodine-soaked cotton wool up his nose to staunch the blood flow.

The crowd anticipated a proper fight as the two sweating teenagers squared up for the third round. But Marc still feared Luc's strength, and after feeling his first proper punches, Luc was no longer as confident about going forwards.

For two and a half minutes the fight was cagey, with neither boy landing a blow worth speaking of. With seconds of the round to go, Marc saw an opening and landed a beautiful shot under Luc's chin.

Luc's head snapped back and his legs wobbled, as the crowd yelled for Marc to finish him off. But the brilliance of the shot surprised Marc as much as anyone and he gave Luc a crucial half-second to steady his legs.

He came back furiously, forcing Marc to back away from a barrage of fast punches. But the shots were fuelled by anger rather than skill.

Right on the bell, Marc landed a blow on the nose. Luc was exhaling at the time of impact and blood spattered Marc's vest, like oil spewing from an overheated engine. As Marc dropped his guard and turned for his stool, Luc hit him full force in the gut.

Kindhe charged in to break the boys apart, but the damage was done. Marc was on his knees, coughing and gasping for air while Luc staggered back to his corner with clogged nostrils and a mist of blood clogging one eye.

Henderson sent his son flying as he shot to his feet. 'That's ridiculously late,' he shouted. 'Give him a second warning.'

Kindhe had already let Luc go back to his corner, but he stepped up and gave the second warning like Henderson said.

'One more and you're out,' Kindhe shouted.

Luc was shattered, but still found the energy to shoot up and point his glove at Henderson.

'Who's the ref, you or the captain?' Luc shouted furiously.

'Second warning,' Kindhe repeated. 'One more and you're out of the fight.'

'Dirty black bastard,' Luc shouted.

For a second Kindhe looked like was about to whack Luc with the back of his hand, but he thought better of it and instead helped PT walk Marc back to his stool.

For the second time, the fight was held up as Marc was given time to recover from an illegal blow.

'Final round,' Kindhe shouted.

The crowd was only twenty-five strong, but they'd all squeezed right up to the mats to get a good view and their noise sounded more like a hundred. After the low blow and the late punch everyone was firmly back on Marc's side.

Luc's nose was bleeding heavily and for the first time since he'd been knocked down in the opening barrage Marc felt like he had a real chance of winning. The caution that marked the third round was out of the window as Marc and Luc charged forwards like rutting stags.

Luc locked an arm around Marc's back, held him close and pounded his body with right jabs. Marc's arms and legs were getting heavy. The constant jabs made breathing impossible and he broke loose with a fierce head butt to the bridge of Luc's already bloody nose.

'Beautiful!' Sam's big brother Joel shouted. 'Now kill the bugger!'

But Kindhe had seen and immediately threw himself between the two fighters. He'd already given Marc a warning for backing out of the ring in round one, now he got a second for the head butt.

'Whoever gets the next warning is disqualified,' Kindhe shouted. 'You've got to behave.'

Both lads had sweat pelting the rubber around their feet as Kindhe gave them the signal to start fighting again. Marc could barely raise his fists, but Luc was livid about the head butt to his already injured nose and staggered forwards, swinging clumsily.

Marc dodged, making Luc stumble comically across the rubber mats, to the amusement of the crowd. Luc didn't give a damn about people hating him, but laughing was different and he glowered at Paul as he stood up.

'What are you laughing at, stick-boy? You want *your* head beaten in?'

With little more than a minute remaining, Kindhe gave the signal to resume fighting. But Luc had his eye on Paul and knew nothing about Marc's first decent punch of the round until it connected with the side of his head.

The crowd whooped as Luc stumbled, but he found a reserve of strength from somewhere and came at Marc with half a dozen strong punches. More through tiredness than anything else, the last of them was another low blow, but Kindhe missed it.

Marc went down on one knee as the crowd screamed about the low blow, but Kindhe had begun a ten-count.

'How could you not see that, you blind dick?' Paul shouted. 'Christ!'

As Kindhe reached eight, Marc was getting back to his feet, but his legs were swaying and Kindhe raised his hands to signal the end of the fight. The crowd hissed as Luc jumped in the air and started cheering.

'I don't give a monkey's what any of you think,' Luc shouted.

Marc found his way back to his corner, but instead of sitting on his stool he picked it up and raised it high over his head. PT tried pulling Marc back, but his sweaty torso slipped through PT's fingers and there was a collective gasp as the stool smashed over Luc's back.

Luc stumbled towards Henderson and McAfferty's chairs in a daze. They both dodged, but Joyce didn't have time to take the brake off her wheelchair and Luc wound up with his bloody face buried in her lap.

Joyce screamed in horror at the blood smeared all over her uniform.

'That was another low blow,' Marc shouted as he charged in for a second shot with the stool, but Kindhe got one of his gigantic arms around Marc's neck as PT lifted his feet off the ground. 'Let me go. I'm gonna kill him.'

Luc rolled to the floor as Joyce shoved his head out of her lap, while little Terence was scared by all the shouting and began sobbing, holding his arms out for someone to pick him up.

'This isn't over, Marc,' Luc shouted, as Takada helped

him up. 'I'm gonna cut your throat.'

Paul and Sam had backed away from the mats while bigger people dealt with the furious and exhausted fighters.

'Put 'em in the ring,' Paul said, half smiling. 'Watch them trade a few punches and step away with their arms around each other's backs.'

'Pledging to stay best friends for ever,' Sam added, as Kindhe and PT pinned Marc against the wall and ordered him to calm down. 'The plan doesn't *quite* seem to have worked out, does it?'

A few metres away, Henderson was trying to comfort his hysterical two-year-old son while simultaneously having an argument with McAfferty.

'Why you two stand idle?' Takada asked, as the squat Japanese instructor approached Paul and Sam with his hands on his hips.

'We thought it best to stay out of the way,' Paul replied.

Takada narrowed his eyes. 'You two to clean up all blood, pull up rubber mats, stack them neatly and wipe my hall floor ready for morning training. Do it well, or I punish.'

Paul and Sam both looked ticked off, but Takada belonged to the *do as I say without question or I'll make you do star jumps until you vomit* school of discipline, so they didn't start a debate.

Forty minutes later the hall was quiet, except for Paul dragging a mop across the floor, and Sam down on his knees using a claw hammer to pull up the last of the nails that had fixed the rubber mats in place. Both looked around as the door creaked, and stood to attention when they saw that it was Henderson.

'Don't stop working on my account,' Henderson said, as he strode in casually with hands in pockets. 'So, tonight wasn't exactly a triumph, was it?'

'No, sir,' Paul said weakly.

'How are the fighters, sir?' Sam asked.

'The USAF doc from the airbase took a look at them. He suggested that we use much thicker training gloves and a proper ring if we decide to repeat this sort of thing. Marc is exhausted, but basically fine. Luc has had three stitches in the bridge of his nose and McAfferty is driving him to the county hospital for a precautionary X-ray.'

Henderson paused, but neither boy said anything.

'I do my best,' Henderson said ruefully. 'But tonight turned into a total farce. I'm not an educator, nor is McAfferty. I'm starting to think we should have a proper teacher to enforce discipline and run the academic side of things here. Maybe I can dig an old headmaster out of retirement, or something.'

There were already enough bossy adults on campus for Paul or Sam's taste, but Henderson looked stressed and neither felt brave enough to disagree.

'You both seem unusually quiet,' Henderson said.

'It's not really our decision sir,' Paul said diplomatically, as his mop slurped about in its metal bucket. 'But I don't think you do a bad job. Every school I've ever been to has gone crazy once in a while.'

'What about the mission, sir?' Sam asked. 'Have you decided who's going? Or will you re-run the final exercise?'

'That's why I came looking for you two,' Henderson said. 'I've got a briefing set for tomorrow afternoon, I'll need you both there. The day after you'll be heading off to receive a little parachute jump refresher course.'

Paul and Sam smiled warily at each other.

'Not quite overjoyed then?' Henderson said.

'No such thing as an easy mission, sir,' Sam said. 'But I'll certainly try my best.'

Paul seemed less sure. 'Sir, I know you're angry with Marc because of what he did to Luc's rifle, but he's a much better shot than I am and he's never put a foot wrong while working undercover.'

Henderson nodded. 'Marc will be coming along too, and Luc, provided his nose isn't broken.'

Sam was confused. 'You've changed it to four snipers, sir?'

Paul looked at Sam and shook his head. 'Saying there were only two places made us all work a heck of a lot harder in training. Isn't that right, sir?'

'No flies on you, are there, Paul?' Henderson said brightly. 'The plan I've been working on requires snipers to cover the underground bunker from all directions. And I'm hoping that you two fresh-faced young chaps will be able to perform a special task, luring some Germans above ground.'

'So when do we set off?' Sam asked.

'I'm still waiting for information on aircraft availability, but if all goes to plan we'll be on French soil by this time next week.'

CHAPTER TWENTY-FOUR

Six days later.

At the green light Charles Henderson pushed off through the hole in Fat Patty's fuselage. While the American bomber flew slow and steady, he was followed at three-second intervals by Marc, Paul, Sam, Luc, Sergeant Goldberg and four chutes attached to aluminium equipment canisters.

Eugene and Rosie's near miss with a Gestapo reception committee was on everyone's mind as they plunged through moonlight. Henderson touched down first, making a perfect landing on overgrown farmland. After releasing his chute he grabbed the compact M3 machine gun strapped to his thigh and glanced about until he was sure he didn't have company.

The latest parachutes used by special operations units

were dyed dark grey, which was near invisible in moonlight. Henderson had a tough time spotting his companions, but he could hear wind catching someone's chute behind a clump of trees less than thirty metres away.

'Marc?' Henderson asked, knowing that he'd been next to jump.

'I nearly landed on top of you,' Marc said, as he came out of the dark, dragging billowing silk behind him. 'Ground feels soft. Shall I start digging a hole for the chutes while you find the others?'

'Makes sense,' Henderson said.

Parachuting in darkness carries risks, from bad landings to the pilot dropping you in the wrong place, but within ten minutes of touchdown Henderson was satisfied that the two abandoned houses on the brow of the next hill were the ones he'd seen in aerial surveillance photos, and injuries could have been far worse than Sam bending his fingers back and Goldberg bashing his leg on an abandoned horseshoe.

'Patty was flying into a headwind the whole way, so we're tight on time,' Henderson told them. 'Sam, help Marc bury the rest of the chutes. Paul, Luc, we need to fan out and head south. We need all four equipment drops, or we'll be stuck until we're resupplied.'

Paul found the first equipment chute two fields over. The aluminium canister was two metres long and had landed nose first, ploughing a long track in the soft ground. He bunched up the chute, then tugged at the ropes, but he couldn't raise it out of the mud and had to call Luc over.

'This must be canister one,' Luc said. 'Henderson and Goldberg sighted two and three. They're just moving on further, trying to hunt down number four.'

As Luc wound the parachute ropes around his wrist and yanked the big canister out of the mud, Paul stared at a house across the field.

'Get round the other side and help me,' Luc said angrily.

'There's washing out behind that cottage,' Paul said. 'And it looks like a vegetable plot. Anyone in there *must* have heard this lot crash down.'

'I don't care,' Luc said, as the canister finally came out of the mud with a big sucking noise.

'I thought this was the coastal exclusion zone,' Paul said. 'There's not supposed to be anyone around.'

'People avoiding labour service, or German deserters,' Luc said dismissively, as he went down on one knee. 'If they were gonna come out shooting they'd have jumped us already and we'll be long gone before they can mouth off.'

The long canister was an ingenious design. As Paul wound ropes around the parachute canopy, Luc used a T-shaped tool to break the canister down into four pieces.

The nose and tail were hollow aluminium designed as shock absorbers that crumpled on impact, while the two cargo-packed central sections had hooks and straps.

They could be carried as a backpack when filled with lightweight items, but canister one contained sniper equipment and ammunition, while most of canister two was filled with a state-of-the-art radio-location device designed to guide bombers to a target. To move this heavy load, Luc and Paul each grabbed a set of small-spoked pram wheels from the nose piece and slid axles through holes in the base of the cargo sections.

'Take this one, it's lighter,' Luc said.

As Paul set off, with the weight of the trolley straining his arms and the narrow wheels carving ruts in the soft ground, Luc stayed back to throw the nose and tail sections in the ditch at the fields' edge.

If the mission had been near to the drop zone they'd have been more thorough about hiding evidence of their landing, but they were over a hundred kilometres from Rennes so it was a question of not leaving anything that might be sighted before sunrise.

As he was about to lob the metal, Luc was startled by a girl squatting in the base of the ditch, less than four metres away. Her age hadn't reached double figures and she was unarmed, but Luc instantly ripped a jagged knife from his belt holster and lunged towards her.

'What did you see?' Luc growled as he held the blade

to her throat.

The girl's nightdress was ripped and she looked like she hadn't washed in a month.

'I heard the bang,' she said, in a voice barely above a squeak. 'I got out of bed to peek.'

'You saw *nothing*,' Luc said firmly. 'Say it.'

'Nothing,' the girl said, as she nodded frantically. 'I won't even tell my brothers.'

'If you do, I'll come back another night,' Luc said.

He toyed with the idea of stabbing the girl, but her family would be angry when they found her dead and might alert the Germans, so he went down his jacket and threw her a small paper twist containing four lemon sherbets.

'Here,' he grunted, as he pushed his knife back into its sheath.

'Vive la France,' the girl whispered, as Luc grabbed the rope handle of his wheeled canister and set off to catch Paul.

*

Once all the parachutes were rolled up and buried in Marc's hole, or packed away under bushes, they jogged east on a deserted country track. The four equipment chutes had dropped eight canisters in total, so Henderson and Goldberg had to carry two while the boys had one each.

It was a muggy night and they all dripped sweat by the

time they sighted their target: a single railway track, winding up a steep hill. Henderson and Marc spun and cocked guns as something crashed through branches behind them, but when they turned it was a boy with his hands held high.

'Don't shoot,' the scared-looking ten-year-old blurted. 'The weather has been good, I'm here hunting squirrels.'

Henderson half smiled as he lowered his weapon. It was a prepared phrase: if the boy had said he was hunting rabbits it would have meant that he'd been captured by the Germans and they'd walked into a trap.

'You must be Justin,' Henderson said. 'I thought we were meeting by the tracks.'

'The coal train went out early tonight and you're late,' Justin explained. 'I climbed up to see if I could spot you.'

'How long have we got?' Henderson asked, as Justin shook his hand, then Goldberg's.

'Fifteen, maybe twenty minutes if we're lucky,' Justin said.

'Any sign of Germans?' Luc asked.

Justin shook his head. 'Been coming out this way for two years. Never seen a German yet, but we're a good ten minutes' walk from the track, so we need to shift.'

Paul was struggling with the combination of the cargo canister and the weight of his own gear, so Justin took his backpack as they set off at a jog.

'In a way it's good that the train is early,' Justin

explained. 'If there's no delays we should get back to my house before daylight.'

The coal train was rumbling somewhere out of sight as they approached the tracks. They'd have to throw the heavy canisters up into the coal wagons and they didn't want to risk smashing the wheels, so there was a mild panic as everyone knelt at the trackside dismantling them.

Henderson and Luc were tallest, so they stood close to the tracks and jointly lobbed the heaviest aluminium canisters up into the coal wagons as they trundled past at walking pace. There was a phenomenal boom as each one landed in an empty metal skip, but Justin reassured them that the driver and guard never heard anything from their positions at opposite ends of the kilometre-long train.

Marc and Goldberg threw the lighter canisters aboard, apart from the one containing the delicate radio beacon which Henderson strapped to his back. Once everyone had boarded, Justin gathered them into a single coal skip, where he gave a quick lesson on dealing with the swirling coal dust when going through tunnels.

'It should be obvious when we arrive at the water tower,' Justin said. 'But I'll whistle just in case.'

As the train crested the steep hill and began picking up speed, everyone moved up the train to reunite with their canisters. Marc found himself sharing the dusty skip with two canisters and Paul.

'You OK?' Marc asked, as train wheels clattered beneath them.

'Eyes full of coal dust and my arms hurt from dragging all that stuff, but so far so good, eh?' Paul said.

CHAPTER TWENTY-FIVE

The train was lit by a purple and orange sunset as it halted. Marc bobbed his head over the end of the coal skip and saw the water tower up by the head of the train.

'Our stop,' Marc told Paul, as he gave him a gentle kick.

After a glance either side to make sure there were no guards or railway workers close to the train, Marc put his palms behind his canister, pushed it up the sloping metal side of the skip, and let it drop down into the gravel alongside the tracks.

There were several similar crashes as everyone threw their canisters out, then they climbed the metal access ladders to leave the skips. As Marc crunched down into the trackside, he saw Justin belting towards him from the front of the train.

'Hurry up,' he ordered. 'I was up front when we stopped. There's two railway cops strolling our way. Get everyone to go down the embankment fast and I'll try and deal with them.'

Justin sprinted off before Marc got a chance to ask how the untrained ten-year-old planned to fend off two policemen.

'Is he OK?' Paul asked, looking along the tracks at Justin running off, as the rest of the team set off down the embankment.

'I don't know,' Marc said.

Paul was behind Sam as the younger boy lost his footing on the steep embankment. Paul's leading foot hit Sam's container, his back foot slipped in the mud and he began ploughing downhill dragged by the weight of his own canister.

There was no major damage, but Paul found himself sprawled in a puddle with the muddy sole of Sam's boot pressed against the back of his neck.

'Nice entrance, little brother,' Rosie said.

Brown water dribbled down Paul's collar as Rosie helped him to his feet. He felt like giving his sister a hug, but she was in a light cotton dress and he was muddy from the embankment and black with coal dust.

'The house is about fifty metres away, through the bushes and to the left,' Rosie explained. 'There's soap and hot water waiting. You need to wash and change quickly, so we can move you to a safe house.'

'Rosie, can you deal with my canister?' Marc asked urgently, as he made a more co-ordinated descent of the hill. 'I need to speak to Henderson.'

'He's already on his way to the house,' Rosie said. 'What's the matter?'

'Justin said he saw railway cops and was going off to deal with them, but I'm not sure what he means by that.'

'They hassle him all the time,' Rosie said. 'I expect he'll tease them into chasing him in the other direction.'

Marc nodded. 'But he's only little. Shouldn't we at least check that he's OK?'

Rosie had a lot of faith in Justin, and it took an outsider's perspective to remind her that he was a young boy with no espionage training.

'Maybe we should,' she agreed, before turning to face Luc and Goldberg, who'd both just arrived at the bottom of the hill.

Goldberg had also seen Justin running off and took charge. 'Luc, use those big muscles and help Rosie get all the canisters out of sight,' he ordered. 'Marc, you're with me.'

Goldberg led Marc back up the embankment. There was no sign of Justin so they crept along the trackside, keeping as low as they could. By the time they'd walked fifty metres, the air was full of steam and the empty coal trucks had begun to move.

When the embankment ended the pair found themselves crossing a bridge, with less than half a metre between a low brick wall and the side of the accelerating train. As the wagons rattled past and the steam cleared, Marc and Goldberg peered around the end of the wall.

There were a couple of railway workers at the water tower seventy metres ahead, but they were more interested in voices they could hear out of sight, behind a disused signal box. Goldberg pointed at himself, then at the near side of the box.

'I'll go there,' he whispered. 'You go around the other end.'

After a glance to make completely sure there was nobody sitting up high in the signal box, Marc dashed over a stretch of dandelions and loose pebbles. Marc heard Justin yelp as he crouched down with his left shoulder against the wooden building.

The voice that came from behind the signal box had the tone of a schoolyard bully. 'We've warned you, Justin. Maybe we should arrest you this time.'

'Remember the first time we put you in our cell?' a different voice with the same tone asked. 'Crying for your mummy when I dunked your head in the toilet bowl?'

Marc peered around the side of the hut for a proper look. The two bullies were thick-set men, dressed in red-piped Railway Police uniform. One was bald, nearing sixty, while the other looked fortyish and must have barely escaped being drafted into the French army before the war.

'Why are you so mean?' Justin asked, as he looked up at his tormentors. 'I give you plenty of coal, don't I?'

The older guard laughed as he shoved Justin up against the box and gave him a punch in the ribs. It wasn't as hard as it could have been, but it was enough to hurt a ten-year-old.

'Your mum must earn plenty scrubbing Boche skid marks,' the older guard said. 'I don't need much coal at this time of year, but I'd better see five francs next time I see you, or you'll get locked up.'

'Might find yourself slipping under a wagon and getting your legs mangled,' the younger one added menacingly, as the older cop gave Justin another slam against the hut.

Marc shook his head as a passenger train whooshed by, tilting him off balance. Justin's situation was rotten, but he couldn't get involved in anything that didn't directly affect the mission.

'Next time I see you I'll pay you five francs,' Justin said meekly, as the noise of the train subsided. 'But you're ripping me off so much, it's hardly worth riding the train any more.'

The older cop slapped Justin so hard that he went down.

'You remember who you are, and who we are,' the younger cop snapped.

As Justin got to his feet he was fighting off tears. Marc put a hand on his throwing knife and almost wished for an excuse to use it.

'Out of our sight,' the older cop said. 'And don't forget our money.'

Justin scrambled away eagerly, but the younger cop tugged on a strap around Justin's shoulder.

'And what's this?' he asked

Marc's jaw dropped: Justin was still wearing the small pack he'd taken from Paul when they'd first met. The older cop's eyes widened, because he knew exactly what it was.

'Where did you find that?' he asked. 'What's inside it?'

When you jump out of an aeroplane, you need two free hands for steering and the parachute, which rules out carrying anything on your back. Any equipment a parachutist carries has to be inside a pocket, or in a sausage-shaped canvas bag strapped to your thigh.

'Where did you find a sausage bag?' the older cop said, as the younger one tugged the strap so hard that Justin's head snapped back. He then used the strap to lift Justin off the ground and swing him head first against the side of the signal hut.

'Stop it,' Justin whined.

'Best to answer us when we speak,' the younger cop shouted.

You couldn't have two untrustworthy cops taking Justin into custody with Paul's equipment, so Marc went for his knife. Goldberg made the same decision a half-second faster and jumped out from the other side of the hut.

'Excuse me, officers,' he said, in French that came with a New York accent.

As the officers turned around, Goldberg fired two shots with a silenced pistol, getting them both between the eyes.

'Jesus,' Justin yelled, hitting the ground as his tormentor dropped him.

The silenced gun pulsed twice more as Goldberg put two clinical shots through the policemen's hearts.

'Oh, God,' Justin said, as he crawled away. He felt queasy even before he dared to look back at the blood and brains splattered all over the wooden hut.

'Justin, you did great,' Marc said, as he offered the boy a hand. 'Don't be scared. Keep your voice low, take slow deep breaths.'

As Justin got up, Goldberg went up three steps and kicked in the padlocked door of the disused signal box.

'How much water have you got in your canteen?' Goldberg asked.

'Not much,' Marc said.

Goldberg pulled a half-full canteen out of his jacket and threw it to Marc. 'Use that to wash the worst of the gunge off the hut. I'll drag the bodies inside. They'll find them eventually, but it should buy us long enough to clear the area.'

As Marc pulled up a handful of grass and used it to wipe down the side of the hut, Goldberg removed the dead cops' watches, wallets and identity papers before dragging them into the signal hut. There wasn't much chance that the cops would think it was a robbery, but there was no harm in trying to make it look that way.

The older cop was twice Goldberg's weight and Justin had regained enough composure to grab his ankles as the American struggled to drag him up the three steps.

The side of the hut cleaned up fairly well, but there was nothing they could do about the pooled blood on the ground. From a distance it didn't look as obvious as two dead bodies on the ground, but the next person to stroll around the back of the signal box would dip their boot in blood.

'Justin, lead us home,' Goldberg said, after a final glance around.

Rather than go back along the tracks, they walked down an overgrown path, crossed a road and reached Justin's house via land behind cottages at the base of the railway embankment.

Inside Justin's home, Luc, Paul and Henderson had ditched their combat gear, scrubbed up and changed into French civilian clothes, while Sam had taken the fourth turn in brown bathwater and was trying to dry off using a ragged and extremely wet towel.

'Good to see you again,' Marc said, when he stepped through to the kitchen and found Edith pouring a big saucepan of boiling water into an iron bathtub. 'Mostly better now?'

'A few scars and headaches. But not too bad,' she said.

As Marc began unbuttoning his coal-black combat gear, Goldberg was updating Henderson on the situation at the signal box.

'Shit happens,' Henderson said, keeping his tone mellow because Justin was clearly in mild shock. 'It's very unlikely that anyone will miss the bodies until we're out of here, so we stick to our plan.'

'Who goes where, exactly?' Luc asked.

Henderson paused for a second. 'Since you're already washed, Rosie can take you and Sam out to Joseph Blanc's house. Take the dirty combat gear and burn it as soon as you get there. Cut off any metal buttons and make sure nothing identifiable remains in the ashes. When Marc and Paul are washed, we'll take the canisters up to Dr Blanc's surgery—'

Rosie interrupted. 'I managed to get hold of a handcart for you. We never get checkpoints around here and it's market day, so nobody will take much notice provided you cover the canisters over with straw. One of the iron bathtubs also belongs to the doctor and she wants it back in time for morning surgery.'

'Excellent,' Henderson said. 'It's risky moving this amount of gear long distance in daylight, so we'll stay at Dr Blanc's surgery until dark.'

'Edith will stay here and help Justin clean up before his mother and younger sisters get home,' Rosie added. 'All being well, we'll carry the canisters out to a spot I've found in the woods after dark.'

CHAPTER TWENTY-SIX

Justin's night-time coal-scavenging trips meant he was used to sleeping through the day.

He needed to pee when he woke just after 4 p.m. The house was empty. His mother was at work and he'd arranged for his little sisters to be out of the way at his aunt's house when Henderson's team arrived, so rather than traipse out to the toilet in the back yard he crossed the room, pulled down the front of his shorts and fired a stream of urine through an open first-floor window, watering plants in the overgrown yard below.

'You mind my damned washing,' the woman who lived in the adjoining cottage shouted, as she shook her wrinkled fist.

'Good afternoon, Madame Vial,' Justin said cheerfully, waving as he continued to pee.

'I had a big yellow streak on my petticoat last washday. Your mother might ignore it, but your father will be home some day and *he'll* sort you out.'

'I'm sure he will,' Justin said, as he tried to hide a grin.

Even in the strongest winds, Justin's pee never came within ten metres of Madame Vial's washing. She was actually a nice old girl, but she was lonely and blamed Justin and his sisters for all sorts of imaginary problems because it gave her something to gossip about.

'Did you see the apples I left by your back door?' Justin asked, as he shook off.

'You're filthy!' Madame Vial said, ignoring the question.

Justin wore a huge smile as he walked back towards his mattress – he wasn't a bad person, but he enjoyed teasing his elderly neighbour more than he should have.

He reckoned it would be another hour before his mum got in from work, but as Justin snuggled back under his filthy bed sheet he heard a squeal, like the brakes of a bus or truck. Since no bus ran out here and French people didn't get a petrol ration it could only be Germans.

There was a lot of shouting outside as he belted downstairs to take a look. He peered through the glass in his front door and panicked at the sight of an open-backed truck, with grizzled troops jumping off the rear platform.

Clearly someone had found the two dead cops and was pissed off about it. Even worse, it didn't look like the sedate middle-aged men who manned the local garrison where his mother worked. They were a rough-looking crew who must have driven in from Rennes. There were also two plain-clothes men, who sent a chill down Justin's back because they looked like Gestapo.

The man in charge was tall, with cropped fair hair and a full-length leather jacket. Justin spoke no German but it didn't take a genius to work out that he was ordering his men to fan out and knock on the doors of the eleven cottages in his street.

Justin's first thought was that he didn't want to face the Gestapo dressed in boxers and vest, so he bolted upstairs to dress. Madame Vial was on her doorstep shouting something as he whipped on a shirt and trousers.

Someone thumped on Justin's front door, and someone was shouting, 'Everybody line up in the street,' in bad French.

Answer the door or try to escape?

Justin pictured the two dead railway cops in his head, as his heart raced. His mum had freaked out when she'd realised that Rosie was from the resistance. She'd reluctantly allowed him to help Rosie, but at that moment Justin was starting to wish that she hadn't.

There was a crash as someone kicked in Justin's front door. The detectives he'd seen in movies always had clever ways of tricking people into saying things they shouldn't, and he was scared that that's what he'd do if they got hold of him.

As two Germans entered the hallway downstairs Justin ran to the window he'd just peed out of, balanced briefly on the window ledge and jumped down into the plants. His own urine spattered his face as the dripping branches sprung backwards, then he started running, terrified that the Germans had sent someone to cover the back of the houses.

If they caught him running it would be highly suspicious. And if they found out that the two dead cops had regularly hassled him for riding the coal train . . .

But whether or not running had been a good idea, Justin was committed to it now. There would almost certainly be Germans coming up the side of the cottages, so he went flat out across thirty metres of open ground and began scrambling up the embankment towards the railway line.

The tall hats of two gendarmes were visible beyond the railway bridge and there was a big gathering of French railwaymen and German soldiers further along by the water tower. A cargo train was trundling in slowly and he decided to cross before it cut him off.

The embankment on the other side of the tracks was steeper, and he had to shuffle down on his bum before jumping off a metre-and-a-half brick wall. It was a sunny

June afternoon and the cargo train cast flickering shadows as Justin found himself in a narrow strip of woodland with the neatly-aligned trees of an orchard stretching into the distance.

After a few seconds with trembling hands tucked under his armpits, taking deep breaths and trying to get his nerves under control, Justin decided that he was probably OK: nobody had seen him escape, and now he could stroll about at normal pace. If anyone stopped him he'd say that he was heading out to pick apples.

The safest option would have been to stay in hiding by the wall, but Justin thought he ought to warn the team hiding inside Dr Blanc's surgery ten minutes' walk away.

*

Marc, Paul, Goldberg and Henderson had spent the day getting on each other's nerves in a windowless second-floor box room. They all tried to sleep, but the equipment and canisters took up most of the floor space, it was stifling hot and as there were no toilet facilities the smell emanating from a rapidly filling chamber pot wasn't great either.

'She's a big girl,' Paul whispered, as they listened to Dr Blanc thumping upstairs towards them. 'I'm bloody starving. I hope she's planning to feed us soon.'

'She said we can move around once her surgery's finished,' Marc said, as he stretched into a yawn. 'Hopefully that's not long now.'

'Mr Henderson,' Dr Blanc shouted.

Henderson opened the door of the tiny room and looked down the stairs.

'Soldiers,' Dr Blanc blurted. 'They must have found the dead railway police.'

'OK, keep calm,' Henderson said, as he reached into the room for his machine gun. 'What are they doing exactly?'

'They've blocked off the intersection. There's about a dozen of them, going from door to door.'

'How many patients in your waiting room?' Henderson asked.

'None. My nurse just left. I saw them arrive as I locked the front door behind her. I was about to call you out for something to eat and drink.'

Henderson glanced at the others. 'I'm going down to look, be ready to move on my mark.'

Dr Blanc was short of breath as she let Henderson by, then followed him downstairs. 'If they find you here,' she said, close to hysterical. 'I have so many patients and there's no other doctor within ten kilometres.'

'If it comes to that, you don't know us,' Henderson said. 'We saw you arrive at your surgery. One of us was injured. We put a gun to your head and forced you to take us inside.'

Henderson peeled back the heavy curtain over the window of Dr Blanc's examination room and didn't like the scene in the street. German army trucks had parked across the road at either end of the small strip of shops and businesses. Soldiers were knocking on doors and ordering everyone to line up in the cobbled street.

'Marc, Paul,' Henderson shouted. 'Go downstairs and try to see if there are any Germans around the back.'

As the boys jumped half a flight of stairs at a time, Henderson peered back through the window, trying to work out if the Germans were being thorough. If they were calling people out into the street they could stay in hiding, but if they were searching inside houses he had a much more serious problem.

But with Germans working from opposite ends of the street and closing fast, he had no choice but to assume the worst.

'How's it looking out back?' Henderson shouted.

'No sign of anything,' Paul shouted back.

'They don't know we're here,' Henderson said. 'They're just putting on a show of force to frighten the locals. But we can't risk them coming inside and finding the canisters. Is the handcart still out back?'

'Yep,' Marc shouted.

'Right,' Henderson said, as he looked up the stairs. 'Sergeant Goldberg, we need to make a break for it. You deal with boys and canisters. I'm going to sneak out and make a distraction to enable you to get away.'

The stairs came alive as Goldberg and the boys raced

up and down. There was a knock at the front door as Paul came down with the last canister and Henderson pulled on a backpack.

'Dr Blanc,' Henderson said. 'Answer the door, but do whatever you can to stop the Germans from coming inside for a few moments.'

As Dr Blanc walked through her ground-floor waiting room towards the surgery door, Henderson, Marc, Paul and Goldberg gathered outside the rear door. Goldberg was loading the last of the canisters on the handcart, and all four had machine guns loaded and slung around their necks.

'What's your plan?' Goldberg asked.

'As soon as you hear something go bang, you three set off with that cart and run like hell. Find somewhere safe, you'll have to improvise. Everyone who makes it meets up with Rosie in the woods at eight, exactly as planned. If I don't make it, you're in charge, Sergeant Goldberg.'

Goldberg was a great shot, but this was the American's first day working undercover and he didn't look comfortable with the idea of running the show.

'You'll do fine, Sergeant,' Henderson said. 'Remember, don't move from here until something blows up.'

As Henderson ran behind the row of small businesses, Marc closed the back door of the surgery and Dr Blanc let the German soldier in at the front.

'I'm sorry for the wait,' she said. 'I thought you were a patient. They turn up at all hours, and I have to be strict unless it's urgent.'

'You're lucky I didn't kick the door in,' the young German said furiously. 'How many others in there?'

'What's this all about?' Dr Blanc asked.

'You don't ask the questions, fatso,' the soldier shouted. 'Everyone must line up in the street for questioning.'

Before Dr Blanc could answer, she heard a huge bang and found herself thrown into the door frame as the entire building jerked sideways. The blast was caused by a full stick of plastic explosive detonating between two buildings less than twenty metres away. Chunks of wood and masonry crashed down as people screamed and glass shattered on both sides of the street.

Marc and Goldberg got pelted with debris as they set off at a sprint, each putting their weight behind one side of the handcart, while Paul strode backwards covering their rear.

Henderson broke cover, close to the truck blocking the graveyard end of the street. He knocked down three Germans with well-aimed shots through the back, then swapped pistol for machine gun and began shooting into the dust cloud caused by the explosion. The aim was to set off panic rather than cause injury, so he fired over the heads of the Gestapo's civilian line-up.

As people screamed and dived for cover, a few soldiers tried to return fire, but couldn't because by the time the dust cleared Henderson had dropped down and rolled under the truck. He placed a grenade in the cobbles directly below the truck's fuel tank, then scrambled towards the graveyard and jumped over its crumbling perimeter wall as the vehicle exploded.

CHAPTER TWENTY-SEVEN

Justin dived behind a hedge as the truck went bang, but was still close enough feel the dry heat against his forehead. After leaving the railway embankment, he'd walked briskly through fields towards the surgery but had only got as far as the alleyway alongside the butcher's shop when Germans arrived.

He'd backed out of the alley as the Germans jumped off their trucks, then crawled rapidly through tall grass until he'd reached the edge of the graveyard with Rosie's words from a few weeks earlier in his head: *A perfect view and half a dozen escape routes if someone comes looking.*

Justin might have been spotted if the soldiers had chased Henderson, but only one German made it around the burning truck. The German didn't fancy going up against a grenade-throwing lunatic and went no further than the edge of the graveyard.

As the soldier jogged back to his colleagues, Justin watched Dr Blanc walking into thick smoke and diesel fumes. One of the men Henderson had shot was still alive, but the Germans had no idea that Blanc was a doctor, and before she could help a rifle butt smashed into the side of her head.

'None of you French bastards move,' the solidly built lieutenant in command shouted, as he strode through smoke brushing chunks of rubble off his uniform. 'Get this rabble lined up. *Somebody* here knows what this is all about.'

But the chaos continued, centring on a blacksmith trying to extinguish a roof fire started by Henderson's stick of explosive.

'Leave it to burn,' the lieutenant shouted. 'Let it be a lesson to people who harbour criminal scum.'

But the blacksmith was desperate to save his business and plunged a bucket into the horse trough outside his shop. The apprentice girl from the butcher's shop said something about fetching a water pump, but the rebellion ended as the lieutenant pulled his pistol and shot the blacksmith in the back.

After a couple of screams, the officer changed position and shot again, this time killing a woman who was rolling about in pain after being struck by a chunk of hot metal from the exploding truck.

'Oh, *now* I have your attention,' the lieutenant said, smirking like a mischievous schoolboy as he swung his pistol about, pointing it at cowering Frenchmen and women. 'Two police officers are killed, then an explosion. Then my men are killed. I *will* get to the truth behind this. Tell me now, or all your lives will be short and agonising.'

Nobody said a word and the officer signalled to his men. 'Come on, line them up.'

Justin had a good view, and noticed that all the soldiers had a certain demeanour. They were much younger than the local garrison. Their boots and uniforms were tatty and most of them had long hair and stubbly beards.

There were a few elderly amongst the civilians, but the rough-hewn soldiers showed no patience with their slowness, dishing out kicks and slaps and even twisting one old man's arm up behind his back.

'Someone here knows,' the officer said, as he looked about, menacing the crowd of about thirty with his pistol.

Dr Blanc had blood streaking down her face from the rifle blow, as the lieutenant closed up on her. In the background, the roof of the blacksmith's shop was now fully ablaze. A central section was sagging and about to collapse into the shop itself.

'What does the fat pudding know?' the officer asked.

Dr Blanc hoped she hadn't been singled out for a reason. 'I just run my surgery,' she said tearfully. 'I've been working all morning. I don't know anything.'

The lieutenant reared up. 'If you're a doctor, why aren't you trying to help my wounded men?'

'I tried,' Dr Blanc hissed, as she pointed to her bloody head. 'That's how I got this.'

The lieutenant was too full of himself to apologise, but the doctor was taken out of the line-up and escorted back to the surgery for her medical bag.

'Liars, all of you,' the officer shouted, as he pointed at the burning blacksmith's shop. 'Either I find out what's been going on here and now, or you'll all be taken into Rennes for Gestapo interrogation.'

The thirty-strong line-up was trembling but stayed silent. Apart from Dr Blanc, none of them knew anything about Henderson's operation.

'We'll need another truck for all our new prisoners,' the lieutenant said. After a dramatic pause he broke into a rumbling laugh and turned to a teenage private. 'While we wait for transportation, why don't you see if starting another fire will jog someone's memory. Schmidt, get your flamethrower. Load the meat from the butcher's shop on to our truck, then set the building on fire. If nobody speaks up, we'll burn the doctor's surgery after that.'

*

The sun was setting as Edith stood in the vegetable plot behind Joseph Blanc's grand house picking beans. There was enough light for her to make out a dust trail on the approach road, and she threw down the beans and sprinted towards the house.

'Rosie,' Edith shouted.

Justin had arrived a few hours earlier and reported on what had happened at the intersection. Edith was on edge and half expected men to jump from the truck and start pushing them around, but instead one of the elderly men from the local garrison stepped down from the driver's seat and walked around the truck to help Dr Blanc disembark on the passenger side.

By the time Rosie came on to the doorstep with Justin behind her, the German truck had pulled into the driveway.

'Everyone stay calm,' Rosie said quietly. 'We've all got papers and nothing's out of order inside the house.'

The doctor looked badly shaken. She had a dressing around her head and her skirt was torn, but the middle-aged soldier treated her decently, and even shook her hand after retrieving her leather doctor's bag from the footwell.

'Those men from Rennes are animals,' the soldier said. 'They make me ashamed to wear this uniform.'

The truck's engine clattered back to life as Dr Blanc walked through the back door of her son's house.

'Are you OK?' Rosie asked. 'Do you need anything?'

'A brandy,' Dr Blanc said, as she crashed breathlessly into a chair in the kitchen. 'Very large.'

As Edith dashed to the living room for the drink, the doctor fixed Rosie with an angry scowl.

'Where's Joseph?' she asked.

'With so many Germans around he was worried about being picked up for deportation. He's gone to Jean and Didier's place in the woods.'

'At least he's safe,' Dr Blanc said, then thanked Edith for the brandy before looking back at Rosie. 'What did your boss think he was doing? His explosion destroyed the blacksmith's shop and with three dead Germans, we're going to have the Gestapo on our backs for months.'

'After you left with the injured German, they took a couple of men away and smashed up the shops and stole a lot of stuff,' Justin said. 'But a bunch of Gestapo men turned up after that and stopped that psychopath lieutenant from burning everything down.'

The doctor looked surprised. 'I didn't even realise you were there.'

'I was hiding in the graveyard,' Justin explained. 'I was trying to warn Henderson, but the Germans got to the intersection before me.'

'Are your family OK?'

Justin nodded. 'Luckily my sisters were away. My

mum's gone to my aunt's house to pick them up now.'

'So what was Henderson playing at?' Dr Blanc asked Rosie accusingly.

'I haven't seen him,' Rosie said. 'But he clearly needed to create a distraction to get the canisters away.'

'But killing three men in cold blood? And the blacksmith's shop is utterly destroyed.'

Rosie considered saying that the resistance had to be ruthless, but Dr Blanc clearly needed calming down and she decided to be diplomatic.

'I'm sure Captain Henderson did no more than he felt he had to,' Rosie said. 'But you can speak to him later when we meet.'

'I've never seen Germans acting brutal like that,' Justin said. 'I was so scared when they took you away.'

'By the time we arrived at the hospital in Rennes, I'd stabilised one of the men Henderson shot,' Dr Blanc explained. 'That probably saved me from being taken to the town jail for interrogation, but the soldier who drove me back from the hospital says that the unit we encountered at the intersection are real thugs. They've spent most of the past year fighting on the Eastern Front. Soldiers there are given free rein to torture and murder any civilians they encounter.'

'They're still floating around as well,' Justin said. 'They set up a checkpoint right near my house.'

Dr Blanc nodded. 'We were stopped three times on

my way from Rennes, even though I was in an army truck being driven by a soldier.'

Edith looked at Rosie. 'We weren't bargaining on checkpoints. What does this mean for the mission?'

'Henderson will have to make a decision on whether to delay the operation,' Rosie said. 'Assuming he made it out of there alive.'

CHAPTER TWENTY-EIGHT

Marc, Paul and Goldberg escaped with all the canisters, hiding out in a barn a few kilometres from the intersection, then moving into the forest after sunset. Although there hadn't been time to discuss routes, Henderson knew where they were heading, so after a few hours hiding out near the railway lines he tracked them down as they set off into the woods.

A meeting had been set for 8 p.m., in the mouth of a cave that forest dwellers Didier and Jean used as an occasional hideout. Henderson took centre stage, lit dramatically by torchlight. Sitting or squatting around him were Goldberg, Paul, Marc, Luc, Sam, Jean, Didier, Rosie, Edith, Justin, Dr Blanc and her son Joseph.

The plan had been for Dr Blanc and Justin's roles in the operation to end after the agents had arrived and taken their equipment into the forest, but Rosie invited them along because they'd witnessed what had happened at the intersection.

'Today has been tough,' Henderson began, deepening his voice in an attempt to instil confidence in new comrades. 'We've seen how plans can go wrong. We've seen how the occupiers can act ruthlessly, and how our own actions can cause suffering to innocent civilians. But every one of us has put our lives on the line to be here. If we back out now, the risks and bloodshed will have all been for nowt.'

There were some enthusiastic murmurs, most notably from Jean, Didier and Justin, but Dr Blanc's discomfort was obvious.

'There's no point hanging around in this business,' Henderson continued. 'My job is to balance risks. The presence of this unpleasant group of soldiers from Rennes and the possibility of additional security checkpoints along our planned escape route makes things more difficult than we'd hoped, but the longer we're in this area the greater the chance that the Germans will find our equipment or unearth some aspect of our operations.

'We also have to co-ordinate with the Ghost network in Paris, and with United States Bomber Command. So, weather permitting, we move ahead as planned on Friday evening. That gives us tomorrow and Thursday for individual briefings, plus a spot of training and final reconnaissance on the bunker site. On Friday those taking part in the mission can eat and relax during the day, so that we're all fit and ready for our little adventure four kilometres east of here.'

Jean, Justin and Didier smirked knowingly.

'I think you mean four kilometres *west*, sir,' Rosie said, as everyone joined the laughter.

'Ahh . . .' Henderson said, glad that it was too dark to see his face redden. 'Well, hopefully I'll have worked out which way I'm supposed to be going by Friday.'

*

While Luc, Goldberg, Henderson and all but the most sensitive equipment spent a humid night in the cave, Paul, Marc and Sam shared more comfortable quarters on the floor of Joseph Blanc's drawing room.

Wednesday's plan was for Rosie to take Henderson and the boys on a fake hunting trip into the forest, in order to get a good look at the bunker site and its surroundings. Goldberg would stay back with Jean and Didier, giving them a brief introduction to weapons handling and espionage techniques.

But Paul's day veered off track before he'd even rolled off the comfortable chaise he'd slept on. There was no sign of Marc, but a note in Marc's hand had been tucked into one of Paul's boots.

Paul,

I can't be this close and not see her. I'm going to Beauvais and I'll be back by Friday latest. Don't get into trouble by trying to cover for me. I'll take my punishment but I have to see Jae.

Your friend,

Marc

Paul and Sam considered a cover-up, but there was no obvious way so Paul handed Henderson the note when Rosie and the six parachutists met up near Jean and Didier's cow shed in the woods.

'Who is she?' Henderson spat.

'Jae Morel, sir,' Paul explained. 'Marc's known her all his life, but he really fell for her when he escaped from prison last year.'

Henderson glowered accusingly at Paul. 'He must have planned this before we left. Can you *honestly* tell me you knew nothing about this?'

'On my parents' graves,' Paul said. 'I know how nuts Marc is about this girl. He sleeps with a lock of her hair under his pillow, but I had no idea that he was going to try something crazy like this.'

'You liar,' Luc said. 'I bet I could get the truth out of Paul if you let me smack him about, Captain.'

Rosie turned towards Luc. 'Shut up, moron. This is serious.'

'Marc's got authentic documentation,' Paul said. 'He escaped from prison camp in Frankfurt and survived on his own, so I'd think he can pull off a trip to Beauvais without major difficulties.'

'That's not the point,' Henderson said. 'Every aspect of this plan has been carefully organised in order to minimise risk. Marc's no fool, but he's putting our lives at additional risk – as well as his own.'

'There's not much we can do,' Rosie said. 'Joseph says there's an early train into Rennes, which connects to the morning express. If things are running on time Marc will be halfway to Paris already.'

Henderson hadn't shaved and ran his hand over a bristly cheek. He was furious at Marc, but hid his anger because he wanted to come across as the unflappable commander.

'Makes no difference,' Henderson said. 'We'll carry on without him.'

'Two other pieces of news,' Rosie said. 'Do you want the good or bad first, sir?'

'I'm not in the mood for games,' Henderson said, with just enough snap to make Rosie stand upright.

'Right,' Rosie said stiffly. 'I received a scheduled radio message from Joyce on campus last night. The good news is that the two-day weather forecast shows clear skies for

Friday night into Saturday morning. Unfortunately, Joyce also received a message from the Ghost circuit in Paris. The Germans have just changed the design of the paperwork required to move foreign labourers around.'

'Changed how?' Henderson asked.

'The new cards are green instead of purple and the layout is completely different,' Rosie said. 'The blanks we've brought with us for the scientists in the bunker are useless. They've also issued a new set of rubber stamps.'

'Blast,' Henderson said, as Luc and Goldberg shook their heads in sympathy.

'The Ghost circuit is doing all it can to either steal or forge sets of the new cards and stamps,' Rosie said.

'How confident are they?'

'They're sure they can get them,' Rosie said. 'Whether they can get them and get twelve sets to us by Friday evening is less certain.'

By this time, Jean and Didier had come out of their shed and caught the end of the conversation. 'What's the matter?' Didier asked.

'Something's always the matter,' Henderson said. 'But it usually sorts itself out in the end.'

*

They'd all seen the bunker in aerial surveillance photographs, but from fifty metres the rusted fence and armed guards sent a tingle down Paul's back.

The Germans had recently tarmacked the single-track road leading to the bunker, enabling it to carry bomb-laden Luftwaffe trucks in all weathers. The mesh fence was topped with three strands of barbed wire. Notices with lightning bolts threatened a shoot to kill policy for anyone who tried climbing in, and hanging for anyone who survived that.

There was a single, gated entrance, manned by two guards. Rosie had made more than a dozen visits to the site and told Henderson that she'd never seen guards patrolling the perimeter, from either inside or outside the fence, but occasionally one of the men on duty at the gate would wander into the trees to urinate in preference to a much longer walk to the guard hut.

The fence formed a rectangle which Rosie had counted as three hundred metres wide and five hundred and sixty deep. The French army had replanted trees to hide the bunker from the air after they'd built it, but the trees inside the fence were all less than ten years old and you could even make out a rough outline because the growth of trees planted above the bunker had been stunted when their roots hit concrete.

Apart from trees there were a couple of dilapidated wooden sheds and a clearing where the scientists came up in pairs to exercise and smoke. The only other indications of life below ground were concrete ventilation shafts poking through the soil and a heavily reinforced reception building.

This reception was the only way down into the bunker and critical to Henderson's planned operation. It was one and a half storeys high and set three hundred metres back from the front gate. On three sides its reinforced concrete roof sloped to the ground in order to deflect any bomb that might hit. The fourth side was a flat wall with two entrances.

The larger entrance went down into a garage where trucks could reverse in to load or unload by a freight elevator, while the smaller entrance was a regular door. In an emergency, or during an air raid, an additional pair of armoured-steel blast doors could slam shut, making the entire building impregnable.

'Have you ever seen them shut?' Henderson asked, as he squatted in the undergrowth next to Rosie.

She nodded. 'From the weight of them, you'd think they'd be slow. But I've been here when an air raid warning goes off and they don't hang about. There's a whoosh of air, and they clang shut within twenty seconds.'

'Not much room for error then,' Henderson said.

'So what's your exact plan?' Rosie asked.

Henderson had briefed the boys before leaving campus, but Rosie had sent her undeveloped photographs back to Britain via the resistance in Paris and since then her only direct communication with campus had been through short radio messages.

'As soon as we found that the notebook was genuine

we put out discreet feelers about the bunker within the French exile community, in both Britain and the USA,' Henderson began, speaking just above a whisper. 'We were lucky enough to track down a French draughtsman in Chicago, who worked on the bunker while it was being built. He's made us a decent drawing from memory, which we've used in conjunction with your notes and photographs of more recent German alterations.

'Our first job is to cut off communications so that nobody can get the message out that the base is under attack. Next we lure as many Germans as possible to the surface and get the snipers to take them out, simultaneously and from a distance. The trickiest part comes next: we've got to storm the base and get into the reception building before someone below ground finds out what's happened and closes those blast doors.

'Once we're below ground, we've got to go room to room until we've killed or secured all the Germans and located the scientists. With so many bombs down there, we can't go in with guns blazing, so we'll use knockout gas. It's absolutely crucial that the Germans don't know we've pulled the scientists out and have no knowledge that this was a resistance raid. So once the bunker is secure, we'll need to drag all the dead bodies inside, set a couple of explosives to go off underground and prime a few German bombs.

'As we leave we set off the homing beacon for the USAF. While we drive towards Paris disguised as German guards escorting a work party, three dozen B-17s will bomb the bunker. It's unlikely that any bombs will break through the reinforced concrete, but the explosives we've left will set off the bombs inside the bunker.'

Rosie nodded. 'So, even if the Americans miss the bunker, the Germans will think that one of their own bombs was triggered accidentally during the air raid?'

'Exactly,' Henderson said. 'Caused by vibration, or whatever. And with hundreds of bombs in storage down there we're hoping that there's gonna be nothing but a big crater and a lot of charred trees in the forest come Saturday morning.'

'And the Germans will think all the scientists died below ground,' Rosie said as she broke into a smile. 'So nobody comes looking for them.'

Henderson nodded.

'It won't be easy,' Rosie said. 'But it's a perfect plan if it works.'

Henderson laughed as he took another glance through his binoculars. 'Of course it'll work,' he joked. 'When have I ever given you kids reason to doubt me?'

CHAPTER TWENTY-NINE

The train from Rennes to Paris took four and a half hours, but on arrival Marc found the platform barricaded and an hour-long queue while Gendarmes checked identity documents and opened every passenger's baggage.

'Is Paris your final destination?' an officer asked, when Marc finally reached the front. He knew his documents were perfect, but still felt uncomfortable as an elderly officer rifled through his identity card, ration card and employment status document.

'I'm visiting a friend in Beauvais.'

'How much money do you have on you?'

'Twenty-two francs.'

'No luggage?'

Marc shook his head. 'I'll be travelling back tomorrow morning.'

As he spoke another train was steaming into the adjacent platform. People opened doors and jumped off before the train stopped moving, so that they could grab a good place in the inspection line.

'Let me see.'

Marc peeled some crumpled francs out of his pocket, along with a return ticket for Rennes.

'Move out,' the gendarme said rudely, as he looked forlornly down his rapidly swelling queue.

There was a German-manned inspection point at the station exit, but Marc skipped it by going down the steps into the Metro. After a short ride under Paris, a mainline train took him fifty minutes out to Beauvais.

The security around the station looked relaxed, but a new pass had been introduced by the Luftwaffe who controlled the area around Beauvais. Marc had left France the previous summer under heavy fire aboard a stolen German fighter plane, so he was more jittery than he'd been in Paris as a Luftwaffe man copied all his identity details into a ledger and then made him empty his pockets.

Marc left the station office with a square of canary-yellow cardboard which allowed him to enter the Luftwaffe zone and a strip of paper with details of how to apply for a special ration card if he wanted to eat or drink during his stay.

The last stretch was an hour's walk. Marc felt his

emotions rise as he ducked past the orphanage where he'd lived for the first twelve years of his life, reaching Morel's farm just before three in the afternoon.

'Are you back to work?' the farm manager asked eagerly. 'I lost four workers to German factories. Three more have gone on the run to avoid being rounded up.'

'Just visiting,' Marc said.

'And who might you be looking for?' the manager asked, before laughing at the absurdity of having to ask. 'You'll find her pulling up potatoes between the cow sheds.'

Marc smiled. Although it was relatively safe in the countryside, there was a war on and until that moment he wasn't even certain Jae was still alive. He bolted off, passing through fields that verged on derelict.

France would face a long and hungry winter if Morel's farm was typical, but aching legs and doom-laden thoughts vanished the instant Marc saw the girl he loved. Jae had grown a couple of centimetres and farm work had built shoulders atop her thin body. To make the moment more perfect, Jae had her back to Marc, so he crept up.

'Need a hand with those?' he asked noisily.

Jae jumped and screamed when she saw who it was. 'Bloody hell!'

They were both crying as they embraced. Marc gulped Jae's smell, the mix of earth and sweat dredging up a million memories of the previous summer.

'I love you so much,' Marc said. 'I've thought about you every day.'

'One of Daddy's Luftwaffe friends mentioned that a plane got stolen,' Jae said. 'But I had no idea if you'd made it back to Britain alive.'

'Our landing was a *bit* bumpy,' Marc said, but tailed off as they joined at the lips.

The next ten minutes was all slurps and groping. Jae was always in Marc's dreams and he half expected to wake up in his campus dorm, breathing Luc's farts. When they finally broke apart, they backed away and stood admiring one another in a state of awe.

'So how's life?' Marc asked.

'Horrible,' Jae said. 'And not just because I miss you. We've got nobody to work the land and Mr Tomas and the requisition authority make our lives hell. He's never liked my dad, and he's really had it in for him since you left last year.'

Marc shook his head at the thought of Tomas. As orphanage director Tomas had made Marc's childhood a misery. When the war began, he'd taken a job with the Nazi Requisition Authority. This much-loathed organisation controlled everything France produced, from trucks to tomatoes, and demanded that an ever increasing share of it was sent to Germany to feed the war effort.

'Tomas constantly has my dad arrested on charges of black-market dealing,' Jae explained. 'It's like the stress is rotting him from inside. He's lost his hair. And he was always thin, but now he's like a ghost.'

'I can only stay one night,' Marc said sadly. 'I'm in France for another mission.'

'Dangerous?' Jae asked.

Marc tried to make light of it. 'When are they *not* dangerous?' he asked. 'But they haven't killed me yet.'

'What a hero,' Jae said, as she gave Marc a kiss. 'I've been arrested too. Three times. The last time Tomas' mob dragged me off the land in my rubber boots. They put me in a room and wouldn't let me go to the toilet, so I peed in a boot and threw it in Tomas' face.'

'Classic,' Marc laughed.

'Daddy told me off. He said I could have got into serious trouble.'

'He's not wrong,' Marc said, but Jae gave him a soft slap across the arm.

'Don't take *his* side. It's OK for you, gallivanting off having adventures. What do I get? Cow shit under my nails and constant backache.'

'But you're the world's sexiest crap-sweeping potato-picker,' Marc said cheekily.

Marc turned and ducked as Jae sent a dry clod of earth skimming over his head. Her next shot disintegrated as it hit him in the back and they threw more stuff at each other until Marc fell over and they started snogging again.

*

Even in bad times a family with as much land as the Morels can eat well. There wasn't much wrong with Pippa's cooking on campus, but Marc preferred French food to English and he bolted down onion soup, beef stew and more wine than was good for him.

Jae had warned Marc that her father looked unwell. The level of Morel's physical decay wasn't nice to see, but it was the change in status that Marc found most poignant.

All through Marc's childhood, Morel had been an aloof and vaguely terrifying man. Slim, well dressed and with the power to do horrible things to scruffy orphan boys with a crush on his only daughter.

But now Morel accepted Marc's position at his table, close to Jae. Morel had drunk too much and candlelight reflected off his bald patch as he listened to Marc's news about the outside world. At fifteen, Marc was beginning to match many adults physically, but he'd never previously encountered a situation where a person of such authority looked up to him.

'What happened to the Luftwaffe officers you had living here?' Marc asked.

'There were several assassinations by communists,' Jae explained. 'All Luftwaffe personnel now have to live on an airbase, or in Beauvais where there's more security.'

'Damned shame too,' Morel added, slurring a little as he drained his fifth glass of wine. 'They were always gentlemen. Plus they scared off Tomas, and got me out of lock-up a couple of times. I mean, how can a man live?'

Morel tailed off before shooting to his feet and erupting into a boozy rant. 'The Requisition Authority sets me a production quota. Then it takes half my men away. Then they arrest me because I've not met my quota and accuse me of selling food on the black market. This farm was *so* beautiful. If my father or grandfather could see the state of things now it would kill them.'

Morel's loud voice caused the cook to peer in from the adjoining kitchen as Jae stood up and put a soothing hand on her father's back.

'Maybe you should go to bed, Daddy,' she said.

'I'll go to the library for a brandy,' he said. Then a flash of the old Morel came through as he pointed accusingly at Marc. 'And I may not be all that I was, but I'll still come at you with a shotgun if you try sticking your penis into my daughter.'

'Daddy,' Jae said, through gritted teeth. 'You're so embarrassing.'

'You're a good boy really,' Morel said, as his tone changed completely. 'Admirable.'

As Jae helped her drunken daddy up the stairs, Marc turned to the cook.

'It's hard seeing him like that,' he told her.

The elderly cook looked at the floor, as if commenting on her boss was some horrible sin. 'The Morel men have always been drinkers, but the harassment and having no workers has done him in.'

Marc licked the cream out of his pudding bowl and drained his wine glass, then waited for Jae at the base of the stairs.

'I didn't realise he'd—'

Jae cut him off by pressing a fingertip to his lips. 'Don't,' she said sadly. 'Everyone talks about my dad *all* the time. I get sick of hearing it.'

Marc thought about saying sorry, but somehow sensed that Jae didn't want him to.

'I know you've got to catch an early train,' Jae said. 'But when I was with you at the lake last summer, I think it was about the happiest I've ever been.'

'The lake,' Marc said, smiling and a little tipsy from the wine he'd drunk with dinner. 'Perfect.'

CHAPTER THIRTY

It was dark as Marc and Jae strolled out. The day had been warm, but the lake water was always cold and night-time brought a chill to the air. They swam naked and came out shivering, then lay against each other on a grass embankment.

They were both virgins. They'd kissed and seen each other naked, but their bodies had only touched through clothes before now. Marc wasn't sure if the manly thing was to try having sex, but he didn't want Jae getting pregnant in the middle of a war and knew that sex had killed off the relationship between Rosie and PT.

When Marc pushed his fingertips between Jae's thighs, he was relieved when her head tilted backwards and she made a barely perceptible, 'No.'

A second swim chilled Marc's lust and after that they

put clothes back on and cuddled. Marc tried to focus on here and now, but there was a clock in his head that he couldn't shut off, constantly telling him how much time there was before he had to leave.

Jae fell asleep with her head in Marc's lap, but he stayed awake watching her breathe, trying to fix the way she looked into his head.

He nudged her awake when the sun poked over the horizon. The smile when she woke up and recognised him sent a sob through his body.

'It's half five,' Marc said. 'I've got to start walking if I'm catching the first train back to Paris.'

A pair of tears raced each other down Jae's cheek as she found her shoes and rubbed a stiff shoulder.

'You OK?'

'Stiff,' Jae said, as she stretched to a yawn. 'I need a day off, but I'll never get one.'

'If all goes well, I'll be back in Paris on Saturday morning,' Marc said, as he held up crossed fingers. 'We might have some spare time before we go back to Britain. I may be able to come here and help for a few days.'

Jae held up her crossed fingers too. 'I hope it's not another year. Will you be in trouble for running away from your unit?'

'Whatever happens to me, you're worth it. Will you walk part of the way into town with me?'

'I'd love to,' Jae said. 'But cows have to be milked.'

Marc could think of nothing better than being with Jae in a muggy stinking cowshed, but he was the best sniper after Goldberg and had to go back. They both broke down completely during their final hug.

'I hate this,' Marc said. 'I'm sorry I've got to go.'

Marc couldn't bear it any longer, and tore himself away. After a few metres he waved, but then he strode without looking back because he was scared that he'd be unable to leave if he saw her again.

There was nobody on the road this early and fifteen minutes brought the orphanage into view. A lot of people knew Marc around here. It was best that they didn't see him, so he dived over a wall and walked behind it for a couple of hundred metres.

When he climbed back, he glanced at a cottage. It was tiny, with a whiff of smoke coming out of the chimney. It was summer, so someone had to be inside cooking and that someone had to be Mr Tomas.

Marc had told Jae that he'd be in Paris by the weekend, but the bunker mission was a huge risk and there was a chance he'd get killed or taken prisoner. He didn't like the idea of being outlived by his former tormentor and he was intrigued by the possibility of an ambush. He'd stayed with Jae until the last possible second and his watch told him he could spare no more than a couple of minutes.

Dry grass crunched underfoot as Marc approached the

cottage. He leaned his shoulder to the whitewashed wall and peeked into the single ground-floor room. Tomas stood in vest and boxers, eating bread with one hand, while stirring a large metal pot on the wood-burning stove in front of him.

The window was half open. Marc was an expert knife thrower and even with his clumsily unbalanced pen-knife he'd have had no problem spearing Tomas' chest from this range. The thought of killing in cold blood troubled Marc, but it was the one way he could help Jae and he detested Tomas more than anyone else on earth.

But Tomas was also one of the most senior Frenchmen working with the Nazi regime. A bloody end might be taken as a sign of resistance activity and lead to German reprisals. So Marc didn't just need to be quick, Tomas' death also had to look natural.

He ran around to the front of the house and gave a playful triple knock on the door. As Tomas swore and turned to answer the knock, Marc dashed back to the window. He opened the leaded pane as quietly as he could, then dropped down into the only room on the ground floor, timing his jump to coincide with Tomas opening his front door.

'Bloody kids,' Tomas shouted, when he saw nobody there. 'Dozy nuns! Can't keep 'em under control.'

Marc grabbed a heavy griddle pan hanging over

the stove, and Tomas caught sight of it as he turned around, kicking the door shut with his bare heel while scratching himself through his boxers.

'You,' Tomas growled as his eyes opening wide. 'You cheeky motherless bastard.'

Tomas had been a middleweight boxer in his prime, and Marc wouldn't be the first cocky orphan to square up and come off worst. But none of those guys had Marc's combat training and as Tomas swung, Marc ducked, bobbed up and smashed him across the temple with a brutal two-handed swing of the pan.

Tomas went down stiff, like a tree trunk. Marc reckoned the force had been enough to crack his skull, but the blow hadn't broken skin so there was no blood.

'That's for every time you thrashed me,' Marc said, wishing Tomas was conscious to hear his words.

Marc went down on one knee, turned back the top of his trousers and broke open a few cotton stitches on the inside. The break in the seam enabled him to push out a tiny L-pill – L for lethal.

After pulling Tomas' jaw open, Marc balanced the pill on one of his rear molars and then closed the jaw up, crunching the pill and releasing a dose of cyanide. Marc had killed a man in a Rennes prison cell using the same technique, so he knew to expect spasms and vomit in his victim's mouth as heart and lungs became paralysed.

But time was short, so rather than watch Tomas' last

moments, Marc rubbed off the skin flakes stuck to the bottom of the griddle pan and hung it back up, then turned his attention to the huge steaming pot.

Marc raised the lid and saw three of the tan-coloured shirts that Tomas wore as part of his Recquisition Authority uniform. As Tomas kicked his last spasms, Marc splashed some of the hot water on to the earth floor, purely to test the pot's weight. He then grabbed Tomas under the arms and dragged him across to the stove, adjusting his position so that it looked like he'd succumbed to a heart attack.

Marc's cover story had Tomas grabbing hold of something as he collapsed, but only managing to grab the heavy pot and bring it down. The water was scalding and Marc was careful not to splash his legs as he drained it over Tomas' head.

The skin instantly blistered and a whiff of hair tonic came up with the steam. The wet shirts slapped the floor as he dropped the large pot. As a finishing touch Marc pressed Tomas' limp palm against the side of the pot, making his flesh sizzle and leaving a burn to confirm that he'd grabbed the pot and pulled it down on himself.

The scene wouldn't stand serious examination, but Marc knew that the Luftwaffe ran the Beauvais area with a fairly gentle touch. They left routine matters to gendarmes and while these French police varied in their degree of loyalty to the Germans, it was unlikely that a country policeman would voice suspicions that might lead to brutal German reprisals against his own community.

Marc backed up as a curtain of steam rose from the earth floor. After a few seconds making sure that he'd made no basic errors and left nothing behind, he checked his watch and backed out into a blaze of low sunlight.

He needed to gain a couple of minutes to be sure of catching the train, but running from a crime scene attracts attention, so he only ran once the orphanage was well out of sight.

Marc had killed before and would have to kill again before the week was out, but he lacked the ruthlessness of Henderson, who could kill and forget it moments later, or the sadistic streak of someone like Luc, who revelled in the vilest things he'd ever done.

Marc knew the faces of everyone he'd killed, but as he bolted downhill with a breeze buffeting his ears he didn't see Tomas' scalded skin. Instead he saw himself as a young boy, with Tomas lashing out mercilessly. And a dozen other boys, who'd cried themselves to sleep as their wounds bled into their bed sheets.

Marc felt strong with his oldest enemy vanquished and the sun on his back. He couldn't stay with Jae, but by killing Tomas he was protecting her. He reached the platform at the same time as the train, but his exhilaration faded as he sat in a half-full carriage steaming towards Paris.

When would he see Jae again? And what would Henderson do when he got back?

*

After making good time, Marc was back for a late-afternoon serving of chicken soup at Joseph Blanc's house.

Henderson was staying in the forest, so he didn't know Marc had returned until the evening. His plan was for everyone involved in the operation to meet near the cave, then walk to the bunker so that he could plot final details, while everyone else got a feel for the place in darkness. But Marc's punishment had to be dealt with first.

'So what do I do?' Henderson asked, wearing his best poker face.

It was just starting to get dark and as Marc and Henderson faced off, Luc, Paul, Sam, Rosie, Edith and Goldberg looked on with varying degrees of interest.

Espionage Research Unit B had twenty agents and Marc was the only one Henderson had formed a close bond with. But this was a double-edged sword, because while Marc hoped Henderson would go easy, there was a chance he'd do the opposite to avoid accusations of favouritism. And it definitely wasn't a good idea being in trouble again so soon after sabotaging Luc's rifle.

'Cat got your tongue?' Henderson asked curtly.

Marc gave a slight shrug and spoke submissively. 'I know I did something wrong, sir. I'll accept whatever punishment you give me.'

Henderson smiled. 'I'm not going to give you a lecture on how you could have endangered our mission by being caught, or having transport problems. You knew the risks when you set off to see your girlfriend and you knew I'd punish you when you returned. But that holds no fear because you're a tough little bugger. I expect you even calculated that I won't punish you too severely one night before a critical mission, and might even forget what happened if the operation goes off well.'

Marc looked down into the undergrowth and didn't speak. Every word Henderson said was true and it was a reminder never to underestimate the captain's intelligence.

'So I'm not going to punish you,' Henderson said.

Marc knew better than to smile as he looked up. 'I'm truly sorry, sir.'

'You do that good-little-boy voice so well,' Henderson said. He laughed, but kept the volume down because sound carried a long way in the forest and there was always a chance of a German patrol. 'You're not sorry. If you had another shot at seeing Jae, you'd do it in a heartbeat. But I *didn't* say you're not going to be punished, I said that *I'm* not the one who'll punish you.'

Marc looked uneasy, but assumed this meant he'd be put through a tough programme of physical jerks by one of the instructors when – or if – he made it back to campus.

'Luc,' Henderson said. 'Get over here.'

A little uneasy became a lot uneasy as Luc stepped forwards. 'Sir?' Luc asked.

'Go to the nearest willow tree,' Henderson began. 'Break a switch off. One about the length of your arm and no thicker than your thumb. Bring it back here, then you can give Marc six of the best on bare buttocks.'

'What!' Marc gasped, as Luc cracked an evil smile.

Paul and Sam didn't like Luc, but they smirked at Henderson's cleverness: Marc was too tough to worry about a caning or a few hours' physical training, but baring his arse and taking a thrashing off Luc in front of everyone would cause humiliation far greater than physical pain.

'He's evil,' Marc told Henderson desperately, as Luc rushed towards the nearest willow. 'You're stronger than him. It'll hurt more if you do it.'

Henderson raised one eyebrow and spoke firmly. 'I'm giving you a direct order to take your punishment,' he said. 'If you disobey, I'll have no choice but to hog-tie you until after tomorrow night's raid, drag you back to Paris with us and then kick you out of my unit when you make it back to England.'

'Bloody hell,' Marc mumbled, and almost followed up with a childish *it's not fair*.

Luc came out of the bushes with half a tree balanced between his arms. It was so ludicrously huge that Paul, Sam, Rosie and Edith couldn't help laughing, even when Marc glowered at them.

'How's that thinner than your thumb?' Henderson asked irritably.

Luc pointed to the tip. 'It's thin up this end.'

Even when Marc was the one in trouble, Henderson had no patience with Luc. He snatched the log from Luc's hands and snapped off the largest branch. 'Use that, you stupid boy.'

Marc gave Henderson a pleading *OK here's when you tell everyone you're joking* look. But this was no gag and he found himself leaning forward, hands on kneecaps and pale white bum on show. Luc had a massive grin on his face as he took a run up and swooshed the willow cane with all the force he could muster.

CHAPTER THIRTY-ONE

The raid on the bunker would involve secret agents, snipers, a dozen members of the Ghost resistance circuit and a squadron of USAF bombers. But at a quarter to six on that Friday morning, its success depended on a ten-year-old boy.

Justin sat on his mattress, coughing up phlegm infused with flecks of coal dust as a small, sticky hand touched his back.

'Are you sick?' Belle asked, with all the earnestness that a three-year-old can muster.

Belle had her own bed and strict orders to stay in it, but Justin was fond of his youngest sister. He'd always let her climb in and cuddle, in preference to the scream-up he'd get if he tried putting her back in her own bed.

'I'm not sick,' Justin said between coughs, as he wiped

a trail of spit on the filthy shirt he was about to pull up his arms. 'Go back to sleep.'

'Mummy might make it better,' Belle said thoughtfully. 'Or send you to Dr Blanc.'

Justin spoke more firmly. 'Belle, go back to sleep.'

'Where are you going?'

'Do you want me to tell Mummy that you slept in my bed?'

Either of Justin's older sisters would have thrown back the threat by saying that they'd tell on him for sneaking out, but Belle had yet to master the subtleties of blackmail and looked scared before lying back down and burrowing under Justin's pillow.

'I won't be long,' he said.

Justin had twisted his mum's arm to get her cooperation when Henderson's team first arrived off the coal train. But the murder of the two railway cops, followed by arson and executions at the intersection had shaken her up and she'd now ordered Justin to stay off the coal train for a few weeks and steer well clear of Rosie.

After creeping downstairs, Justin cut through a gloomy kitchen and leaned out of the front door to look for checkpoints. Following the railway cop murders the thuggish German soldiers had put up several temporary checkpoints, including one less than fifty metres from Justin's house.

For two and a half days they'd searched, slapped and harassed anyone going near the railway line or intersection, but they'd tired of their games. The checkpoints had been taken down the previous afternoon, and there was no sign of them returning.

Justin's mum slept at the rear of the ground floor, so rather than take the direct route through the house he straddled a low wall and crossed a patch of shaggy grass to reach the railway line.

He took a furtive glance along the tracks. There was no sign of soldiers or railway cops, but the elderly man who worked the water tower was peering along the tracks, so apparently a train was expected soon.

Justin had no timepiece of his own, so he'd taken his dead grandfather's pocket watch from a locked drawer the previous night. The worst his mum ever did was shout and whack him with her wooden hairbrush. That didn't worry him, but she'd most likely start crying if her dad's watch went missing, so, after using it to confirm that the train was due in fifteen minutes, he made sure to carefully rebutton his shirt pocket.

He felt hungry and tired and a big yawn set off another round of coughing. The first train was a cargo train that didn't stop at the water tower. The one he was here for came in twenty minutes late, which was frustrating because the longer he was gone, the more likely it was that his mum would be awake when he got back.

Once the passenger train had filled its tank with water, the driver let out a blast of steam and took off the brake. Justin became certain it was the right train when it set off slower than you'd expect it to. He only got a glimpse into the driver's cab as it rolled past, but he saw the stoker downing his coal shovel and sending a small leather case pirouetting through the air.

The train's momentum and the steep embankment meant that the case flew some distance, ending up near the back wall of Madame Vial's garden. Although Justin had thrown thousands of coal sacks down the embankment, today felt scarier because Rosie had warned him that the Germans would try to cultivate spies, and notices had been posted at the intersection offering two thousand francs and the return of a prisoner of war to anyone coming forward with information about resistance activity.

It was fortunate it had been warm and dry for most of the last week, because the spot where the case landed was often muddy. As the sound of the passenger train receded, Justin walked briskly back to his house with the case tucked under his arm.

When he got indoors he heard his mother coming down the hallway, and hastily tucked the case behind a coat stand.

'Why are you out at this hour?' she asked brusquely, hands on hips and still in her nightdress.

'I couldn't stop coughing,' Justin said. 'I didn't want to wake the girls, so I went out for some air.'

'Any sign of the Germans?'

'No,' Justin said, as his mother took a step closer. The case wasn't completely out of sight so he took a step himself to stop her getting too close.

'I worry about your chest and all that coal dust,' Justin's mum said, as she gave her son a kiss on the forehead. 'I don't want you riding that train any more.'

'We'll need the money once winter comes,' Justin said. 'Remember how expensive everything got last year?'

'I'll think of something. There's plenty of places short of men. Maybe I can get a second job or something.'

*

There were more early risers at Joseph Blanc's house. Rosie's final radio sked was at 6:30 a.m. The Germans had expert teams dedicated to hunting down resistance radio signals, so before each transmission she'd always take the suitcase-sized radio two kilometres up into the woods, using a different location each time.

Rosie was used to lugging the transmitter, heavy battery and fifty metres of coiled aerial wire on her own, but for this final transmission she had Paul, Sam and Edith along to share the load.

After stretching the aerial across the ground and giving the set ten minutes for the valves to get warm, Rosie transmitted an encrypted Morse code message. She said that all was well, that the local security had apparently died back to normal levels and that the mission would go ahead.

The response came in groups of five random letters. Rosie would normally take these back to the house for decoding, but today she worked with Paul, using a printed silk decoding sheet, while Sam and Edith dug a hole.

'It all looks good,' Rosie said, when the message was done. 'Clear weather is predicted. Fifty US bombers will attack Rennes tonight, with half diverting towards the bunker if they get the signal from our beacon. The Ghost network says that the documents were successfully placed on the train. Joyce and everyone else on campus wishes us luck.'

'We'll need it,' Paul added, as he set a lighted match to the small square of silk with Rosie's codes printed on it.

The thin fabric had a special coating that made it burn in a flash.

'Edith's got to leave for her train,' Rosie told Sam. 'Do you need a hand finishing the hole?

Sam shook his head, always keen to show that he didn't need help from older agents.

'Make sure that the radio case is closed so that no dirt gets in,' Rosie said. 'There's a slim chance we'll have to come and dig the radio back up if things go wrong. And cover the hole with branches after you fill it in.'

Sam tutted. 'Rosie, I'm not an idiot. Go do *your* job.'

Edith and Sam hugged briefly. If things went to plan they wouldn't see each other again until after the operation.

'Good luck tonight,' Edith told Sam. 'Perhaps I'll see you again in Paris.'

'I hope so,' Sam replied.

'And when you get back to the house, tell Marc that I hope his bum's feeling better,' Edith said.

Sam laughed. 'I'm sure he'll be able to sit down by now.'

Rosie had spent many hours lugging the radio set back and forth, and many more tinkering to keep it working. She liked the idea of never seeing the blasted thing again as she set off towards Justin's house with Paul and Edith in tow.

Paul teased Edith gently as they walked. 'Am I detecting a little chemistry between Sam and yourself?'

'He's younger than you,' Rosie noted, as Edith turned bright red.

'Oh, wrap up,' Edith said, before laughing uneasily. 'He's really nice, but he's a kid.'

'We've actually got the same thing in a slightly older model back in England,' Rosie said. 'His brother Joel looks just like him.'

'How old?' Edith asked keenly, realising that she stood less chance of further embarrassment if she played along with the joke.

'Fourteen,' Paul said.

Justin's house and the railway station were half an hour's walk. When the trio got within a hundred metres of the little street of cottages they were pleased to find no sign of Germans. But there was still a possibility that the soldiers were hiding out, so Rosie gave the pistol tucked into her jacket to Paul and walked the last stretch on her own.

'This way,' Justin whispered, giving Rosie a fright as she got within twenty paces of his house.

'Something wrong?' Rosie asked, as she glanced about suspiciously. 'Did you get the packet?'

He nodded. 'Got 'em fine, but I didn't realise my mum was off work today. If she sees you she'll wring my neck.'

Justin led Rosie up to a battered tin shed in the garden of a cottage two doors from his own.

'Don't sweat,' Justin said. 'People see me here all the time.'

Rosie understood when Justin opened a tin shed stacked high with sacks of coal.

'I stash the coal here, 'cos it's the butcher's house and nobody messes with him,' Justin explained. 'He gets free coal and I don't have to worry about people nicking my stock.'

'Clever,' Rosie said. 'You're quite the businessman. I bet you're gonna end up running your own factory some day.'

Justin smiled as he pulled out a sack about one third full. He held it open, showing Rosie the document case inside.

'Just be sure to wipe all the coal dust off before you unzip it. It's all in there. Fifteen blank forms, and three rubber stamps.'

'Fifteen?' Rosie said.

Justin shrugged. 'Spares I guess, in case you mess one up.'

'Makes sense,' Rosie said, as she pulled an envelope out of her jacket. 'Henderson asked me to give you this, in thanks for all you've done. It's a thousand francs, plus two gold ingots.'

'Gold?' Justin said, as he peeked into the envelope and smiled at the money.

'Currency is nothing more than toilet paper in a crisis,' Rosie explained. 'Gold is always worth something, because you can't make any more of it.'

Justin smiled as he took the envelope, but his eyes looked sad. 'You're sure there's nothing I can do tonight?'

'You've more than done your bit, mate,' Rosie said. 'If it wasn't for you, Edith would be dead. We'd never have met Dr Blanc and found out about the bunker. And you introduced me to Jean and Didier, who've been brilliant forest guides.'

'Are those two still going to Paris with you?'

Rosie nodded. 'They're on the run and the forest is likely to be crawling with Germans if the bunker gets blown up. We've fixed up new identities and medical exemption certificates so they can't be sent to Germany.'

'I'll probably never see you again,' Justin said, as a tear welled in his eye.

He was such a smart, resourceful character that you only remembered his age when something like this happened.

'I wish I could carry on helping,' Justin sniffed. 'I want to be a proper member of the resistance, like you or Sam.'

'We know where you are if we need you,' Rosie said. 'But your real job is to look out for your mum and your sisters. Be careful when you're crawling around on trains in the dark, and be sensible with that money. People will ask where it came from if you start splashing out, and it's going to be a long, hungry winter so you have to make it last.'

'I'll be sensible,' Justin agreed.

'If tonight's a success, I'd bet this raid will be world famous,' Rosie said. 'They might even pin a medal on you after the war.'

Justin still felt really sad, but raised one cheeky eyebrow. 'You try not to get yourself killed.'

'I'll do my best,' Rosie said, as she grabbed the coal sack. 'See you at the medal ceremony.'

'Buckingham Palace or Château de Versailles?' Justin asked.

'Both, I reckon,' Rosie laughed.

Rosie was glad she'd cheered Justin up, but felt anxious about the mission as she walked away.

'Something the matter?' Paul asked, catching his sister's expression when they met up again.

'Did he not get them?' Edith added.

'It's all fine,' Rosie said. 'I was just thinking about something.'

'Right,' Edith said, sighing with relief. 'I'll walk across to the station. My train to Rennes is due soon. When I make contact, I'll tell Ghost that we got the documents and everything's set for tonight.'

'I'll let everyone back at the house know Justin got the new documents,' Paul said, as he gave Rosie her pistol back. 'Goldberg and Luc should be there getting the locator beacon and sniper equipment ready by the time I get back. And you're sure you don't fancy popping back to cook our lunch?'

'I'm sure the six of you won't starve without my cooking for one day,' Rosie said, narrowing her eyes slightly. Paul regarded his comment as a joke, but Rosie resented the way that she always ended up doing cooking and laundry because she was a girl. 'I'll go meet Henderson in the woods and tell him everything's ready to roll.'

CHAPTER THIRTY-TWO

'You know your jobs,' Henderson said, as he looked at his wristwatch.

They formed a circle of nine, crouching amidst moss and tree roots, three hundred metres from the bunker: Henderson, Goldberg, Rosie, Paul, Marc, Sam, Luc, Jean and Didier. Despite the forecast of clear weather, wispy cloud blotted out the moon and an on-off drizzle would make sniping tricky.

'Let's synchronise our watches,' Henderson said. 'Remember, the bomber crews are at risk while they're circling and the Germans will smell a rat if they're up there for too long. We *have* to keep this on schedule.'

As everyone pulled up sleeves to expose wristwatches, or took out a pocket watch, Henderson studied the second hand of his own timepiece.

'11:07 dead, on my mark,' he said. A few seconds later, 'Mark,' was followed by clicks as people pushed in their watch crowns to set them running.

Everyone shook hands with everyone else before they split into teams. Goldberg went left; Sam and Paul headed to a position near the bunker's front gate; Henderson, Marc and Luc went to the right side. Rosie stayed where she was and had to warm up the homing beacon, while Jean and Didier stayed with her because they had no role in the first phase of the operation.

It was important that none of the base guards alerted the local garrison, so the first job was cutting communications and fell to Henderson's team. The trio didn't speak as they crunched through the woodland, dressed in black commando gear with their faces darkened with coal dust. Marc and Luc had sniper rifles over their shoulders, pistols, knives and grenades hooked to their belts, and backpacks loaded with everything from gas masks to emergency ration packs.

The bunker was connected by a single telephone line and a radio. Cutting the telephone was easy, because the French had destroyed the underground phone line before abandoning the bunker during the invasion. Rather than dig a new trench through several kilometres of woodland, the Germans had strung their replacement cable through the treetops.

Luc shimmied up a tree a hundred metres from the

perimeter fence, snipped the line with a pair of wire cutters and threw both ends to the ground. While Luc climbed, Marc had unzipped his pack and removed the bulkiest item from it: a battery-powered field telephone that dated back to the Great War. After pulling the line leading into the base out of the branches, Marc squatted by a tree trunk and used a knife to strip insulation from the wires.

The base radio was harder to get at. While Marc connected the phone up using his pen-knife and a small screwdriver, Luc and Henderson headed for the base perimeter. Rosie had all but confirmed that the perimeter was never patrolled, but they stayed low just in case, as they used giant bolt-cutters to snip the wire fence.

'You crawl, I'll cover,' Henderson said, once they had a decent gap.

While Henderson sat inside the fence with his pistol ready, Luc sprinted fifty metres through the trees towards an aeriel. The thing was rusty and had partly tipped over in the wind.

The base of the aerial was enclosed in a metal cabinet. Luc had a crowbar ready to break the cabinet open, but all it needed was a good tug and a sweep of his boot to clear away mulch that had built up around the opening since its last service.

Once he was in, Luc slid the hooked end of the

crowbar behind wires soldered to the aerial's base and ripped them out.

'All good,' Luc whispered, when he got back to Henderson.

Seconds later they were back with Marc, who proudly held the phone up so that Henderson could hear a vague hum on the line.

'I'll make the call in a couple of minutes,' Henderson said. 'Marc, tell the gate team we're ready for their bit, then circle around and join up with Goldberg.'

'Aye-aye, captain,' Marc said, before scrambling off.

*

While the rest of the team came in combat gear, Sam approached the perimeter gate dressed like a typical French boy and carrying a hunting knife and a blood-stained cloth bag with a dead rabbit poking out of the top.

'Excuse me, sir,' Sam said, sounding meek and anxious as he aimed his voice towards a guard hut. 'Do you speak a little French?'

There were two guards in a small wooden hut, set five metres back from the mesh gate.

'Buzz off,' a man with a cigarette between his lips shouted. 'If you make me come out there, I'll arrest you for breaking curfew.'

Germany didn't waste good men on remote bunkers. The guard was an elderly fellow, with a platform under one boot to compensate for one leg shorter than the other.

'I'm really sorry, sir,' Sam continued, as he faked a sniffle. 'I know I shouldn't be out this late. But we were hunting. We got lost and my friend hurt his leg. He's bleeding badly. *Please* help me.'

The German didn't understand much French, but Sam's boyish face and hysterical tone was enough to send him limping towards the gate. Paul watched through the sight of a sniper rifle from a hundred and ten metres out. This wasn't his moment to shoot, but it was the first German he'd seen between his crosshairs and the thought of killing an elderly disabled German didn't fill him with glee.

Sam kept up the hysterical spiel as he led the German into the woods, towards his imaginary injured friend. The German's slow walk hadn't been factored into the plan, and it took Sam twice as long as he'd expected to reach a small clearing seventy metres from the fence.

'What is this?' the German asked.

As the guard looked about suspiciously, Sam reached into the fork of a tree and picked out a silenced pistol. He'd played this moment in his head since he'd heard Henderson's first detailed briefing and it felt dreamlike as he gave a double tap on the trigger, putting one bullet through the German's head and one through his heart.

This was Sam's first mission. He'd not killed before and had to suppress a shaking hand as he pulled up his shirt and tucked the gun into a holster. While the

German bled out, Sam grabbed his kitbag from behind the tree. He pulled on a black combat jacket stuffed with grenades and sniper ammunition, before digging his fingertips into the earth and smearing some across his cheeks as camouflage.

*

Henderson sat with the field telephone in his lap while Luc kept lookout. When it was time, he pressed the only button to make the phone at the other end of the cable ring.

'Hello,' someone said.

'This is Beauvais headquarters,' Henderson said, responding in perfectly-accented German. 'Are you having difficulty with your aerial? We've had no response to our urgent request for an inventory report.'

The man sounded confused. 'Our radio is only used in an emergency.'

'It was not *your* emergency,' Henderson said irritably. 'Our telephone system has been sabotaged. An urgent request was sent to you by radio.'

'Err . . .' the man said, sounding like someone who wished he'd not picked the phone up. 'Can I get the base commandant to call you?'

'No,' Henderson snapped back. 'Our telephones are still erratic and I am calling from a street telephone. Get someone monitoring your radio transmissions. The signal will be repeated in five minutes and I suggest that you act upon the instructions promptly this time.'

'It takes longer than that to warm the receiver up,' the guard said.

'Very well, ten minutes. And the group commander expects an immediate acknowledgement of our request.'

Henderson slammed the phone down, and gave Luc a smile. 'Now let's see if they take our bait. Get into your sniping position and be ready to fire on my signal.'

*

Henderson's plan to get as many Germans as possible above ground took a few minutes to start moving. As soon as the radio set had warmed up inside the bunker, its operator realised that the aerial was faulty and two Luftwaffe men came out into the drizzle.

They soon discovered that the aerial cabinet had been sabotaged and then tracked Luc's boot prints to the hole in the wire fence. One German stood around looking clueless while his colleague rushed back inside to tell someone senior.

By this time the guard who'd remained on the gate had grown increasingly suspicious about the prolonged absence of his colleague. He couldn't leave the main gate unattended, so he used the phone in the guard hut to call up two more men who could help him search.

Paul watched them emerge from the bunker, knowing that Sam would also be able to see from his shooting position more than a hundred metres west. While those two covered the front of the compound, Marc and Goldberg had excellent firing positions from higher ground to the west, while Luc worked from a position close to Henderson in the east.

Henderson balanced in a tree to get a better view through his binoculars and was delighted when the base commandant, another Luftwaffe man and an army sergeant came out of the bunker's only entrance.

Rosie had estimated that there were twelve Luftwaffe and four army guards manning the base at any one time. Getting nine of them above ground was as good as it was likely to get and now it was time for the snipers to do their stuff.

CHAPTER THIRTY-THREE

Henderson unscrewed the silencer from his pistol and dropped it into his pocket before firing two noisy shots into the air.

'Good luck,' Rosie told Jean and Didier as the double bang sent birds into the sky.

Sniper shots cracked off as Jean and Didier pulled on gas masks and set off at a run towards the base, with machine guns swinging from their necks and a heavy gas cylinder held between them.

Luc rattled off two quick kills, getting two men standing by the sabotaged aerial. Marc and Goldberg had to deal with the three moving targets, walking briskly towards the aerial. Two went down with clean headshots, but Marc had to finish the base commander with a shot in the back as he broke into a run.

In front of the base, a moment's hesitation from Paul meant that Sam took out the victim in his scope before he'd pulled the trigger. Paul's next target made a run towards the guard hut. It's easier to hit a target when they're still so he turned his aim towards the hut's door and waited for his victim to get there.

For all his angst about killing, when the moment came Paul focused his mind as Goldberg had taught and shot beautifully, hitting his man in the back of the head with such force that his body tore the unopened door off its hinges.

While Paul reloaded, Sam took out the last German standing above ground.

Henderson surveyed the scene with binoculars before giving a shout of, 'Clear,' and beginning to pull on a gas mask.

The sniping had been crucial in reducing the number of Germans in the bunker, but the next phase of the mission was the most dangerous. They had to storm the bunker entrance and get a team inside before anyone still below ground smelled a rat and shut the blast doors.

While Paul and Sam stayed back as sniper cover, Jean and Didier charged through the main gate with their gas cylinder. Luc and Henderson reached the bunker entrance a couple of seconds before them, while Marc and Goldberg were well behind, because they had to stop and cut a hole in the fence on their side of the perimeter.

'On go,' Henderson said, keeping low as he put his hand on the door. 'Three, two, one, go.'

Luc covered with his gun and Didier had the gas cylinder ready to blast as Henderson charged in first. He kept his back to the wall as he entered and shuffled down a narrow corridor with a short run of metal steps at the far end.

A pistol shot rang out when Henderson reached the top step. The aim was off, but it hit the wall close to his head and a chunk of flying plaster smashed into his cheek.

'Give me some gas,' Luc shouted, as he dragged Henderson out of the way.

As Didier aimed a jet of light blue gas down the staircase, Luc poked his machine gun barrel around the stairs and squeezed off a few shots. When the blast ended there was another sound: the hiss of large hydraulic jacks as the armoured-steel doors closed behind them.

'Sir?' Luc said, looking to Henderson for orders.

But Henderson was in a daze, clutching his face with blood spattered across the inside of his visor. The rubble had punched clean through his gas mask and cheek, leaving his mouth filled with tooth splinters and bits of masonry.

Jean and Didier had little training and no experience, Marc and Goldberg stood no chance of getting inside before the blast doors slammed, so it was all down to Luc.

'Stay close,' Luc told Didier, as the blast doors made a doom-laden clang.

The base wasn't heavily manned so Luc doubted there were any more than one or two bodies near the base of the stairs, but with no route out he had to act fast, because more would arrive and corner him if he gave them time.

In a normal raid, Luc would have lobbed a grenade down the stairs and backed up, but the stairs led into a garage and for all he knew he'd be setting off an explosion under a truck loaded with bombs.

Luc's only realistic option was to jump down the stairs and hope that the gas had either slowed his opponents or forced them to back off. He landed with a clank of metal, and glanced through the window of his gas mask at dim orangey bulbs and a bluish haze.

He tiptoed around the garage. It was big enough for six trucks but currently only held two, plus a tatty car up on jacks. As he kept his back to the wall, Luc looked for any sign of movement under the parked trucks. It was close range and his machine gun was an indiscriminate weapon, so he pulled his silenced pistol from a belt holster as he watched shadows.

He'd reached the cab of the last truck when he heard a coughing sound close by. He spun and dived behind the truck as a man took aim from the other end of the garage. Luc hit the floor, flat on his chest. He took aim between the tyres and shot the German in the ankle.

As the German yelled, Luc crawled rapidly under the truck and finished him off with a shot through the chest.

'Jean, Didier,' he yelled. 'Get down here and cover me.'

Luc studied the dead German. The gas cylinder contained water, concentrated pepper oil and ether. The mixture was supposed to cause breathing difficulties and drowsiness, but judging by the man's horribly swollen eyes the cocktail was more potent than the way Henderson had described it during the detailed briefing.

'Try to find some controls,' Luc said, as he approached a winding staircase. 'Levers, buttons, whatever. Get those blast doors back open or we're shit out of luck.'

As Jean and Didier hunted, Luc moved towards a spiral staircase which ran around the outside of a cargo lift. According to the French draughtsman that Henderson had tracked down, the bunker was designed as a place to store weapons, safe from the threat of German bombs. The design was quick-and-cheap, with one entrance, one lift and one set of stairs leading down to a cavernous storage area.

'Zweig, why have you closed the door?' someone down below shouted in German. 'Don't you know the commandant is still out there?'

Luc's German was far from perfect, but his accent was passable and he hoped that the echo on the stairs might hide the fact that he wasn't Zweig. 'The commandant wants everyone out searching.'

As Luc said this, Jean pulled on a lever and the doors started opening again.

Marc was first in, and was shocked by the sight of Henderson slumped against the narrow corridor wall, almost unconscious. But before he could worry about that he heard Luc's pathetic attempts to lure more Germans up the stairs.

Marc's German was excellent and he rushed towards the stairs and shouted authoritatively. 'The commandant is going ballistic,' Marc shouted. 'I've just reopened the doors. He wants every free man up here searching the woods.'

'Who's that?' the man at the bottom shouted.

Marc deliberately didn't reply. There was no sound of footsteps on the stairs, but just as Marc and Luc started to assume that the Germans down below were suspicious, the lift began moving upwards.

'Henderson should survive, but he's away with the fairies at the moment,' Goldberg said. He stared aghast at the lift. 'Are they *really* that stupid?'

'I reckon Luc's number one man for massacring Germans coming out of a lift,' Marc said. 'Shall we go down and flush the rest out?'

'You bet,' Goldberg said. 'Didier, we might need gas. Come with us.'

The lift was designed for strength not speed, and Marc watched its rusty drive cable shudder inside the wire cage as he raced down ninety stairs behind Goldberg.

'*Hello*, boys,' Luc said, when the lift juddered to a halt in front of him.

The front of the lift was a folding metal gate, so the men inside could see Luc as he pushed the muzzle of his gun between the bars. He swelled with joy as five desperate Germans either lunged for their own weapons or tried shoving another man in front of them.

'This one's for my parents,' Luc stated.

Luc squeezed his machine gun trigger, spraying rounds from point blank range until there was nothing but dead bodies and a stream of blood draining from one corner and spattering the floor of the lift shaft twenty metres below.

Luc was clutching his fists and grinning madly as he backed away, dropping his clip and fitting on a fresh one. Jean looked completely horrified.

'No mercy for Nazi scum,' Luc told Jean, as he slapped him on the back. 'Signal the boys out front, then deal with the trucks. Make sure the engines run. Make sure the tanks are full and clear out any junk in the back. I'm going downstairs to back up the others.'

CHAPTER THIRTY-FOUR

Paul and Sam had watched from their sniping positions in front of the base as the huge blast doors closed and reopened. Handheld radios were too bulky and highly vulnerable to German interception, so the pair had no way of knowing what the situation was below ground until Jean came out and signalled with a torch.

Two flashes would have meant that the bunker had been secured, but he gave a single which meant it was safe to move in, but that the operation was still underway.

Paul slung his rifle over his shoulder, leaving Sam as the last sniper to cover any surprise movements on the base. After jogging to Sam's position and checking that he was OK, Paul ran a couple of hundred metres back to Rosie in the clearing.

She'd taken the locator beacon out of her pack, connected the battery and switched it into the warm-up position. The device was the size of a couple of loaves of bread. It contained two transmitters, with a rotating dish aerial on top and a package of high-explosive booby traps at the bottom to destroy the top-secret device if a bomb didn't get it first.

Once activated the first transmitter would send a radio pulse which could be picked up from over fifty kilometres away. The second short-range transmitter sent out a series of directional radio beams. A bomber fitted with a compatible receiver unit could fly along the path of these beams, and receive precise information on their distance to the target.

'What's going on?' Rosie asked, when Paul got close.

'It's as clear as mud,' Paul said. 'But we got the single flash from Jean, so they must be making progress.'

'I know we had it working earlier at the house,' Rosie said, as she stared at the contraption anxiously. 'But the pounding it's taken must have knocked a connection loose. It's switched out of warm-up mode twice already.'

'Too late to start tinkering with it now,' Paul said, as he stared at the transmitter's army-green casing. 'It'll either work or it won't.'

'I don't want it to get bumped,' Rosie said. 'I'll carry the transmitter. You take my backpack and gun.'

*

Marc did sums as he crept down the spiral stairs behind Didier and Goldberg. He hadn't seen every kill, but reckoned they'd sniped eight to ten Germans above ground, Sam had taken one out in the forest and there'd been a few more in the lift.

'Can't be more than three bad guys left down here,' Marc whispered.

'Sounds right,' Goldberg agreed. 'I'll lead. Marc, cover my back with the silenced pistol. Didier, keep the gas ready.'

The stairs ended at a broad corridor, with a pair of battered miniature forklift trucks parked at the far end. Rooms branched off on either side, each with doors wide enough for cargo pallets, while the air was heavy with aromas of bad plumbing and cigarettes.

There was no sign of life, but most of the doors did have small portholes. Dr Blanc had told them that she'd treated the suicidal scientist in the penultimate room on the right-hand side of the corridor, and had briefly glanced into the laboratory directly opposite.

Within seconds of Marc reaching the bunker floor, Luc had caught up.

'Got five of 'em,' he said proudly.

Goldberg ordered Luc to stand by the lift shaft, covering the length of the corridor while he and Marc walked down, peering into the rooms on each side as they passed.

The rooms seemed more like tunnels. Each went back more than sixty metres and was ten metres wide, with the only light coming from a line of bare bulbs strung down the centre.

The first room Marc peered into was full of metal crates filled with fighter-plane ammo, his next had sinister-looking racks containing hundreds of bombs and the third was crammed with all the junk the French had left behind, from waterproof ponchos to ancient wooden-handled grenades.

Goldberg had reached the dorm and laboratory when a bolt snapped on a much smaller door directly behind him. Cigarette smoke billowed as an elderly man strolled out, adjusting braces attached to drab green army trousers.

By the time Goldberg had turned to face the door, Marc had shot the man through the chest. The pudgy figure stumbled back into the toilet, clattering into a bucket filled with brooms and mops.

The range was nothing, but aiming wasn't easy with gas masks on and Goldberg nodded appreciatively.

As Goldberg approached the scientists' dorm, Marc looked into the laboratory. The main lights were off, but there were several indicator lights and the glow of valves visible through the grilles of electrical equipment.

'Get ready,' Goldberg said, as he made a *come here* sign in Didier's direction. 'Have the gas ready, just in case, but try and avoid using it. We don't want to have to carry these scientists out on our backs.'

Goldberg pushed the door handle down, and booted it inwards before spinning out and pressing his back to the corridor wall. He'd expected a blast of gunfire or some heroic German charge, but all he got was a strong whiff of body odour and a couple of sleepy moans about making less noise.

Marc reached around the doorway and flipped light switches when his hand found them. The men inside were on metal-framed bunks and began yawning and shielding their eyes. Goldberg charged in with his machine gun ready, but there was no sign of soldiers or Luftwaffe.

Goldberg pulled up his gas mask. 'Where are the Germans?' he shouted.

A man in the top bunk nearest the door stared at Goldberg's commando gear as he felt about for a set of wire-rimmed glasses.

'I think the Boche all went up top for something,' the man said. 'Something connected to your presence, I'd imagine.'

Goldberg looked surprised, as Marc made sure there were no Nazis under the beds, or hiding behind the lockers at the end of the room.

'They left you completely unguarded?' Goldberg asked.

The man with the glasses nodded as he swung his

feet over the side of the bed. 'We don't give the Germans any trouble,' he explained. 'Best not to mess with men armed with machine guns, don't you think?'

The plan had been for Henderson to tell the scientists what would happen next, but he was up top with a mouthful of busted teeth. As French wasn't Goldberg's first language, the job fell to Marc.

'Listen up,' Marc said, clapping his hands to fix everyone's attention as he put down his backpack.

'Have the Americans landed?' a fat man rolling off one of the rear bunks asked.

'No such luck,' Marc said, as he realised that the men down here probably didn't get much news. 'We're part of a resistance group. You need to listen carefully. The base guards are either dead or hiding out in one of the other rooms. We have high-quality false documentation that will enable you to travel to Paris, disguised as a team of labourers. Once there you'll be split into pairs and you'll begin carefully planned journeys to Allied territory.

'I need you to move quickly and quietly. Pack a few personal belongings, but *nothing* that contains your real identity. You can also go—'

Marc was interrupted by the sound of a bullet ricocheting off bricks. Goldberg looked out and saw that Luc had shot a Luftwaffe officer who'd been hiding in the laboratory.

Boo and Joyce had dug up pictures of many of the

scientists named in the notebook, mostly from the group photographs traditionally taken at the end of big scientific conferences. Luc recognised his victim as the German project director, Dr Hans Lutz.

'Got another Nazi!' Luc shouted cheerfully. 'Guess the big boss didn't want to go upstairs and get his hands dirty.'

'When we're certain it's safe, you can also go across the hall to the laboratory,' Marc continued, trying to assert himself above an atmosphere of fear and shock. 'You can each take a small quantity of scientific notes, along with any equipment that you feel is of high value. But we only have two trucks and whatever you take, you've got to be able to carry by yourselves. I also need to take up-to-date photographs of each of you, which I'll develop en route and attach to the blank documentation.'

'Are you here because Jaulin passed his notebook to that fat doctor?' a lanky man dressed in socks and undershorts asked. It was understandable that the scientists had mixed feelings about the sudden shocking arrival of the resistance, but this fellow sounded outright hostile.

'Yes, we got the notebook,' Marc said. 'We'll have plenty of time to explain when we're on the road. What matters now is that you pack up and leave as quickly as possible.'

'Escaping sounds damned dangerous to me,' the lanky

man said. 'What if we don't want to leave?'

Goldberg didn't like the man's tone and spoke angrily. 'We're here because we were led to believe that you're French scientists being forced to work on a German military project. If you *want* to stay here and continue working for the Nazis, that makes you traitors and war criminals and I'll have no option but to execute you.'

Another man nodded in agreement with lanky, but most of the others were either neutral or stared at him in disbelief.

'What right have you to do this?' the lanky man ranted furiously. 'You're American. Are you working with the authority of the French government in exile, or for American imperialist ends?'

'What about our families?' another man asked. 'If we escape they could be persecuted.'

Marc had a lot more sympathy with this last question. 'We're going to set this place to blow before we leave. Shortly after that, twenty-five American bombers will wipe this place off the face of earth. Nobody will come looking because the Germans will think you're all dead.'

'So our families will think we're dead?'

'Possibly,' Marc said. 'But think how happy they'll be when they find you're not.'

Some of the scientists laughed nervously.

'We've put our lives on the line to save you,' Goldberg added indignantly. 'If it wasn't for what's in your big brains you'd die down here, like other Nazi prisoners who die every night in Allied bombing raids.'

But the lanky man still wasn't having it. 'You have no legitimacy,' he said, as he got right in Goldberg's face. 'You Americans want to steal our technology. You're no better than the Germans.'

Goldberg wasn't a big man, but he was tough and his patience had run out. He stepped forward and smashed the skinny Frenchman in the mouth with the metal butt of his machine gun, then floored him with a knockout punch to the temple.

'He stays here and he'll be dead in an hour,' Goldberg told the others. 'Now start packing. This is a war and I'm not your mother, so no more shit from any of you.'

If anyone still had doubts, none of the scientists dared show them as they started getting dressed and packing up. Marc had taken a pocket camera and a pack of flashbulbs out of his pack, and began taking identity photographs with each man standing in front of a bare wall.

'We're glad you're here,' one man said, as Marc lined him up in a wire-frame viewfinder. 'What we do here has been eating me up. Jaulin spent weeks drawing and hiding that notebook. He'll be over the moon when he gets back from the toilet.'

Another man laughed before butting in. 'Old Jaulin can spend half a day in that toilet. I don't know how he stands the smell.'

Marc's eyebrows shot up. 'Jaulin's not here?' he asked, as he did a quick count and realised that there were ten men moving and one unconscious.

Jaulin was a brilliant scientist. Joyce had found pictures of him, but Marc only now made a connection between the grey-haired scientist in a spotted bow tie he'd seen in a photo on campus and the man in German army trousers who he'd shot emerging from the toilet.

Marc felt like spewing, but before he could tell anyone what had happened, he heard Luc shout from the base of the stairs.

'Rosie and stick-boy have arrived with the beacon.'

Goldberg let three scientists cross the hall into the laboratory to pick up their research notes before turning to Marc.

'How long do you need down here?' Goldberg asked, as the next man in the photo queue stepped up to the wall.

'Only a couple of minutes for the pictures,' Marc said. 'Lift's a bloody mess and some of the guys are pretty old, so it's gonna take a while to get them up the stairs.'

'Fifteen minutes sound about right?' Goldberg said.

'Should be plenty of time,' Marc said.

Goldberg shouted down the hallway. 'Luc, tell them to turn the beacon on in twelve minutes. We should be at least a mile from here before the bombers arrive.'

CHAPTER THIRTY-FIVE

The scientists' fake identity documents had to be ready for the first German checkpoint they encountered, so as soon as the photographs were done Marc pulled the film from the camera and worked with his hands in a light-proof bag, unravelling the film from its roll before dropping it into an insulated metal pot filled with warm developing fluid.

It would take seventeen minutes for the film negatives to develop, after which the canister would be flushed with distilled water. Then he'd add a bleaching agent for a few minutes, flush the canister again and finally add a fixing chemical to stop the negatives from fading.

To make photos from these negatives Marc would then have to make contact prints on to light-sensitive paper using a handheld enlarger and repeat the develop/bleach/fix process on the paper itself. It was a process he'd practised dozens of times in the campus darkroom, but never with the added stress of a mission going on in the background.

While Marc concentrated on photographs, Didier helped two exuberant Jewish scientists carry a chunky wooden mock-up of an FZG-76 nose cone, fitted with the latest prototype of its guidance system, up the spiral stairs.

Other scientists followed, carrying up a mixture of personal items, blueprints and scientific equipment. The lift remained operational after the machine gun blasts, but nobody had the appetite to clean out the gore and even the weakest of the scientists chose ninety-four steps over balancing on mangled corpses.

When Marc was satisfied with the film, he placed the darkroom bag and developing cylinder inside his backpack, then checked his watch, making a mental note of when he had to start the bleaching phase.

'Everyone out,' Marc shouted, as he leaned into the laboratory. 'Time to leave.'

There was nobody in the lab, but the dorm still contained an elderly scientist called Wallanger, who was hovering over the man Goldberg had knocked out.

'He's a big mouth,' Wallanger told Marc. 'There was no need for that, he'd have settled down.'

'Maybe,' Marc said ruefully. 'But dozens of people will put their lives on the line to smuggle you lot out of

France. We can't take chances with someone who isn't on our side. And you'd better get upstairs. Make sure you grab a set of overalls before you board the truck.'

'Getting too old for adventures,' Wallanger said, as he picked up a battered leather case. 'How old are you anyway?'

'Nowhere near as old as I feel right now,' Marc replied, feeling a surge of emotion as he snatched Wallanger's case. 'I can't leave anyone who knows our plan alive, just in case the bombs don't go off. So *please* don't make me shoot you. I'll carry your case. Our friends in Paris know you're elderly and I can promise they'll look after you.'

As Wallanger toddled reluctantly down the hallway, Marc felt tears welling as he pointed his pistol at the lanky fellow lying unconscious on the floor. He turned away before taking two silenced shots, killing the second of the twelve scientists he was supposed to be rescuing.

A bearded physicist called Rivest almost bowled Marc over as he stepped into the corridor. 'Why are you back down here?' Marc roared furiously. 'I'm *trying* to clear you bastards out.'

'I forgot an important notebook.'

'Well, hurry up,' Marc shouted. 'We've got to be out of here in *three* minutes.'

Rivest looked wary, realising that his life was in the hands of a highly stressed fifteen-year-old who was waving a pistol around while tears streaked down his face.

Marc picked up Wallanger's case and his own backpack. He headed towards the stairs, but stopped and wiped his cheek before stepping into the bomb-storage room.

'How's it going?' he asked.

Luc and Goldberg stood over a bomb rack. They'd set timed plastic explosive charges in four places, and now they were screwing sympathetic fuses into giant 1000kg Hermann bombs.

In theory, any American bomb going off directly above the bunker would set off a shockwave and trigger the sympathetic fuses in half a dozen large bombs. But the air raid was purely a deception designed to ensure that the Germans didn't come looking for the scientists, so even if all twenty-five bombers missed, the plastic explosives were a failsafe that would trigger the bombs fifteen minutes later.

Whatever set the Hermanns off, their blast would generate enough heat to detonate every other bomb in the room and leave nothing but a large crater in the middle of a forest.

'These fuses we brought from England are shit,' Luc told Marc angrily. 'Whoever machined them made them a fraction too big. It's taking way longer than we thought to screw them in the detonator shafts.'

'Just a couple more now though,' Goldberg said, trying to calm Luc down, because angry psychos and bombs are rarely a good mix. 'Tell everyone to board the trucks and start the engines. They can drive out the instant we jump in the back.'

'Right,' Marc said. 'I'll grab my shit and run up now.'

Rivest was helping the elderly Wallanger up the spiral stairs as Marc came back into the corridor. He bounded past the pair and caught an anxious shout from Paul as he neared the top.

'What's going on?' Paul screamed. 'Why are those idiots still down there?'

Marc glanced at his watch and looked mystified. 'We're OK. The bombers won't get here until after the beacon's switched on.'

'The beacon's been on for ten minutes,' Paul said.

'You what?' Marc shouted. 'Why did you turn it on?'

'Luc shouted up the stairs.'

'He *told* you to turn it on in twelve minutes,' Marc said. 'Shit!'

'I didn't hear twelve minutes.'

'I bloody did,' Marc said. 'I was right there when Luc shouted.'

Marc had reached the garage by this time. Sam, Jean and Didier had dragged in the bodies killed by sniper shots and piled them up at the base of the metal staircase. This way, they'd get blown up and the Germans wouldn't find bodies with gunshot wounds. Eight scientists sat in one truck looking anxious, while

Henderson was in the other, with Rosie knelt over him giving first aid.

'Get that truckload of scientists out of here, now,' Marc said, as he put Wallanger's case down and threw off his backpack, shedding weight so that he could move as fast as possible. 'I'm going back down.'

'Planes could be here any second,' Paul said.

Didier shouted from up by the garage doors. 'I think I can hear them.'

Planes on a bombing run fly at over two hundred kilometres per hour, so unless Didier was hearing planes from a very long way off Marc had no chance of warning Luc and Goldberg in time. But Marc wasn't thinking rationally after shooting the two scientists and he headed back down, even though it was probably a suicide mission.

As Marc set off, Didier was climbing into the truck to drive the scientists out of the garage.

'You two run,' Marc screamed, as he pushed past Rivest and Wallanger, a dozen stairs from the top. 'Luc, Goldberg. Get up here now.'

Paul was shouting from up top. 'Marc, we're leaving. Three planes sighted, we're moving out *right* now.'

Marc gripped the banisters on either side of the staircase and leapt three steps at a time, all the while screaming for Luc and Goldberg. Even in his panicked state Marc saw the irony that he despised one of the people he was rushing to save.

His thoughts were all jumbled: he thought about Jae, he imagined a fireball shooting up the staircase. Then he missed a step and twisted his ankle, but he had too much adrenaline in his system to feel the pain.

'They've set the beacon, planes are coming,' Marc screamed, when he burst through the door of the bomb room.

In the back of Marc's mind, he was beginning to think that if Didier really had seen three bombers, he should be dead by now, or should at least have heard some bombs going off nearby.

'What moron set the beacon?' Goldberg yelled. 'They should just be turning it on *now*.'

'We've done five out of six,' Luc said. 'It should be enough.'

Goldberg hesitated as Marc turned to race back up the stairs. 'You said you've got two baby daughters back in New York,' Marc told the American. 'If you ever want to see them again, you'd better shift.'

CHAPTER-THIRTY SIX

Henderson looked up at Rosie as he lay across the slatted wooden floor of a canvas-sided German army truck. She'd put five stitches in his holed right cheek before stuffing the inside of his mouth with bandage. She'd also ordered him to press another wodge of bandage hard against the outside of his cheek to stop the blood flow.

'Uah uop,' Henderson said. 'Uop uop.'

Henderson was used to running the show. Not knowing what was going on was as much of a torture as the missing teeth and the hole in his face.

'I can't understand you,' Rosie said. 'You've got to keep your mouth still until a scab forms.'

As Rosie spoke, Jean started the truck engine, and scientists Rivest and Wallanger were clambering over Henderson's legs.

'Leave now,' Paul said, as he slammed the truck's rear flap. 'Drive about a kilometre. We'll try catching you up. The photographic stuff is in Marc's pack, if we don't make it try to rescue the negatives.'

'What about you?' Rosie asked.

'If I don't stay, Marc will think we've abandoned them when they get up here.'

Rosie wanted to say something to her brother, but Jean was terrified that he was about to get blown up and floored the gas pedal.

As the truck shot up the ramp and out into the night, Paul moved up to the exit, figuring he might stand some chance of surviving if he broke towards the woods when he heard planes passing over. After half a minute, with no more sign of planes, Paul felt a rumbling under his boots and saw red in the sky.

It looked as if the USAF's diversionary raid on Rennes had started. Paul now suspected that the three aircraft Didier had spotted a couple of minutes earlier had been German night fighters sent out to intercept them. But even though that had been a false alarm, the beacon had now been running for over fifteen minutes and this was the last place on Earth Paul wanted to be.

'They've bloody abandoned us,' Luc shouted furiously, as he came around the top of the stairs with Marc and Goldberg and saw the trucks gone.

Paul shouted from the doorway. 'I'm here. I sent the

truck out into the woods for safety, but we can run and pick it up.'

'You deaf shit,' Luc roared, when he got close to Paul. 'Twelve minutes I said. If we do make it out of here alive, I'm going to kill you.'

'It's tough to hear up the stairs with the echo,' Paul protested.

'You two argue, I'm running,' Goldberg said, as he set off for the main gate at a sprint.

By the time they'd reached the fence the Americans really were on their way. Twenty-five four-engined bombers, minus however many had been shot down en-route. The entire sky seemed to vibrate with the hum of propellers.

Paul was slowest, and Marc's kit was already in the truck, so he took Paul's backpack when they were a hundred metres past the exit gate and gave him an encouraging shove.

'I'm sorry about the beacon,' Paul said. 'I didn't hear.'

Luckily Rosie had ordered Jean to stop a few metres down the road, rather than the full kilometre that Paul had suggested. Rosie stood by the rear canopy and caught the four running figures in the beam of her torch.

'Come on,' she screamed, as Jean put the truck in gear.

The first six bombers swept overhead in pairs, each releasing thirty-two five-hundred-pound bombs when their aimers pushed a button. Marc's ankle was starting to swell and he was last into the truck, hauled aboard by Rosie.

'Drive,' Wallanger shouted frantically, as he banged on the metal partition behind Jean in the driver's seat.

The first bombs landed as Jean moved into second gear. There was a tangle of arms and legs in the back and Henderson cursed as Paul trod on his hand.

'I need my bag,' Marc shouted, as he crawled up to the back. 'I've got to get the film out of the developer or they'll turn out black.'

Despite the beacon, the first bombs fell well wide, shaking the ground and silhouetting the trees against brilliant orange flashes. At least one fell close to the road, and they all sprawled to the floor as shards of bark speared the truck's canvas awning.

It was fortunate that the Americans didn't trigger the sympathetic fuses until the truck was another half-kilometre along the road, because when it happened it made one of the biggest bangs that the world had ever seen.

From the driver's seat, Jean felt the back of the truck lift up and watched the tarmac ripple as if it was water. The sky blazed white and the heat from the fireball was so intense that treetops ignited.

In the back everyone screamed and grabbed each other. For a few horrific seconds, they were all convinced that the explosion was going to engulf them, but the light and heat did fade, and somehow Jean had kept the truck on the road, even while he'd been blinded.

'Some fireworks,' Luc said, as he peered over the truck's rear flap, ears still ringing from the blast. His bad boy act meant he didn't smile much, but he exchanged helpless grins with Rosie because they'd both expected to die.

*

The drive from Rennes to Paris took six hours and since it was after curfew the two German army trucks cruised empty roads with no speed limit.

The original plan was for Henderson to drive the lead truck, dressed in German army uniform. Fortunately German manpower shortages meant that it wasn't uncommon for Frenchmen to drive military vehicles, especially ones filled with forced labourers dressed in grubby overalls.

Marc's photos came out fine and the Ghost circuit had done a beautiful job providing forged or stolen documents. The first test came after two hours, when both trucks pulled into a roadside fuel depot to fill up.

Jean and Didier were ready with wodges of military documentation and permits, but the lone soldier on guard waved them towards a roadside tanker and told them to get on with things.

A more thorough check came on the outskirts of Paris. Two German privates went through the individual workers' documents and shone torches in the back of the vehicle. They were suspicious when they saw Henderson's bandaged face, but the documents said they were a construction crew and the hole in his cheek was explained away as a painful encounter with a swinging pickaxe.

'OK, get out of here,' one of the privates said.

Everyone was relieved, because a physical search would have revealed weapons, notebooks and scientific equipment.

It was 7 a.m. Saturday as the trucks reached Paris's western suburbs and split up. Each one had three drop-off points for the scientists. Originally a pair of scientists were to be dropped at each location, but as two had died, two men were dropped singly.

After leaving the trucks, the scientists would be met by associates of the Ghost circuit. Each drop was different. One pair had to enter a barber's shop and ask for Daisy, one was given a Metro ticket and told to report to the station's lost luggage office, and another pair were told to join a short queue outside a public baths.

They'd all be bathed, shaved, given new clothes and civilian identity papers before setting off on the next phase of carefully planned escape routes. Some would spend a week or more in a safe house, others would be on trains heading towards the Swiss border by lunchtime.

Their chances of making it to Allied territory were excellent. They'd have money, documents and experienced guides from a well-run resistance circuit. Most important of all, the Germans thought they'd all died inside the bunker so nobody was out looking for them.

After the drop-offs, the two trucks met up at a meat warehouse. What little meat was available in Paris came through the black market, so the meat hooks hung bare and only metal wheel rims remained from porter's handcarts that had been chopped up for firewood.

'Leave the scientists' notes and equipment from the laboratory,' a man dressed like an undertaker told them politely. 'It will be picked up by Lysander and should arrive in Britain before the scientists.'

'Upp ruh uh,' Henderson said, as he found his feet and wobbled slightly.

'I don't have a stretcher, but I could bring out a coffin,' the undertaker suggested.

Nobody could understand a word Henderson said, but it was pretty clear he didn't like the idea of travelling in a coffin and although he was lightheaded from the blood loss he managed to walk OK with one arm around Luc's back.

'I'll arrange for a doctor,' the undertaker said. 'We have an excellent man and decent medical supplies thanks to American equipment drops.'

The undertaker led Henderson, Goldberg, Marc, Paul, Luc, Sam, Rosie, Jean and Didier across the empty marketplace and down some steps to a cellar. The walls to the next building had been knocked through and they emerged into the mortuary beneath the undertaker's shop.

Then it was up three floors to a luxurious top-floor apartment. They'd made more noise on the stairs than they should have and Edith opened the door before they reached the landing.

'How did it go?' she asked.

'Could have gone a lot worse,' Paul said, as he stepped in and breathed real coffee and bread baking.

'Paul's getting his ears syringed when we get back to campus,' Marc added before crashing into an armchair and yelling with pain.

'You don't sound so good either,' Edith said.

'It's not good,' Marc explained. 'My ankle hurts if I stand up, but my arse stings when I sit down.'

There were some laughs at Marc's expense as Maxine Clere came in from the kitchen and Luc laid Henderson out on a sofa.

'Henderson's not as bad as he looks,' Rosie told Maxine. 'But I took three loose teeth out of his mouth so he'll need a dentist as well as a doctor.'

Maxine gave Henderson the gentlest of kisses on his good cheek. Henderson smiled for an instant, but any movement of his face was painful and he'd decided to give up trying to speak because it hurt like hell and nobody understood a word.

'I might just prefer Henderson like this,' Maxine said. 'Can't usually get a word in when you're around.'

Luc grunted. 'I'd heard you preferred Henderson naked in your bed.'

He wouldn't have dared say that if Henderson was healthy. Maxine looked uncomfortable. Marc, Rosie and Paul couldn't help smirking.

'I can't stay,' Maxine said. 'But I've arranged for everything you need. Hot water, towels, clothes, food, identity documents. Don't go out. Keep the noise down and try not to flush the toilet too much because the people downstairs might wonder who you are.'

Rosie looked at the undertaker. 'You'll get the doctor here soon?'

He nodded. 'Hopefully half an hour.'

Marc looked at Maxine as she pulled on a navy coat that seemed too heavy for a July morning.

'What happens next?' Marc asked.

'If you wish to return to Britain it can be arranged,' Maxine said. 'But if any of you want to stay, I'm sure I can keep you busy.'

Marc wanted to stay because it meant he'd be close to Jae. For the others, the decision would be more complex.

'Think it over,' Maxine said, as she pulled out long

hair trapped under the collar of her coat. 'Right now you're exhausted. Wash, sleep, eat and relax.'

The undertaker politely opened the door for Maxine to leave.

'Oh,' Maxine said, turning back when she was halfway out of the door. 'I forgot to say: welcome to Paris!'

EPILOGUE

FZG-76

Hitler eventually renamed FZG-76 the V1. On 13 June 1944 it became the first of his much-hyped victory weapons to be used in anger.

Over the following eighty days, 8,554 V1 pilotless bombs were aimed at London, killing over 6,000 people and injuring 17,000 more. But by this time Allied troops had invaded Northern France and by September 1944 all V1 launch sites capable of targeting Britain had been captured or bombed to destruction.

Once Britain was out of range, V1s were launched against targets in Holland and Belgium. The last V1 to be used in anger was fired towards the Dutch port of Antwerp on 29 March 1945.

HIRAM GOLDBERG

Two years after the successful destruction of the bunker near

Rennes, Sergeant Hiram Goldberg returned home to his family in New York, where he wrote a memoir about his work as a sniper attached to the US Army Intelligence service. Like all ex-servicemen, Goldberg was required to submit his book to the US Army censorship office before trying to get it published.

In an internal memorandum, the office produced a list of reasons why all references to the bunker raid should be removed from Goldberg's book:

MEMORANDUM–TOP SECRET

REF: GoldbergHC/Intelligence Memoir/0045816
DATE: 8/22/47

RE: CHAPTERS 8–13 RENNES BUNKER RAID

After further discussion and meeting of 8/17/47 decision taken that none of material contained in chapters on Rennes Bunker Raid is currently considered publishable. Reasons as below:

1. Cap Charles Henderson's use of chemical spray during military operation was clear breach of 1928 Geneva Protocol. Henderson used the cylinder without

UK or US authorisation and the matter is still under investigation.

Any admission to use of chemical weapons during war, even unauthorised, likely to result in significant and undesirable publicity for UK/US military.

2. Of nine bunker scientists who made it out of France, seven now work in United States on USAF rocket-guidance systems programmes. These men regarded as targets for Russian espionage and any publicity relating to them best avoided. Also, British/French still believed sore and feel that US 'poached' these scientists from under their noses at the end of the war.

3. Version of guidance system removed from bunker was more advanced than unit deployed in the finished V1 flying bomb. Key technologies taken from this unit remain secret and are still probably unknown to Soviet Russia.

4. Although Espionage Research Unit B disbanded late 1944, UK remains keen to hush up matters relating to use of underage persons in espionage ops.

A new unit reporting to the British Secret Intelligence Service named CHERUB is experimenting with use of boys in peacetime intelligence operations. CIA currently studies this project with interest and may implement similar unit of its own at some point. For such unit to be effective, it is imperative no publicity be given to use of underage agents.

NOTE ON DEALING WITH GOLDBERG

Take all reasonable steps to ensure that Goldberg's book is not published in <u>ANY</u> form. It is not desirable for a man involved in such a sensitive operation to attain any public notoriety.

Goldberg is a family man, with good service record, wounded at Battle of Okinawa and decorated on two occasions.

Suggest matter be discussed with him face to face using carrot/stick approach:

<u>Carrot</u>: Appeal to patriotism, offer further military decoration if felt necessary and suggest censorship office can assist in finding a publisher for his work.

<u>Stick</u>: Stress possible loss of military pension, possibility of court martial and imprisonment for any breach relating to release of military secrets. If

Goldberg remains difficult, hint at possibility of 'tax problems' and 'bad publicity' for Goldberg family's New York cigar stores.

Signed
Major JT Banasyznski.
US Army Censorship Office

Sergeant Goldberg died in 2007. His book was never published and the only known copy was destroyed in a mysterious apartment fire in 1949.

SCORCHED EARTH
SUMMER 1944

As Allied soldiers prepare to land in France, Marc and his friends must destroy a battalion of German tanks that could halt the invasion in its tracks.

The tide of war has turned against the Nazis, but desperation has made them more brutal than ever.

Henderson's Boys' final mission will be their most dangerous. With food and weapons in short supply, survival is the biggest challenge of all.

PLUS, FIND OUT WHAT HAPPENS TO ALL THE CHARACTERS AFTER THE WAR ENDS:

Who is arrested for his part in a bank robbery ...
... who becomes a multi-millionaire ...
... who gets married at age sixteen ...
and who becomes a member of the House of Lords ...?

READ ON FOR AN EXCLUSIVE FIRST CHAPTER OF
SCORCHED EARTH

CHAPTER ONE

Monday, June 5th 1944

'Mondays have never liked me,' Paul Clarke said, trying to keep cheerful as his face creased with pain.

The fifteen-year-old had turned his ankle and skidded down an embankment. A khaki backpack cushioned the muddy slide, but he had dark streaks down his trousers and puddle water trickling into his boot.

'Nice slide?' Luc Mayefski asked, offering a hand as rain pelted their waxed jackets.

The teenagers' hands couldn't have been more different. Paul's slender fingers linked with a great ham fist, and even with 30 kilos of explosive in Paul's pack, Luc didn't strain as he tugged his skinny cohort out of the mud.

If it had just been the pair of them Luc would have taken the piss out of Paul's tumble, but these trained members of Charles Henderson's Espionage Research Unit B (CHERUB) had to show a united front for the benefit of their inexperienced companions, Michel and Daniel.

Michel was an eighteen-year-old Maquis. Nine months' living in the woods had left him stringy, with wild hair and a wire tourniquet holding on the sole of his right boot. His brother Daniel was only eleven. Their father was a prisoner in Germany and their mother had vanished after being arrested by the Gestapo. Daniel had chosen to live on the run with his brother, rather than be dumped at an orphanage.

'Are your explosives OK?' Daniel asked, as Paul joined the brothers on a muddy track at the base of the wooded embankment.

'Plastic explosive is stable,' Paul explained, as he tested his ankle and decided he could walk off the pain. 'You can safely cut it, mould it. It wouldn't blow up if you hit it with a hammer.'

Luc checked his compass and led off, eyes squinting as the early sun shot between tree trunks. Even with the rain Luc was sweating and he liked the earthy forest smell and the little squelch each time his boot landed.

Paul and Michel were suffering after 15 kilometres under heavy packs, but Daniel had done them proud.

He'd walked all night, but refused to stop even when doubled up with a stitch.

Luc had been out this way on a recon trip two days earlier, and he turned off track at a point he'd marked by pushing two sticks into the soft ground.

'There's a good view down from this ridge,' Luc explained, as he led the way. 'But keep quiet. The sound carries across the valley and we're not far from the guard.'

'If there is one,' Paul added.

The undergrowth was dense and Michel lifted his brother over a fast stream carrying the overnight rain. As Daniel got set down, Paul was touched by the way Michel put an arm around his little brother's back and kissed his cheek.

'Proud of you,' Michel whispered.

Daniel smiled, then squirmed away, embarrassed, when he realised Paul was looking.

After a dozen more paces, Luc crouched and pushed branches aside. He'd opened a view over a ledge into a steep-walled valley cut into chalkstone. Water dripped off leaves on to Paul's neck as he peered at two sets of train tracks running along the valley's base. Sixty metres to his right, the tracks entered the mouth of a tunnel blasted through the steep hillside.

'You'd never be able to bomb this from the air,' Luc whispered, as he slid a pair of German Zeiss binoculars from their case. After wiping condensation off the lenses, he raised them to his eyes and looked towards a wooden guard hut near the tunnel mouth. The magnified view showed no sign of life and a padlock on the door.

'We're in luck,' Luc said.

The tunnel formed part of a main line running north from Paris, taking trains to Calais on the Channel coast, or forking east into Belgium and Germany. The Germans had built guard huts at the ends of hundreds of important bridges and tunnels, but only had enough manpower to staff a fraction of them.

'Nice binoculars,' Paul noted, as Luc passed them over. 'Where'd you get them?'

'Drunk Osttruppen[1],' Luc explained. 'They'd swap the uniform on their backs for a bottle of brandy.'

Paul backed away from the ledge as Luc glanced at his pocket watch. 'If there's a guard at the other end, we'll sneak up and take him out from behind. Our target train is due to reach the tunnel at around seven a.m. That gives us half an hour to lay explosives along the tunnel and get in position, but with air raids and

---

[1]Osttruppen – German soldiers recruited from occupied countries such as Russia, Ukraine and Poland. Most volunteered to avoid starvation in labour camps. Osttruppen were regarded as poor soldiers and were usually given lowly duties such as emptying latrines, burying bodies and working as servants to senior officers.

sabotage, there's no guarantee that any train will run on time. Especially one that's come all the way from Hanover.'

As Luc spoke, Paul slid canvas straps off his badly-chafed shoulders and moaned with relief as his pack settled in the undergrowth. An exploratory finger under the shirt collar came out bloody, but there was no time for first aid.

After unbuckling the pack, Paul took out two grubby cloth sacks. They seemed to be half full of potatoes, but the uneven lumps were plastic explosive, linked with detonator cord like a string of giant Christmas lights.

Paul looked at Michel. 'Remember what Henderson said. The weakest part of the tunnel is around the mouth, so pack plenty around there.'

As Luc and Michel each grabbed one of Paul's sacks and slung it over their shoulders alongside their own heavy packs, Paul looked at Daniel and tried to sound upbeat. 'Ready to hike?'

The brothers quickly hugged, then Luc gave Daniel his binoculars before leading Michel along the side of the valley.

'You break those and I'll break you,' Luc warned.

As there was no guard, Luc and Michel faced an easy journey down to the tunnel mouth using uneven steps carved into the chalkstone. When they reached the mouth, their task was to unravel the chains of explosive along the tunnel's 300-metre length and retreat to a safe distance, ready to trigger them.

Meantime, Paul and Daniel had to find a vantage point atop the forested hill through which the tunnel cut. Once in position, they had to identify their target: a 600-metre-long cargo train carrying twenty Tiger II tanks, dozens of 88-mm artillery guns and enough spare parts and ammunition to keep the 108th Heavy Panzer Battalion functioning for several weeks.

Since handing over the explosives, the weight of Paul's pack had dropped from 30 kilos to less than four. The bread, cheese and apples that had spent the night at the bottom were squashed, but the two lads scoffed eagerly and shared a canteen of milk as they followed a track to the top of the hill.

Two trains steamed south through the tunnel as they walked and Paul was glad to be up here in fresh air, rather than laying explosives along the dank, soot-filled tunnel.

'Hope they're OK,' Daniel said warily, as he eyed plumes of smoke billowing from either end of the tunnel.

'You have to keep low and put a wet cloth over your face,' Paul said. 'It's not fun, but they'll survive.'

Daniel stopped worrying when he found a bend in the narrow footpath, and spotted another marker from Luc's recon trip. The dense forest made trainspotting hopeless from ground level, but Luc said he'd climbed to a position where he could see trains approaching along several kilometres of snaking track.

The eleven-year-old wasn't just along for the ride. Growing up in Paris, Daniel had earned a reputation as a daredevil, clambering over rooftops, diving off bridges and breaking both arms when he'd leapt between two balconies for a dare. After joining the Maquis in the woods north of Paris, Daniel made a name for himself as a forest lookout, able to climb branches too slim to hold an adult's weight.

'I'll have to lose all this gear,' Daniel said. 'Put it in your pack in case we need to make a quick getaway.'

Paul didn't like taking orders from an eleven-year-old, but Daniel was a good kid and he watched the youngster pull off his boots and strip down to a stocky frame, clad in grotty vest and undershorts. Regular climbing had toughened Daniel's skin and he looked more ape than human as he launched himself into the branches with Luc's binoculars swinging from his neck.

'Careful,' Paul warned, as Daniel vanished into the leafy canopy, becoming nothing but rustling sounds and occasional shifts in the early sunlight.

Paul burrowed down his pack and found the phosphorous grenade he'd use to warn Luc and Michel when they spotted their target. Twenty metres up, Daniel swung his leg over a fork, clamped the thick branch between his thighs and wiped a palm smeared in bird crap down the front of his vest.

'Slippery, but the view's great,' Daniel said, happy with himself as he stared over the treetops at fields, villages and a clear view of the railway tracks approaching both ends of the tunnel. 'Why don't you hop up and join me?'

25% OFF ALL
HENDERSON'S BOYS BOOKS!

How far would you go in the fight against the world's deadliest
and most feared army?

Withstand torture at the hands of an officer desperate to get
information out of you?

Befriend the enemy in an attempt to sabotage their campaign, knowing if you
were caught you would be killed?

Parachute jump out of a plane moments after you discovered your
equipment wasn't fitted properly?

For Henderson's Boys, this is only the beginning.

Now you can join them on all their missions with a 25% discount!

Go to www.hodderchildrens.co.uk/hendersonsboys

and enter promotional code HB25

THE ESCAPE
Robert Muchamore

Hitler's army is advancing towards Paris, and amidst the chaos, two British children are being hunted by German agents. British spy Charles Henderson tries to reach them first, but he can only do it with the help of a twelve-year-old French orphan.

The British secret service is about to discover that kids working undercover will help to win the war.

www.hendersonsboys.com

Hodder Children's Books

EAGLE DAY

Robert Muchamore

Charles Henderson is the last British spy left in occupied France in 1940. He and his four young agents are playing a dangerous game: translating for the German high command and sending information back to Britain about Nazi plans to invade England.

Their lives are on the line, but the stakes couldn't possibly be higher.

Book 2 – OUT NOW

GREY WOLVES

Robert Muchamore

German submarines are prowling the North Atlantic, sinking ships filled with the food, fuel and weapons that Britain needs to survive.

With the Royal Navy losing the war at sea, six young agents must sneak into Nazi-occupied Europe and sabotage a submarine base on France's western coast.

If the submarines aren't stopped, the British people will starve.

Book 4 – OUT NOW

Also available as an ebook

www.hendersonsboys.com

Hodder Children's Books

CHERUB

THE RECRUIT Robert Muchamore #1 International Bestselling Author

CLASS A Robert Muchamore #1 International Bestselling Author

MAXIMUM SECURITY Robert Muchamore #1 International Bestselling Author

THE KILLING Robert Muchamore #1 International Bestselling Author

DIVINE MADNESS Robert Muchamore #1 International Bestselling Author

MAN vs BEAST Robert Muchamore #1 International Bestselling Author

THE FALL Robert Muchamore #1 International Bestselling Author

MAD DOGS Robert Muchamore #1 International Bestselling Author

THE SLEEPWALKER Robert Muchamore #1 International Bestselling Author

THE GENERAL Robert Muchamore #1 International Bestselling Author

BRIGANDS M.C. Robert Muchamore #1 International Bestselling Author

SHADOW WAVE Robert Muchamore #1 International Bestselling Author

PEOPLE'S REPUBLIC Robert Muchamore

GUARDIAN ANGEL Robert Muchamore

BLACK FRIDAY Robert Muchamore

WWW.CHERUBCAMPUS.COM

h
Hodder
Children's
Books

CHERUB

THE RECRUIT
Robert Muchamore

A terrorist doesn't let strangers in her flat because they might be undercover police or intelligence agents, but her children bring their mates home and they run all over the place. The terrorist doesn't know that one of these kids has bugged every room in her house, made copies of all her computer files and stolen her address book. The kid works for CHERUB.

CHERUB agents are aged between ten and seventeen. They live in the real world, slipping under adult radar and getting information that sends criminals and terrorists to jail.

WWW.CHERUBCAMPUS.COM

Hodder
Children's
Books

THE BATTLE OF THE BANDS IS ON.

Jay plays guitar, writes songs and dreams of being a rock star. But his ambitions are stifled by seven siblings and a terrible drummer.

Summer works hard at school, looks after her nan and has a one-in-a-million singing voice. But can her talent triumph over her nerves?

Dylan is happiest lying on his bunk smoking, but his school rugby coach has other ideas, and Dylan reluctantly joins a band to avoid crunching tackles and icy mud.

THEY'RE ABOUT TO ENTER THE BIGGEST BATTLE OF THEIR LIVES.

AND THERE'S EVERYTHING TO PLAY FOR.

www.rockwar.com

Hodder Children's Books